## PRAISE FOR PATRICK HYDE!

"Patrick Hyde does for Washington DC what Dashiell Hammett did for San Francisco."

> Katherine Neville,  author of *The Eight*
> and *The Magic Circle*

"A sharp, tough, fast-moving legal thriller."

> -Daniel Stashower, Edgar winning author
> of *The Beautiful Cigar Girl: Mary
> Rogers, Edgar Allen Poe and the
> Inventions of Murder*

"…Patrick Hyde has hit a home run…"

> -Don Bruns, author of *South Beach
> Shakedown*

"A great read."

> -Robert Gussin, author of *Trash Talk*

"Hyde's entertaining edgy debut shines like a highly polished gem."

> -Ellen Crosby, author of *The Merlot Murders:
> A Wine Country Mystery*

"The book reeks with the scent of a Washington that you don't get in civics class or see from the Tour Mobile… Patrick Hyde spent years working in the criminal justice system, and it shows in his writing.

> -Clyde Linsley,  author of *Die Like a Hero*
> and *Saving Louisa*

"A great first novel—a fast-paced legal thriller that lets the reader explore the sharp mind of a street-wise lawyer-detective. Hyde's descriptions are masterful."

> -Alan Simon, author of *To Live Among
> Wolves*

"Patrick Hyde explodes onto the legal thriller scene with Stuart Clay, an unforgettable hero who plunges headlong into danger and intrigue."

> -Patricia Gussin, author of *Shadow of Death*

*For Noreen Wald*

Published in the United States by
Beckham Publications Group, Inc.
P.O. Box 4066, Silver Spring, MD 20914
First Edition

The characters and events in this book are fictitious. Any similarity to real persons, living or dead, is coincidental and not intended by the author.

Library of Congress Control Number: 2006926333

ISBN: 0-931761-61-1

10987654321

# The Only Pure Thing

"IT TAKES NERVE TO LIVE IN THIS WORLD"
                                    –John Dos Passos
                                    *The 42$^{nd}$ Parallel*


"Say I help you. What then?"
                                    –Tameka Starnes

The author gratefully acknowledges the help of the following people: Attorneys Stephen Brennwald, Richard Gilbert, DeMaurice Smith, and Willie Alexander. Private Investigators George Steel, Dwayne Stanton, and Trevor Hewick. Editorial Maven Extraordinaire Bonner Menking. Lynda Hill, Megan Plyler, John Jasper, Dorothy Patton, Derek Lowe and Michael Yockel. Also thanks to Barry Beckham, Noreen Wald, Michael Connelly, Darren Coleman and Les Green. My greatest thanks, as always, is to Carolyn and Madeleine.

# The Only Pure Thing

## A Stuart Clay Mystery

## Patrick Hyde

THE **Beckham**
PUBLICATIONS GROUP, INC.
Silver Spring

# CHAPTER 1

MURDER is like real estate. The key to it all is location, location, location. Kill a poor guy in the back streets of Washington, D.C., and they sigh and moan about life in the naked city. But kill a businessman in Georgetown, and you assault commerce. Everyone is pretty nervous right now, so when commerce is assaulted, the prosecution swoops down to guard our nation's capital. If you're the one they finger, you had better have an attorney like me.

Cleveland's need for my services began with Benny's trip to Georgetown's hottest nightspot. By all accounts Benny Batiste had a wonderful time on his late-night jaunt to the Potomac Club. Unfortunately, things took a tumble when Benny walked out the door. Somebody cut his head off in the parking lot.

I inherited Benny's problem a few hours later. Within minutes of his untimely demise, police scoured the city in search of the lady who left the club clutching Benny's arm. Instead, they found Cleveland Barnes, pushing a shopping cart of empty cans down M Street. Mind you, recycle bin theft was no big crime in the District of Columbia. The officers fixed on something else. Cleveland

1

wore a green army raincoat, a battered top hat, and bloodied Bally loafers. As the police discovered Benny without a head or shoes, Cleveland had big trouble, and I didn't sleep.

5:03 A.M. I'd spent the night catching up on paperwork after a three-week trial, and hoped to rest a few hours before going to court. But no such luck.

The cell phone blared. I flicked it open, and he spoke before I could.

"Attorney Stuart Clay?"

"Howard?" Howard Reynolds, Director of the Criminal Justice Act office.

"You're the on-call CJA defender this month," he said. There's been a grisly murder, the public defender has a conflict, and we need you now."

"Not the on-call until September. For God's sake, it's July."

"I know the month," Howard barked back. "This is an emergency, and the Felony One judge on the case wants to appoint you. What part of that don't you understand?"

I paused several seconds, tried to focus. Don't bicker. Foolish for a CJA lawyer to cross Howard Reynolds at any hour. The judge picked me and nothing else mattered.

"Sorry, man. Long night." I sighed and sat up. "A name would help."

"Barnes." His voice lightened. "Cleveland Barnes. They got him wearing the dead man's Bally loafers! Now they're waiting for you, Mr. Clay. Okay?"

"Sure, but I—"

"Sorry Clay, I've got other fish to fry. You wouldn't believe last night's lockup!"

The line went dead.

# CHAPTER 2

DONNING yesterday's shirt and still-knotted tie, I ignored the wrinkled cloth and sour smell, sipped cold coffee from a Styrofoam cup, and stepped into my loafers. Had to stuff the exhaustion. Somewhere. Reaching inside my shirt pocket I found a strand of black licorice, stuck it in my mouth, and gave a determined chomp. Truth is, I knew when I chose this life that 5:00 A.M. phone calls came with the turf.

The fax machine whirred. Howard's cover sheet and police department "PD reports" printed out and came to rest in a stack beside the computer screen. I grabbed my suit coat off the hook on the door, stuffed the faxed pages into the inside pocket, and headed for the elevator.

Seconds later, my rumpled soul and mortal coil passed through the Indiana Avenue exit of 603 Pennsylvania Avenue, north building. I headed across Sixth Street toward the brooding shadow of the D.C. Superior Courthouse, a building that never slept, a building I called Paradise. The concrete form jutted up among the Victorian houses in Judiciary Square. Inside, eighty-

3

five judges and twenty-five magistrate judges tried to assert order over a sixty-three-square-mile parcel of land named the District of Columbia.

I walked through the metal detector, bid how-do to graying marshals, and made my way down toward the lockup. My steps echoed off escalators that wouldn't turn on until 6:00 A.M. Reaching C level, I nodded to another three marshals and an Assistant U.S. Attorney scurrying toward the office where the next day's cases were prepared for presentation in court. I headed down a brightly lit hallway for 200 feet and entered the U.S. Marshal's block.

A yawning marshal sniffed my bar card.

"Mr. Clay," he growled. "I'll warn you, it's a full house. I can't wait for this damned hot weather to break."

He pointed to an orange metal door. An electronic lock buzzed. I pushed the thick door open, and followed the marshal down a long gray corridor toward a place we called the bullpen.

I knew what awaited me. A July night in the district produced a free-fire zone in many of the crumbling Victorian blocks and public housing projects. Street corners, back lots, and playgrounds teamed with the disenfranchised, young black, white, and Latin faces looking for a rush, looking for sex, looking to pull a vaporous smile off a sticky rock smoldering in a tin-foil pipe. These places and people were deadly, yet the seekers came, possessed by both a need for excitement and a nihilistic doubt of all tomorrows. They hung out, talked, smoked, searched for something missing in the day life. Guns were as common as crack dealers handing out little baggies for folded bills. It was normal to witness multiple drug sales, normal to hear the wail of sirens and see the strut of young flesh, normal to hear the sputter of gunfire and view a body fall and a crowd disperse, followed by the cry of "five-O" and the flash of speeding police cars.

The mean streets were raked and groomed—managed, not tamed—by stressed-out cops who fought back the dark tide. Now, in the nearness of morning, the court prepared to assert order back over the mean streets, back over the darkness darker than night. It happened in this building, on this floor, at this place. My gut tensed as the stench and noise of the newly arrested ratcheted upward.

We reached the bullpen. I stared through the bars at Dante's Inferno.

A smirking old man wriggled out of his jumpsuit, raised both arms and howled in laughter at a marshal. Shaking his fist, the marshal hissed into a handheld transmitter for backup. Laughs and catcalls filled the humid air, echoed back through barred cages and off the greasy concrete floor and walls. Inside several divided cages, the mad tide roared. Most in orange suits. Some in white. Some in blue. One in a filthy rain coat. Dozens of the newly arrested congregated in large cells: all shapes, sizes, and colors, more than 200 men and women, strangely awake and excited, reeking the sour stench of street life.

My guide steered me toward another orange door. Another marshal waved from inside a Plexiglas and iron-framed kiosk. I heard the electronic lock buzz. We entered solitary confinement.

Halfway down the gray hall, past several metal doors with portal windows, we stopped. He grabbed a collection of long, thick keys chained to his belt. Clutching the right key, he drove it into the dry lock works and twisted. The marshal opened the door and revealed a chained, handcuffed man seated behind a rickety table.

Pointy dark eyes shone through foliage of crow's feet, gray beard wire, and badly matted Rasta locks. He wore an orange jumpsuit and oversized paper slippers. Certainly not Bally's. I took him to be about fifty-eight, weathered and filthy—but lucid.

After the marshal left and the door clanged shut, the man stared straight at me. Shock surged up my spine. His eyes flickered wildly, and then came back into focus.

He grinned and nodded.

"Running my cart by the Georgetown bars, Snick. Just running my cart. The man just messing with me while I was running my cart."

"What cart?" I tucked a business card into the pocket above his chained hands, sat across from him, and took out my notepad.

"My cart! Run it to find my stuff. My stuff! To serve my holy bridge people! Just minding my own business and the man locked me up!"

"Is that how you got the shoes?" I recalled the few facts Howard had given and pulled out the PD reports that he'd faxed.

"Uh-huh."

"Where were they when you found them?"

His eyes darted away, up to the door, and then returned to me.

"Put it this way, Snick, since they made you my lawyer." He tried to lean over the table and then he whispered. "The dude didn't need them any more."

"You took shoes off a dead guy?"

"Off part of him," he shrugged.

"Part of him?" I waited.

"Dude's head was elsewhere." He said the last word with the inflection of a late-night televangelist. "Elsewhere." He said it again and stared at me. "On top of a parking meter."

# CHAPTER 3

"BAGHDAD on the Potomac?" I imagined the headline. My stomach turned as I thought of the head. Alas, poor Yorick. And in Georgetown?

"Don't you understand that touching a crime scene is a felony?" I said. "You put a bull's-eye on your forehead, and then seem surprised when they pop you with an arrest."

"Dude was altered when I got there, Snick." He stared at me, launching another odd word. "Altered!" He said again, with a strange accent.

"Did you see anyone with him?"

"No sir, too dark in that lot. Just talking to a whore, then I see the dude."

"Was anyone with you when you saw him?"

"Cracker, are you deaf?" He glared at me. "I said the whore. Tiffannie! But she split. Plus there were some kids playing on upside down buckets by the club door. Tap Dancing. But they weren't really with me."

"Did Tiffannie see the body? She was with you when you

discovered the body?"

"I think so."

I wrote the name down.

"How long had you been talking with her?"

"Ten minutes. Maybe more. Ran into her on M Street by the gold-dome bank. She walked with me."

"And what then?"

"Like I said. She split."

"What did you do?"

"I went closer and pulled the beauties off his feet. Then I split too. Going back to the bridge people."

"Who are bridge people?" I braced.

"I live under the Key Bridge."

"Okay." I'd heard that people lived there.

"My people live under the bridge. My people! It is our spiritual right. Ducky. Zebra. Snapper. Shark. They'll tell about me," he said proudly.

"I'll remember the names." Lord knows I would. "I'll find them. But who are they?"

"We're New Columbians, Snick! People think we're stupid trash living under a bridge, but they'll see who we are. Just like Francis Key saw."

He glared at me bitterly. I wondered, bitter enough to kill?

"Why do you call me 'Snick'?" I had to ask. We'd get to Francis Key in a moment.

"That was always your name."

"Always? When always? We just met."

He broke into a broad grin and cocked his head back, laughing up at the ceiling.

"Come on, Snick. I knew you right off, so don't game me. Since we first met—1835 in Lafayette Square. Remember?"

# CHAPTER 4

WHAT did I remember? Indeed I did recall something about Lafayette Square and the year 1835, but I also remembered the rules for seeking a psychiatric study. The bottom line issues concerned whether Cleveland was oriented in reality enough to assist in his own defense.

Obviously, Cleveland lived in his own world. That could be a big problem. But, on the other hand, craziness went with the turf. The so-called forensic screenings were more often than not a forty-day stay at St. Elizabeth's Hospital with no real change at the end. I didn't want this.

Cleveland could still function, could communicate, and seemed to understand his situation. Plus he provided a plausible legal defense: *street person takes shoes off murder victim but didn't do the murder.* Though it was hard to get a bail bond in a murder case like this one, Cleveland had given me this plausible trial defense. My job as appointed counsel required that I prepare a response to the first reading of whatever prompted the police to make an arrest. To answer competently, I needed facts and an idea to frame a defense. Crazy or not, Cleveland had already given me what I needed.

We talked. Cleveland admitted to a long list of arrests and claimed to have a sister in the ministry that often came to his rescue. Panhandling, trespassing in abandoned buildings, shoplifting in all-night drugstores, and other misdemeanors. I could confirm the old cases and family ties when Pretrial Services opened at 9:00 A.M.

Ironically, his criminal past helped. Cleveland had a history of silly misdemeanors like robbing cans from a recycle bin, but no history of violent crime. He lived off discards. He lived under a bridge. His connection with reality seemed marginal, and perhaps that faulty connection resulted in his swiping shoes off a dead body. So what? These facts didn't prove murder.

Unfortunately, we had a greater problem. The economy and terrorism weighed on Cleveland's fate. I could hear the distant fizzle of bromides at the Board of Trade. They might contemplate the loss to tourism and business travel to Georgetown. That could hurt restaurant trade, boutique traffic, and cost jobs and tax base. The powers that be would want to head off bad publicity with quick case closure. Capture the bad guy and bring him to justice. But who was the bad guy? Was it this recycle-bin bandit?

Studying my intrepid client, I sighed and resolved. Guilty or innocent, my job was the same. No quick fixes on my watch.

I explained protocol to Cleveland. As a repeat player he probably already knew the drill, but I couldn't assume so. Above all, I warned Cleveland not to waive his right to silence. He must not talk to the police and must never say anything in open court unless expressly told to by me. Loose lips sank defendants.

Closing my folder, I stood and nodded to Cleveland.

"I'll get back to you later in the morning. Arraignment is at 11:00 A.M. Stay cool."

"Get me out, Snick. I got work to do!" He spoke quietly, despairing at the chains around his arms and wrists.

I rapped twice on the cell door. Within seconds the door swung open, and a troll-sized marshal motioned me out, slammed the door shut, and locked it, then escorted me back through the bullpen. As I walked away, I thought about Cleveland, 1835 and Lafayette Park. Cleveland's comment tweaked a memory. Had I met him before?

# CHAPTER 5

I FELT much better than a forty-something guy with no sleep had a right to feel. That was a benefit of trial work. You're constantly shocked into the next adrenaline surge. You ride the rush, by God, and I loved it.

Nonetheless, I had to gussy-up for court. Crossing Sixth Street, I entered 603 Pennsylvania Avenue and took the elevator to the seventh floor, returning to the law firm of Mitchell & Strong, otherwise known as the Factory. Things were still quiet. The skeleton crew consisted of a few security guards, squinting secretaries doing overflow work, and needy, red-eyed associates starving to please somebody, somewhere, sometime, somehow.

Then there was me, the prosecutor who resigned from the U.S. Attorney's Office and joined the CJA Panel. I punched out a Witness Protection administrator who had expelled my witness from the program without as much as a word of notice to me. The next day, my witness was found hanging from a green garden hose. Because of these circumstances, my license to practice law survived what the Bar Counsel's admonishment referred to as a "lapse in good judgment due to extreme stress." I completed a 100-hour course on anger management. Thereafter, the Mitchell partners brought me on as a criminal law go-to guy in matters that involved the municipal courts.

I liked my new job, but the hours were grueling. Today, after my all-nighter in the office, I needed to run my six-foot, three-inch hulk through the wash and wax.

Grabbing a suit bag and shaving kit, I headed for C sublevel, where the firm's gym included showers and a sauna. The elevator opened onto a beige-and-tan marble foyer, edged in lines of orange and black pearl. I picked up a *Washington Post* from a stack of fresh newspapers on a side table by the locker room door.

Disrobed and seated on the third row of the redwood sauna, I read and sweated gallons. Benny's murder hadn't made the news yet. I expected the late edition to carry a feature article.

Forty minutes later I pushed through the revolving door onto the 600 block of Pennsylvania Avenue, again heading east towards Paradise. The morning gridlock churned in front of the metal detectors at the court's entrance.

Crowds lined up to go through scanning. Complaints spilled out like angry prayers. The uninitiated or out of control grouched at burly marshals. An elderly citizen with missing choppers sputtered, "Hell with that," and stomped off cursing to herself. An out-of-town lawyer in a pin-striped Armani suit alternatively checked his gold Rolex and briefcase, asking no one in particular how attorneys could appear on time with such delays.

In the midst of it all, a few dozen regulars gazed on. They laughed, smoked, shook off the latest hangovers, leaned against the brick barricades to observe this daily promenade. For them, and for me, this was another day in Paradise. Those lucky enough to be above ground should not complain. They should thank God and didn't because they were too inexperienced to conceive of the real danger around them. I envied their naiveté.

By and by I made my way through a metal detector. Cleared to pass, I waded through the crowded court halls to the escalators ratcheting downward to the lower levels.

A large crowd huddled around a dimly lit bulletin board known as the Wailing Wall. This cloister of the misbegotten included the families, friends, and lovers of the accused. They eyed the *new drop*—a withered, hanging list that told of those just arrested and their alleged crimes.

I slid through these citizens, instinctively breathing through my mouth to avoid the acrid smell of anxiety, fear, and alcohol sweat. Peering over the shoulder of an obese blonde woman in a skin-tight T-shirt, I searched for my notice of appointment. There, on line sixty-two, the case report read:

**CLEVELAND BARNES—883565-MURDER I, THEFT I, AND ANY OTHER OFFENSE—STUART GATZ CLAY, BAR NO. 399183**

I squeezed past and copied from another column reporting the name of the arresting officer and the police district. I expected the case to be based at the second district, but the officer's name surprised me: Detective Rhondo Touhey out of VCU, the Violent Crimes Unit. My best friend, almost best man, and sparring partner at Fifth Street's Falcon Karate School.

I walked across the hall to the Pretrial Services Agency, known as the PSA, a large facility with computers eternally spewing out reports stating the vital statistics, addresses, and prior arrests and convictions of persons in the lockup. PSA seemed to be staffed by some of the finest looking women in the city. Today's group proved to be no exception. I spotted Carmen Alavaro, a statuesque Latina about five feet, five inches with long black hair tied back in a ponytail and a jolliness that defied the dour surroundings of criminal court. Her almond eyes lit up from across the room, and she pointed a petite index finger at a big stack of reports, declaring, "He's in there, Stuart." She turned around to take more reports off the printer, but ventured a sly grin over her shoulder. She knew I'd still be looking.

Thumbing through a stack on an unattended counter, I grabbed Cleveland's report. An eight-page printout listed various aliases, former addresses, convictions, and other information about Cleveland Barnes. Known family reported as Ivyroot Malveaux of 403 46th Place, S.E. in the District of Columbia. On page four I found a listing of forensic data reflecting a two-year stint at St. Elizabeth's Hospital following a diagnosis of schizophrenia.

I'd have to check the computer in the lawyers lounge to confirm the information in this report on the Clerk of Court's information system. I waived goodbye to *mi amiga*. Before heading for the lawyers' lounge I ducked into the CJA mailroom, flicked open my cell phone, found the name RHONDO in my directory, and punched the "send" button. He picked up on the first ring.

"Rhondo."

"What's up, Kentucky?" His Jamaican baritone filled my ear.

"I'm defense on Cleveland Barnes. Give me a statement?"

"They put you on Barnes?"

"God must be punishing one of us. Probably you. Did you see the rap sheet on Cleveland Barnes? Ever occur to you that he's just a street man that stole some shoes? I mean--"

"Don't mean to cut you off, Stuart, but I've got to meet Special Detail papering. We'll talk later. Take it from me, my man. This thing isn't about a pair of shoes."

"Could you clarify that obtuse remark. My man?"

"Later, dude." My *good friend* hung up on me.

# CHAPTER 6

NOT about a pair of shoes? I jerked the door to the mailroom open and nearly collided with a lady reaching for the doorknob. "Sorry." I nodded and stomped past her, pledging to hunt Rhondo down. If the case wasn't about shoes, he would bloody well tell me what it was about!

But first I had to compare the court's criminal division records with the PSA sheet. I headed for the computer in the lawyers' lounge.

The halls teamed with anxious folk waiting for arraignment proceedings to begin. An additional stream of people headed in and out of the Pretrial Services' drug-testing facility. Husky marshals wearing off-the-rack suits mingled with women from Pretrial Services, all in a mosey to their newest task. Three young toughs careened down the hall in unison, stepping to some unseen choreographer. A thin old fellow sporting Coke-bottle glasses asked everyone in sight if they knew the attorney appointed for his grandson. A young black man with blue jeans falling off his rear-end played with a chirping little boy. A bearded man wearing orange prison clothes sat in a wheelchair swami-style, with legs and arms crossed, while an older marshal pushed him down the hall. The orange clad *swami* scowled at everyone walking by and hissed obscenities at the old man transporting him. These and others flew by, slipped into my subconscious with a bang and clatter. I opened the door to the lawyers' lounge.

What a mess! Newspapers lay all over rickety tables and chairs, and the rug was a tie-dye of coffee spills and who knows what else. A wall-length bulletin board contained dozens of old outdated postings with no conceivable importance. Attorneys mingled in groups of two and three, complaining about nasty black robes and sneaky prosecutors, making the most of tattered metal and vinyl couches and chairs, two battered conference tables, and three telephones.

Harry White slept under an open newspaper. He snoozed on an old couch against the far wall. From across the room, I could smell the wheeze of stale whiskey breath blowing out from beneath a withered sports page. Harry was no dummy, but liquor proved a great equalizer among the tragically afflicted. Harry's presence warned us all. We could join the dinosaurs, more extinct than ever because of the CJA Panel oversight, could fall down into that tar pit, could tumble face first into dreams, and then forget that we had any dreams at all.

While I waited in line for the computer, I transcribed police department and court file numbers and PSA codes into my files. After several minutes my turn came. I logged on. File links to the District of Columbia Criminal Information System (CIS) database filled the screen. Each listed Cleveland's name, police department identification, or PDID, number, as well as birth date, a number for the particular case, the charges, the disposition, and the sentence imposed by the court. It took several minutes and I had to restart the computer once, but I printed out all of Cleveland's court records.

Obviously, Cleveland had issues. The PSA and CIS records indicated that he'd been charged in thirty-two misdemeanor crimes ranging from shoplifting to trespassing. He'd been convicted in twenty-seven of these cases. But still, he never had a single violent crime. Not a single one!

A thump on my right shoulder broke concentration.

"Are you Lawyer Clay? The CJA man said that Clay was big

and dark haired like you and that I'd find him in this room." An unseen Louisiana Cajun drawl filled my ears.

"That's me." I turned around. An attractive older woman stared at me. She wore a long white dress, a bright multi-colored scarf knitted through a yard of straightened hair, and had the same piercing eyes as my new client. She held out her hand and, as I shook it, an odd shiver passed up my spine. Something popped and crackled in my skull.

"I'm Cleveland's sister, Ivyroot Malveaux," she drawled. "You can call me Ruthie. This is my friend Amanda, Amanda Sewell." She pointed to a woman beside her. "We've come for Cleveland."

Amanda nodded. Probably around the same age as her companion, but without the same spark.

I stood up from the computer, yielded my chair to the next of four lawyers waiting to search records. The one behind her started bickering about whose turn it was. I stuffed the printed sheets into my briefcase, and thanked Ruthie and Amanda for coming to court.

We headed across the hall to the largest interview room available in Paradise, the courthouse cafeteria. This study in green paisley vinyl and matching carpet pile sometimes smelled like wet dog. Today a humid ambiance from the kitchen filled the room with an aroma of cardiac-arresting meats. Luckily, we weren't eating.

We needed a table away from the police and anyone else who might intentionally or accidentally hear us. I settled on a spot in an outside corner of the room where two glass dividers joined. Recalling my discussion with Cleveland, I opened my notebook, reviewed a few notes, and tried to conceal puzzlement.

"Cleveland said that you were a minister." She didn't fit my idea of a minister.

"I'm a mambo."

"I beg your pardon?"

"A mambo, lawyer Clay. A Voodoo priestess."

"Voodoo?" I studied her face. Not a joke.

"Let's not get into it too much," she sighed. "Voodoo is very misunderstood."

"Well, please explain just a little." Since the misunderstanding parties included me. "It might come up if you want to have Cleveland stay at your home while this case is going on."

"That is exactly what I want, for Cleveland to come home. My home is stable. Voodoo is a religion like any other. There are believers like Amanda and I all over this country. African slaves founded Voodoo to combine tribal magical practices with Catholicism. We feel a certain voice, a certain power, a spiritual tie that is much more immediate than normal Christianity. That power is around us right now and makes things happen in our midst. To celebrate that voice, we started the Capital City Voodoo Society."

"I see." I didn't see at all.

What I did see were two warm bodies. They might vouch for a street guy who needed any friend he could find. Please, I prayed, let's move on.

"We're not crazy, lawyer Clay." Amanda said. "Voodoo combines two very powerful religions. History put our people in that combination. Our faith makes sense of it."

"I understand," I replied. "Or at least I understand enough so that if the issue comes up in court I can explain it. But let's talk about the case. Cleveland has been arrested for murder. I need your help. I need information on him and somebody to vouch for his ties to the community."

"My brother's a lot of things, lawyer Clay. He's sick in his head. Gets drunk and preaches. But he is not a killer. I'll tell that judge man myself!"

"That's right, lawyer," Amanda chimed. "Cleavey drinks too much and says some strange words. That boy wouldn't hurt a fly."

"Do you think they are going to convict him of murder?" Ruthie frowned and wound hair around her index finger.

"Too early to say," I replied. "Certainly not today. Today they present Cleveland to the court, read a summary of key facts, and decide bail. They won't convict him of anything."

"But do you think they will convict him?" Ruthie persisted. "Does the DA have a case?"

"Not on what I have seen so far. Cleveland was arrested wearing the shoes of a murdered man. Doesn't prove murder. He was out hunting for throwaways and he found some shoes."

"Where did he find the shoes?" Ruthie asked the obvious.

"I'm not at liberty to discuss that," I said. "Let's talk about Cleveland. Did he grow up here?"

Ruthie pursed her lips in annoyance. She wanted to know

where Cleveland found the shoes, but I couldn't discuss it. She studied me with mild reproach, but said nothing.

"We're not from D.C. We came from Louisiana in 1973. Met Amanda here and her man Wendell—God rest his soul. We went to work in Wendell's grocery, but Cleavey was always in trouble."

"Grocery? Do you mean Sewell Produce?" I knew the store.

"That's right. I had to be strong for us both. Cleveland constantly got into trouble."

"You own Sewell Produce over on Rhode Island Avenue NE?" I turned to Amanda, and she nodded. "Don't you sponsor a basketball team in the D.C. Youth League?"

"My son is in charge of that."

"And he's Adrian Sewell, a tall, thin guy that looks like a GQ model?" I smiled.

"That's my son." Amanda smiled back. "And Cleveland is Adrian's godfather."

"Adrian once served as a character witness in one of my criminal trials," I said. It never ceased to amaze me what a small town D.C. really was.

We talked for several minutes, tracing Cleveland's life from 1973 to the present. Both women cared about Cleveland, but lamented his uncanny ability to get himself into trouble. Lots of minor things added up over the years, became enough to exhaust the people around him. Even so, these two would help if they could. I wrote fast, collecting as much detail as they could give me. Ruthie offered to appear before the magistrate judge in C-10, if necessary, and eagerly agreed to let Cleveland stay with her if he were released.

The conversation proved helpful because they explained a lot about my new client's past and could possibly serve as custodians for Cleveland, at some time in the future if not today. But I had several things to do before the calendar call—had to go to the U.S. Attorney's courthouse office, had to meet again with Cleveland.

We agreed to continue discussions after the court hearing. As I started to walk away, Ruthie asked me to wait for a moment.

"What is it?" I said. "Sorry to run, but I really have a lot more to do on this case before it is called in court."

"Just a moment." Ruthie raised her hand, seeming to collect her words. She stared away for a moment, then focused her eyes on me. "Lawyer Clay. I need to say something, need to make something clear. Cleveland has his faults, but he couldn't have done this. If they try to make a scapegoat out of my sick brother, we will not take it lying down. I promise you that we will vindicate our rights!"

"What does that mean?" Vindication is a fickle thing, and I wanted a heads-up.

"It means," she said, in a matter-of-fact tone, "if they don't do the right thing by Cleveland, I will shut this courthouse down."

# CHAPTER 7

My cell phone rang and flashed "JACK PAYNE." The senior partner at Mitchell & Strong. My boss. Had to take his call.

Ruthie's eyes burned into me.

"We've got to talk some more before you do anything," I said. "But please. Hold on a second." I hurried over to the rear wall of windows by the C Street exit, where phone reception was best.

"Jack?" Hoped we hadn't lost connection.

"Hello, Stuart. It's Muriel." Jack's throaty assistant. "I know you're busy, but it's about the Cleveland Barnes case."

"You already heard about the new case?" How the devil?

"Judge Robideaux called the boss. The news people are already pounding the judge for answers and he wants to make sure that man gets a fair defense."

"So the judge called my boss to complain about me?"

"It's not like that, Stuart. Not at all."

"Okay, sorry. It's not about me, right?" Like hell it wasn't. But a Felony One judge had to feel a special burden to make sure an accused murderer got decent help in a case like this one. I turned from the window. Ruthie and Amanda didn't follow me out of the cafeteria and were nowhere to be seen.

"Not that the judge doesn't have faith in you." Muriel added. "But the government will probably come at this with several attorneys, you know. So Jack committed to giving you a pro bono backup second counsel from the firm."

"A second lawyer for free, huh? Wow." Not unprecedented, but unusual. "Somebody from our firm?" An uncomfortable sensation climbed up my back.

"Parcival Diel. He used to work for the Prince George's county public defender's office. Plenty of experience."

"Percy a PD?" My neck knotted. Public defender, indeed! Percy Diel was the son of the firm's largest client. A lot of people at the Factory wondered if Percy had ever worked at anything ever in his life.

"You've got a meeting with Mr. Diel this afternoon at 2:30 to discuss the arrangement. Call me if we need to move it."

"Thanks, Muriel. I'll take it up with Mr. Barnes. He has to consent, you know."

"Really? Fancy that."

"So long, Muriel." I snapped the phone shut. "Yes, *really*, Muriel. Fancy that," I muttered to myself.

I peeked into the cafeteria and lawyers' lounge. No sign of Ruthie and Amanda. Had to find them later.

Co-counsel? I rolled the term around on my tongue. Didn't much like it. Shaking off the frustration, I made my way to the courthouse office of the U.S. Attorney. Had to find Rhondo and see if he had more of the police reports on Cleveland.

A maze of coatless prosecutors, cops, and secretaries worked behind bulletproof glass, crouched over two dozen desks and computer screens in a large open room. No receptionist. I waited. After a few minutes Sergeant G.G. Nelson turned around from a prosecutor seated at a computer and noticed me.

G.G. could have easily been mistaken for an ill-nourished homeless person. A superior mind with a superior mask, this first-rate detective proved to be one of the best undercover cops around and one of the best martial artists I'd ever sparred with. G.G. needed his fighting skills to survive. He often worked deep undercover with people who would kill him in a hot second. Now shooting at me with his index finger, G.G. walked over to the window and slid open the document slot.

"Dude!" He reached over the counter and shook my hand.

"Been here all night, man?"

G.G. grinned at me through his ten-day shadow.

"Wish I'd spent my night someplace this safe. Who are you hunting for?"

"Rhondo Touhey. I represent Cleveland Barnes on a murder at the Potomac Club over in the Second District. Rhondo's the man. Any idea who the prosecutor is?"

"Rhondo's doing paperwork and getting some warrants signed. Check C-10. That's a Homicide and Major Crime Section case. I don't know which assistant is assigned to the 2D beat." G.G. turned around to the sea of desks. "Petey? Who's got the Potomac Club murder?"

Assistant U. S. Attorney Peter Mathis peered up from his pile of paper and squinted at me. We'd done a few trials across from one another about four years back. He looked exhausted.

"Clay." Peter squinted. "You defense?"

"Yeah."

He studied me for a moment, and then shook his head.

"It's Lisa Stein, man. What you wanted to hear, right?"

"I'll live with it. Thanks." Just what I wanted, indeed: a major case against the ex-fiancé I hadn't spoken to in four years. I half-saluted through the glass and headed off for courtroom C-10.

Lisa Stein. Throughout the late '90s, Lisa and I had been cohorts doing homicide and violent crime trials in the U.S. Attorney's office. She came from a well-to-do family that probably wanted her in corporate America. I'd come into the office as a made-over high school dropout from Kentucky. Juries liked us. Somehow, we clicked on other levels. After two years I proposed marriage. I thought we'd spend our lives chasing bad guys together, but a bureaucrat and a garden hose brought everything crashing down.

Nineteen-year-old Tameka Starnes lived in Wheeler Road's Liberty housing project, a drug-infested development in Southeast Washington. She watched gang murders out of her bedroom window. As the prosecutor on one of those murders, I went door to door with my investigators looking for someone who saw the killing. Shy Tameka stepped forward to identify the gang members in my case and a half-dozen other murders. She feared for her life, but wanted to do the right thing. I coaxed her, quietly pled with her, and explained that the system couldn't operate unless citizens stepped forward to tell the truth. Finally, Tameka agreed to testify. She'd be a golden witness.

Word of Tameka's cooperation somehow made it to the street, and she feared for her life. I got her into the Witness Protection Program. Initially, it looked like everything would work. Tameka lived in a motel out in College Park, Maryland and spent her days watching soap operas. She'd been strictly forbidden to return to D.C., and that worked okay. Then another problem popped up. To be in witness protection, Tameka had to drug test. She tested positive for marijuana. Tameka said it was caused by secondhand smoke from when a new boyfriend from the motel came to visit. No matter.

"Three strikes and she's out," the administrator in charge had said.

"You do that and she's dead," I'd replied.

For several maddening weeks, I tried to resolve the situation. In the end, they expelled Tameka, and with no warning to me.

After being unceremoniously expelled from the Witness Protection Program on a Wednesday evening, Tameka was last seen in College Park, walking down University Boulevard in the direction of Adelphi, Maryland. Early Thursday morning a jogger found her little body hanging by a garden hose at a picnic stop on Beach Drive in Washington, D.C.'s Rock Creek Park.

The witness I persuaded to testify relied on my word, but I couldn't deliver. She stood up to evil and got a garden hose noose for thanks.

No witness, no case. The defendants responsible for the murder in my case, and at least seven others, smirked as they strutted out of the courtroom. By then, I'd resigned—after punching the genius who sent Tameka to her death. Then the inevitable happened when I gained acceptance to the CJA Panel. Lisa handed my ring back. Hadn't spoken to me since.

I'd avoided Lisa for four years and expected she'd done the same. Now this. But I couldn't let it interfere. Had to focus.

If they filed papers on the case and charged Cleveland, Lisa would seek to lock up Cleveland until trial. Had to try and block that. Not very likely that I would succeed given the pretrial release laws that applied in a murder case. Still, I had to try.

"Counselor," Chief Clerk Lester Peabody called to me as I

walked into courtroom C-10. He had a head the size of a bowling ball, no neck, and a five-foot, ten-inch frame that probably weighed in at over 300 pounds. Lester dressed impeccably in custom shirts, leather suspenders, and jeweled cufflinks. He had good humor, patience, and the iron personality needed to preside over courtroom C-10. He could be your best friend until he was your worst enemy—but he only became your enemy if you insulted the dignity and decorum of the court.

"So the catfish were jumping last night." I walked up the aisle between rows of mostly-empty benches.

"You know it," Lester said. "We've got a hell of a big lockup. Look at this stack of case files." He gestured at the table in front of his raised desk. A half dozen clerks busily organized what looked to be more than a hundred legal-sized manila folders. One folder per case. Before the morning ended, each case would be carefully announced by Lester, each prisoner would be presented, and the U.S. Attorney would charge or dismiss the case against each defendant.

"Howard Reynolds summoned me bright and early, and I've been around since 5:20 this morning." I continued down the carpeted aisle.

"Heard all about that, counselor. Pretty unusual, but a lot of people had their sleep interrupted last night." Lester raised his brows. "Including the chief of police and the medical examiner. I bet you even the mayor got woke up. I'm sure our morning will be interesting." He gestured at the front left pew.

Kirby Barron, the *Washington Post* illustrator, sat in the front row with his open kit of sketching pencils and a large paper pad, ready to draw. He showed up on high-profile cases because cameras were barred from court. Already he'd sketched the judge's bench, Lester's station in front of it, the array of counsel tables, and the door that led from the lockup to the courtroom.

Rhondo was nowhere to be seen. I decided to check outside, but first had to store my briefcase. I moved into the audience area onto a walkway between the Plexiglas divider and the front row of benches, and then stored my twenty-five-pound briefcase underneath. Back at the rear exit, I paused and studied the courtroom, wondered what would unfold. Then I pushed through the double doors, collided with Lisa Stein, and crashed to the floor.

# CHAPTER 8

"NICE to run into you." I sat up and eyed the coffee stains on my white shirt. "Still take two creams and an Equal?"

"God, I'm sorry. Are you okay?"

"It's the business we're in." Sort of true. Maybe this bit would get me some pretrial discovery. "The dry cleaner's tab will go on the Barnes bill."

"So you know I'm on the Cleveland Barnes case?" She brushed a lock of thick brown hair behind her ear. "You don't want me off the case because of . . . before?"

She studied me, ill at ease, trying to address the issue of our broken engagement interfering in the case without showing any feelings about that failed relationship.

"I'm not going to object, Lisa." I stood up, tried to blot up some of the coffee with my handkerchief. "I know you're not going to cut me any breaks. You know I'm not giving you any. Expect the fight of your life."

She studied me for a moment, saying nothing. Mean as it sounded, I suddenly realized that I didn't have feelings to hide—

other than relief that I didn't marry someone as traditional as Lisa. It never would have worked, and I'd have messed up her life and my own.

"I'm glad you won't object," she frowned.

"Got time to discuss it? I have a right to know what you're alleging happened."

"You don't want to go change that?" She pointed at my sopping shirt.

"Nope. What you can tell me is more important."

"Just for a minute." She glanced at her watch and wheeled the black litigation case to the corner of the room. "I don't want to be late when the Magistrate judge comes in. We don't have the statement of facts from the police yet, but I can tell you about it." She frowned again, motioned me over.

"You mean a statement from Rhondo Touhey, right?" I walked over close to her.

"Right. From Rhondo. Do you want to hear my unofficial summary?"

I nodded yes.

"Okay, here goes. The murder victim was a New York businessman on a night out at the Potomac Club. We think he was there with a prostitute but she hasn't been located. Woman in her early twenties, attractive blonde. He got drunk. She gave him oral sex under the table."

"Some businessman," I said. "What then?"

"I guess the crowd and staff just ignored what they were doing. The two didn't really bother anyone. After an hour and a half and several drinks, they paid up and left together. Minutes later, a college student walking down the sidewalk finds Batiste's head on a parking meter. The body was in the parking lot. No sign of the woman. Maybe the lady left him at the door. Maybe not. None of the cars in the lot belonged to him. No car keys recovered. All we know is that somebody got him in the parking lot. No witnesses yet. No murder weapon recovered, but, judging from the serration, it had to be an ax or a damned heavy sword.

"The head was completely cut off," she continued. "I'm told this is not a simple thing to do. Somebody mounted it on a parking meter. I'm told this would have been hard as well. Your client got arrested about twenty minutes after the estimated time of death. He was wearing the decedent's shoes."

"Any statements?"

She reviewed notes and papers in the case file. The manila folder seemed fresh, but the file was very thick for a new case. Too thick.

"Don't have exact quotes," she waffled. "Your client said something about being on a mission for Mabutek and seeking justice for the people who founded the District of Columbia."

"Doesn't sound like a confession?"

"Might be a motive or a war cry," she said.

Decapitations for Mabutek? Nothing in Cleveland's past supported this.

"Why the fat file, Lisa? The guy hasn't been dead a dozen hours yet."

"Ask me something I can answer, Stuart. The Court of Appeals doesn't require the government to disclose facts based on having a fat file, and I'm in a rush."

"Regardless of your rush, the Court of Appeals does have rules requiring you to share evidence including the documentary evidence—which you are apparently carrying. What is it?" I pointed at the file.

"I'm not saying I'm carrying anything." She stepped back. "You got suspicions? Get me a letter demanding a conference with a bill of particulars. I'll review it."

"Nothing like a nice chat among old friends." Her posturing started to annoy me.

"Nice chat?" Lisa's eyes narrowed. "Look, Stuart, you're the one who walked. Don't talk to me about nice anything."

"Sorry for valuing the life of Tameka Starnes," I hissed back. "More prosecutors ought to buck the stupid rules in that office. Now do you have any physical evidence?"

"Okay, Perry Mason. How about a pair of bloody shoes?"

"I'm aware of the shoes." I ignored her tone. "What else?"

"Nothing else now. You know Judge Robideaux is going to lock me into giving you everything you can legally ask for, and we both know you're going to ask for everything. So what's the rush?"

"The rush, as you well know, is because of conditions of release and evidence that shows how strong your case is or is not. I assume that you'll want to jail Barnes until trial?"

"Wouldn't you?"

"No." I locked my eyes on hers now, wondering if this case would turn into payback against me. "I wouldn't want him jailed. Not if I thought he was just some poor street guy that needed something to put on his feet!" I tried to keep her looking at me but she broke away. So I continued.

"You have a requirement to give me a statement of probable cause for this arrest. I'd appreciate that before the hearing. For what it's worth, I've verified his community ties and address."

"Right," Lisa said. "You and I both know an address is the least of this guy's problems." She swung around suddenly, stuck her file in the black litigation case, and tilted the case onto its rollers. "See you later."

"Remember the statement of probable cause, Lisa. I don't want to take the court's time reading it during the hearing."

Saying nothing, Lisa wheeled her case past me and through the doors into courtroom C-10. Her fragrance teased my nostrils as it always did, but now it felt like a soppy memory. I studied the luscious form moving beneath the gray business suit. It hurt to watch her pull that black box down the aisle. But I'd travel no aisles with Lisa.

The black box moved out of sight.

# CHAPTER 9

TURNING to walk away, my thoughts raced from the old to the new as I spotted my investigator Cyndi Oh strutting down the hallway toward the cafeteria, sporting her go-to-court blue business blouse and skirt. This Asian lady's legs could cause a mistrial, and her curves could stop a train, but that only began to describe Cyndi's appeal. She was smart, funny, and had a thing for me. Or so it seemed in recent days. And maybe I had a thing for her, too.

My intrepid investigator held a third degree black belt and belonged to the same dojo as Rhondo and I did. In fact, her family started the school. Cyndi thrived in the street world. She left a paralegal job at the Department of Justice headquarters to do criminal defense investigation.

An ocean of citizens sporting clip-on juror badges slowed my advance toward Cyndi. Even so, the crowd seemed to part for her, and she sauntered through like a runway model. Brushing long black hair off her pretty face, Cyndi flicked a wave and winked.

"Counselor?" I said. "You giving an opening statement

today?" She was a statement, all right.

"Very funny. Did Tyrone's bail brief get filed?"

"Finished it around 4:30 this morning. It's in my bag to take up after a C-10 hearing. Listen, I have a major new case. Guy got capped up by the Potomac Club."

"Don't you just hate it when that happens?" She made a slicing motion across her throat. "Actually saw that in the paper. We're in for a ride on that one."

"The paper? Which one?"

"Final Edition of the *Post.* In the metro section. Our man Fred Collins. Says your dead guy bought it outside the Potomac Club. There was unspecified reference to some other evidence linking the guy arrested to the crime. Sounds pretty grisly. Also said the dead man was with some New York trucking company. Hinted around about a suspicious relationship with a certain organization in which everyone's name ends in a vowel."

"The Mafia?"

"Right."

"Now there is a defense for my street person—the killing was mob-related!"

"Yeah, really." She squinted. "Surprised you hadn't heard, Stuart. You've got to read the article."

"Damn straight! But we're in front of Godzilla in fifteen minutes. Got the *Post*?" I didn't have time to go outside and buy one at the paper machine.

"Sure. Just follow me for a second."

"Right. Any cops named?"

"Your buddy Rhondo-mon and his partner Zeus is on it too."

"Zeus would be automatic." Homicides in D.C. were always worked by partners. Jesus "Zeus" Martinez was a brainy muscleman teamed with Rhondo.

"The *Post* said that a lot of the Second District techs and Mobile Crime Unit guys were also at the scene, and the chief tech threw some of the blue suits from downtown out of the taped-off area. Claimed they were compromising the evidence. Over here," she pointed.

Moving through the crowd into the cafeteria, we went to the closest uncluttered tabletop. Cyndi opened her briefcase, pulled out a copy of the *Post*, and handed it to me.

"Merry Christmas. Who's your *persecutor*?"

31

"The prosecutor, spelled p-r-o-s, is one Lisa Stein."

"My favorite over-the-hill cheerleader!" Cyndi knew Lisa was my ex-fiancée. "Too damned wholesome for my taste. But go to it, big guy. Just don't go fraternizing with the enemy." She outlined a bulge over her stomach. "It might complicate things—in more ways than one."

"Smart ass!" More ways than one? I studied her twinkling eyes. "What brings you to Paradise, anyway?"

"Hockmeyer's got a cocaine distribution trial with Judge Adams. Fifth time up. The *persecutor* assigned is in trial already, so our jury selection is on hold at the moment. Probably wind up getting continued at lunch. While we're waiting I'll have two status hearings with Hockmeyer."

"Okay. What's the trial your prosecutor is doing?" I needed to get Cyndi away from the other attorney she worked for. If the prosecutor stayed busy in another trial, chances of a continuance were excellent.

"It's DeMaurice Jones against Melvin Dillard and Patty Newborn in that 7-Eleven robbery-murder trial. They got Big Reggie as their judge and it's a pretty ugly case. From what I could see, the defendants were sunk and must have gone to trial because the only plea offer was to life without parole. I think Dillard and Newborn have several post-trial motions already cooked up and some custom-made jury instructions that will give the Court of Appeals something to think about no matter who wins."

"So you don't think Hockmeyer and Jones are going to trial today?"

"Not likely."

"If the cocaine distribution trial gets continued, can you go to Georgetown with me after my hearing? I could use you today and probably this evening."

"Of course. As I say, my guess is that I'll get out at noon. But I got to get back up there now, Stuart." She squeezed my arm and winked again, then launched off. I watched her disappear into the crowd.

I sat on a green vinyl bench and thumbed through the *Post* until I found the article:

**NEW YORK BUSINESSMAN**
**DECAPITATED IN GEORGETOWN**

The *Post* relayed basic information about the murder and stated that Benny was seen leaving the club with an unknown woman. Seen by whom? The reporter, Fred Collins, had interviewed me several times when I'd been president of the trial lawyers. Later, he joined the Falcon Dojo where a few dozen defense attorneys, prosecutors, and cops learned to defend themselves. Now Fred was family. I made a note to call him later. Likely that we'd have information to swap on the case.

Cyndi had given an accurate account of the article. Benny Batiste worked as a manager at Seabreeze Trucking, located in the Bronx borough of New York. In 2000, he'd been an un-indicted codefendant in a smuggling prosecution filed against members of the Spilotro Family. I smirked to myself. These were among the "few facts" Lisa had overlooked mentioning, but no doubt knew about. This explained at least some of the bulk in her new court jacket. Not information about the defendant, but, most likely, information about the victim.

The article went on to say that a defendant, identified only as a homeless man, had been arrested. He was to be formally presented to a magistrate judge in D.C. Superior Court today.

I smiled to myself thinking of all the ways we could use the Mafia angle in our defense. Street people weren't typically used as hit men. So who else had it in for Benny? What was Benny's business in town? Was the missing woman competition or the competition's soldier? Who did he come to see? Certainly not Cleveland Barnes!

# CHAPTER 10

To hell with Rhondo. Things looked better for Cleveland. I'd have a lot to throw into the vat of trial preparation. After the morning's hearing, I'd need to get a complete background portrait of Benny Batiste and comb the crime scene and neighborhood.

11:07 A.M. Being late for court could be deadly in Paradise, even in C-10, where there were lots of preliminary matters. I rushed back, hoping to slip behind the courtroom to the holding cell and talk to Cleveland while the D.C. Corporation Counsel's calendar was called. Assistant Marshal Whitey Jacobs, a tall, fit African-American man, waived me back.

"Attorney coming back to see prisoner in holding cell G!" he called down the hall.

"Roger." A speaker blast emitted a burst of static, and an electric lock released. I pushed it open, passing into a large open cell structure. A group of deputies sat behind a raised glass-enclosed structure looking like sports announcers in a stadium. Before them was a large room divided into a variety of waiting cells with about 200 prisoners divided into rooms made of three walls of iron bars and a concrete back wall.

Marshals led prisoners to the hallway leading to C-10. Soon it would begin. Surging forward, inching forward, everything pulsed now with a certain rhythm and anticipation, a steady flow of orange suits working their way toward the door and into arraignment court like widgets on a moving belt.

I waved at the marshals behind the glass, hoping for direction to Cleveland. He had to be close by. One fellow wearing earphones and a microphone waved back and pointed to a cell on the far wall. Cell G6, temporary home of Cleveland Barnes.

Walking over, I nodded to Cleveland. He smiled back, this time saying nothing.

What was he thinking? Rather than jump into the follow-up interview drill, I stood and looked at him and waited. We studied each other.

Three minutes later Cleveland spoke.

"I believe you are a New Columbian."

"Maybe I am," I said, though I had no idea what he meant.

"I can feel you are." He pointed to a bump on his left elbow. "I got one growing here, you see. Here's the tip of its left heel, but he isn't ready yet."

"That's interesting," I responded, again considering the dismal possibility of a psychiatric screening. Did I have much of a choice? I thought of the questions a judge would ask. "Got to go over some stuff, Cleveland. First, where do you live?"

"Under the Key Bridge with my people. I keep the TV hooked up to the boathouse." He grinned. "You could say I'm the master of entertainment!" He laughed.

"What?"

"I got a TV under the bridge," Cleveland announced. "A wide screener hooked to electric and satellite."

"Great. Do you have any family in the area?"

"One sister."

"What's her name?"

"Her name is Ivyroot Malveaux."

"Any nickname?"

"Ruthie."

"What year is it?"

"2007. What's your problem, Snick?"

"What city are we in?"

"It's Washington, D.C. Come on, man."

"Don't worry about it. I have to ask." But I'd guess, as the psychiatrists put it, that Cleveland would be found "oriented to time and place." He had some pretty odd ideas, but we would probably make it through the presentment hearing.

"Are you a vet?" I chided myself. Missed this one before. Sometimes the Pretrial Services reports were wrong.

"Sort of."

"What do you mean by 'sort of?'"

"I fight in all the wars. They just keep happening. You should know that by now!" His voice began to rise, and I felt his hostility. Looking behind me, I made sure the marshals weren't too close.

"Why should I know it?" I pressed him.

"Don't jive me, Snick. I see it. I see the rays in that aura. You are one of us from back in Lafayette Square and Georgia. You remembered 1835. You are a New Columbian!"

# CHAPTER 11

"WHAT'S that mean?" I stared at Cleveland.

"Counselor, we have to clear the block." A short red-haired marshal with a flattop tugged at my sleeve. "Magistrate judge's on her way down."

I reminded Cleveland not to say a word in court. He smiled.

I hurried out of lockup and back into the courtroom. Several reporters from the *Post,* the *Washington Times,* and other papers congregated in the left front benches. Her honor had not yet emerged from chambers. I slid back to the right front bench, sat down, and pulled my briefcase out from beneath.

Over the next five minutes a few hundred people streamed into C-10 and filled the audience seats. Aside from the press, the first two rows were filled mostly by CJA lawyers, the contract attorneys who handled more than 80 percent of the criminal cases in the District. They were an ocean of blue, gray, and tan suits and cordovan brief bags. Behind the CJA lawyers were ten rows of benches now seating the wives and babies' mommas—the latter being a common reference to the unmarried mothers who came to court carrying the young children of a defendant. Then there were the real mommas, the occasional grandparent, and other family members of the arrested come to offer what help they could.

Inside the well of the court, two prosecutors worked with a paralegal around a table stacked with case files. Lisa would come later with the special detail crew, the elite soldiers of the prosecution.

Half a dozen large marshals of both sexes mulled around the court bar and the bulletproof windows. As usual, they were better tailored than most of the lawyers.

Without warning, Lester barked out: "All rise! Attorneys having matters before the Honorable Irene Jones please come to order. This honorable court is now in session."

Magistrate Judge Jones swooped up to her bench from a curtain behind the bench and bid good morning to the crowd and four clerks seated before her. With the voice and style of a forty-something valley girl, this black robe had wavy reddish hair, good looks, and as even a temper as one could expect in the legal conveyor belt of arraignment court, where even the best of us were known to get a might bit testy. I sort of liked her, but she could be ferocious and, to honor this trait, I'd nicknamed her Godzilla.

Leaning over her bench, the magistrate judge spoke to a young female clerk then turned to her right and conversed with a Pretrial Services worker and a young man who I surmised was her legal assistant. Meanwhile, the door to lockup opened and two marshals led the first of the prisoners to seats along the wall.

The standard routine began with the calling of minor criminal cases, and would slowly lead to the ranks of kidnap and violent crimes. The D.C. Corporation Counsel prosecuted the minor offenses, which typically carried a maximum of ninety days in prison. The U.S. Attorney's office handled everything else.

Lester adjusted a microphone with his massive hand, nodded at the head marshal, looked back to the magistrate judge, then turned around and began the drill.

"Calling the D.C. list, lockup sixteen. Gene Baker." A marshal raised up lockup sixteen, a street person with reddish skin, long sandy hair and beard, and a torn-up corduroy coat. "Mr. Baker, the charges against you have been dropped by the District of Columbia. You are free to go."

"But wait," Baker cried. "This case has greater societal implications. This is part of a conspiracy of the Pods!"

"I said you're free to go, Mr. Baker." Lester fumed. Two burly marshals escorted the mumbling man out through the courtroom.

Next came a prostitute in a tight black skirt who shook and winked at the audience.

"District of Columbia versus Marvin Tubbs." Lester read a charging document for solicitation, loitering, and assault on the police officer who tried to get Marvin to move away from the intersection where he'd been knocking the windows of cars stopped at the light. In view of Marvin's long record of sex and drug offenses, these new charges resulted in imposition of a $500 bond.

Next came five-foot-three Sean Michael Garrety, frequently arrested while skinny-dipping in the Navy Veterans' fountain. I'd represented Sean on two occasions. Today a junior colleague had the honor. The Magistrate judge sent this fellow packing after charges were dismissed, and he waived to me as he happily tromped down the aisle toward the double doors.

The case call transitioned into more serious charges. Lester proceeded to call the main course of the morning lockups—felony assaults with handguns and knives, distributions of crack cocaine and heroin, car thefts and burglaries.

Cuffed recruits marched out from the lockup, were pointed to seats in a row of heavily guarded chairs, and then brought before the court. Some got set free. Many went back to the lockup. Row after row were seated and then brought up to the bar in ones and twos and occasional teams. Prosecutors grabbed file after legal file, made arguments for release, third party custody, or detention with or without bond. Defense attorneys recited address and employment confirmations, argued about the weakness of charging documents. The magistrate judge said little, as succeeding rows of the orange suited were seated in the well, brought to the bar, and *processed*.

Row after row they came—mostly sullen young men with blank stares, pawns in a war against civilization, guilty or innocent, now bystanders to a debate on their own liberty. Row after row they came, like bit players in a beggar's opera titled *Law*. Row after row—before yuppie lawyers, bureaucrats, and an overworked black robe. Row after row—in this choreography of process, this conveyor belt of justice. Hopefully, it guarded the rights of the accused. Certainly, it cleared the deck.

"Counselor Clay, you're up!" Lester barked and pointed at me. "Your case has been called and the magistrate judge is waiting."

# CHAPTER 12

"So glad you could join us, Mr. Clay." Godzilla glared down from the bench. Lisa stood on the left-hand side of the presentment table. I considered mentioning the hour at which I arrived in court, but ate the thought. No bickering with the black robe.

"Good morning, your honor. I was just going over the details of the case." I took my place on the right side of the table. Two marshals led Cleveland out, placed him to my right. Even though the poor fellow's shackles practically prevented him from walking, the marshals were on edge and poised for trouble.

Quiet fell over the room as the morning's biggest attraction began to unfold. Lester opened the folder and took out the charging paper as if it were a razor-sharp blade now readied for loading in the guillotine's grooved scaffold. He carefully handed the blade to me. Then he announced: "Calling the case of United States versus Cleveland F. Barnes, felony case number 62062-0C, Attorney Stuart Gatz Clay for the defendant. Mr. Barnes stands before this court charged with one count of murder-while-armed, one count of theft one, and one count of robbery. Mr. Barnes, you are advised that you do not have to say anything, that anything you say can be used against you, and that you are entitled to an attorney. Counsel, how do you wish to proceed?"

"On behalf of Mr. Barnes," I stated, "we waive further formal reading and request a preliminary hearing, and release on personal recognizance or third party custody.

"I have confirmed Mr. Barnes' address and community ties and I believe his sister is in the courtroom today, and Mr. Barnes may reside with her during—"

"Mr. Clay." Magistrate judge Jones held up the thick Pretrial Services printout. "Your client has a significant mental health history. Significant, Mr. Clay. Are you seeking a forensic examination?"

"Not at this time, your honor." No wasted forty days at St. E's on my watch! I heard a tearing noise as Lisa separated the multiple copies of what I suspected was page two of police department form 163—the Gerstein Statement of probable cause. She handed one copy up to the judge and gave me a copy, and not a single second before she had to. So much for collegiality, I thought. Lisa probably had the document in her hand when we spoke in the hall and just wouldn't give it up until the last possible second.

"Good afternoon, your honor," she said. "Lisa Stein for the United States. The government is seeking preventive detention for commission of this violent murder, and we tender our written statement at this time. In addition, we are seeking a probation hold based on Mr. Barnes' violation of a condition of probation by being rearrested. Mr. Barnes is on probation in case M-72227-05 in which he pled guilty to one count of shoplifting."

"Let's take a moment to review the Gerstein." The magistrate judge squinted. I studied the form and noticed Rhondo's signature at 6:47 A.M. in the morning. Now he sat in a chair behind the prosecutors' table stroking his Van Dyke beard. I read the proffer of facts: "On July 27th at approximately 2:30A.M., Witness-1 called 911, and reported seeing a severed human head mounted on a parking meter in the vicinity of 2600 Water Street, N.W. and Cecil's Alley, beneath the Whitehurst Freeway, which is in the District of Columbia. Homicide Detective Rhondo Touhey and Officer Jesus Martin of the MPDC Violent Crime Unit were dispatched to the scene, finding a severed human head at the above location and a headless torso approximately fifteen feet away inside the vicinity of a pebble-and-clam shell covered parking lot. The lot surface around the torso was wet and discolored with liquid that proved to be decedent's blood. Investigation further revealed that the torso was shoeless. Documentation found on the torso identified decedent as Benito Batiste of an address in the Bronx borough of New York City. The top of the right hand of decedent bore a cordovan ink stamp spelling the words 'Potomac Club.'

"At approximately 2:55 A.M., Second District Officer Barry Acres observed defendant, Cleveland Barnes, pushing a shopping cart containing empty cans in the 3200 block of M Street, N.W., adjacent to the stairway leading up to Prospect Street, also in the District of Columbia. Upon inspection the officer discovered that Barnes wore Bally brand loafers with significant blood stains on their tops and soles.

"Mr. Barnes was at this time patted down and placed under arrest. Following Miranda warnings and the signature of a PD 47 statement of Miranda rights, Barnes stated that he had found the shoes in an alley off of K Street, N.W. He further stated that he was collecting materials for the New Columbians, a community residing underneath the Key Bridge. In response to questioning, Mr. Barnes denied all knowledge of the decedent but became extremely agitated. He stated, in verbatim quote, that 'the New Columbians live off the throw aways of the oppressors but some day we will rise up.'

"Prior to being placed in the patrol car for transport Mr. Barnes was subject to a second, more thorough search for weapons and contraband. At this time a leather pouch was found inside Mr. Barnes' left trouser leg. The pouch contained $733 in assorted bills and a gold and ivory cigarette lighter with the words, 'from Kim to Benny, 8/3/89.' Upon further questioning, Mr. Barnes claimed that he had also found the cash and lighter in an alley off of K Street.

"All of these events took place in the District of Columbia."

Her honor sniffed loudly and stared down at me, waiting for a response. In a murder case the government generally got to hold the accused pursuant to legal presumptions set forth in the District of Columbia bail statute. With a violent crime there was a presumption of dangerousness, a presumption that no conditions of release would protect the community from the accused. My job was to present our side in the best possible light, and to see what facts I could find out from the opposition.

"What do you say, Mr. Clay?" She stared down.

"Your honor, we don't believe that this statement of probable cause satisfies the requirements of the law. A man was murdered outdoors, and the police found the defendant wearing some shoes and had some property that he found on the street. We already know defendant forages for discards left outdoors. So what does this prove? Nothing. We need more evidence from the government, your honor. I move the court to order release of investigative notes and witness interviews from the arresting officer."

"This is a criminal presentment counselor, not a rule sixteen discovery hearing." She said.

"But this evidence bears on probable cause, your honor. We tender to the court a clipping from today's Metro section and ask the court to take judicial notice of it. The decedent was a man with some substantial organized crime ties. More significantly for our purposes, at this juncture, there is no link between my client and the decedent, no admission of guilt, no showing of guilty knowledge, no fingerprint, no showing of—"

"Possession of recently stolen property creates an inference that the possessor took it," the Magistrate judge said. "How do you answer the inference?"

"The government is alleging murder, robbery, and theft—not receipt of stolen goods. And obviously murder is the big issue, not theft." I grappled for words. "We aren't here for a mechanical recitation of principle. This court has an ethical obligation to determine probable cause for the charged crime alleged based on the facts alleged. There is no showing of probable cause for robbery or anything remotely related to it."

"Your honor," Lisa interjected, "the government's adamant position is that this defendant is dangerous, that the community can't be protected from him without his detention, and that he should be detained."

"Well just hold on right there," Cleveland cried out. "Can I say something, judge?"

I cringed.

43

# CHAPTER **13**

"COURT'S indulgence. Mr. Barnes and I must confer briefly." The back of my right hand had covered his mouth and shoved against a mat of beard wire. As Magistrate-Judge Jones studied us, I smelled something horrid and felt Cleveland's hot, wet breath pulsing over the exact spot on my hand where a Potomac Club doorman had put a burgundy stamp on Benny's hand. Would our case soon be headless too? Cleveland could kill us right here. Everyone knew it. You could have heard a pin drop. The judge pointed at me.

"Granted," her honor ruled. She turned on a husher to produce static noise blocking the sound of my words with Cleveland. Still, I cupped both hands over Cleveland's left ear, rested my chin on my thumbs, and whispered, "Don't do this, man. Don't let loose words for the government to use."

Cleveland started to speak, so I cupped my hands into his stinky beard and held my ear close.

"Don't worry, Snick. It's on me. It's on me."

Oh joy, I thought. It's on him. Won't that make it right? I shook my head and nudged Cleveland's left ear with my cupped hands once again and continued.

"Don't be a fool. Please don't talk. No matter what you say, it's a mistake. The government will twist it around and use it against you."

I stepped back, tightlipped, and looked up at the judge.

"Could the court pass this matter for five minutes, your Honor? We need to confer about—"

"Denied. You've had your conference and the docket is bulging. What does your client want to do?"

"I'd like to reopen the issue of a forensic evaluation for competency and—"

"Denied," Godzilla fumed. "The prisoner doesn't become incompetent because he wants to exercise his constitutional right to speak. For the last time, Mr. Clay, what does your client want to do?"

"We note our objection to the court's rulings. But in view of your rulings, Mr. Barnes will have to tell the court his wishes." This statement made my record for any appeals of the court's ruling. "Mr. Barnes has my advice. If he disagrees with it, perhaps he would like another counsel appointed."

Maybe I would like another client!

I turned to Cleveland again. He grinned at me and spoke.

"He's a good lawyer, your honor. Give him a break!"

The audience burst into laughter. Lisa smirked at me, and someone in the audience shouted, "Don't lock up that lawyer, Judge Irene!"

A marshal stepped over and tapped a nightstick against the Plexiglas and pointed severely at an unseen person. We turned back around, and Cleveland continued.

"Your honor, I'm a New Columbian. We reside under Key Bridge and make due on what folks toss out. Sorry if I get excited, but the only thing I do is to prepare for our savior, our Mabutek to come and save his people. Just like the rest of you all believe in Jesus. We don't hurt anybody. I just found some shoes and stuff that someone threw away. That's all I want to say."

And that was enough.

Cleveland smiled at me with a clear sense of satisfaction. I prepared for the inevitable, waiting to see how the court and prosecutor would find a way to cast these scant words in the most damaging light possible. I was not disappointed.

Lisa started to speak, but the magistrate judge held up her hand. Sitting silently above us, her honor studied Cleveland as though he were something that had just grown on her judicial Petri Dish. She took up her pen and wrote several lines in a red leather ledger. After a few minutes she closed the book and spoke: "I find that Mr. Barnes has given a cogent explanation and defense of his circumstances. The substance of his statements confirms his ability to reason abstractly, understand the charges against him, and present a defense. I find that he is lucid and articulate. I find he is therefore competent to answer charges of murder, robbery, and theft. The statement of probable cause is sufficient and the defendant will be held without bond pending hearing before Judge Robideaux on July 30."

Her honor slid off the bench, and went through the curtained doorway behind the podium. Lester barked "this honorable court stands adjourned for a brief recess."

Before I could say a word, the marshals pulled Cleveland back from the dimly lit table and blocked me when I tried to follow. "No legal visits," one said. "Closed for prisoner transport." Cleveland disappeared behind the door. I turned back to Lisa.

"Thanks for sharing your documents out in the hall, colleague. And congratulations on your brilliant victory. Was that six words or seven that I heard you say?"

"Just seven," she retorted. "Having dead guy's stuff equals probable cause. Or if you need another one, try this: we caught the bad guy red footed."

# CHAPTER 14

"HEX upon you, you goddam woman!" Ruthie shrieked as she marched down the aisle toward Lisa. Ruthie held her arms up with palms wide open, then pointed her fingers straight like weapons. "Hex upon you by the power of Saint Domingue. By the power of all that crawls in the earth!"

"Hey!" Lester's shout made the Plexiglas dividers shake, and he suddenly became a 300-pound ball of fury flying into the aisle. "No shouting in this court!" he shouted. "No shouting in this honorable court!"

Half a dozen marshals swarmed around Lisa, ready to pounce on anyone who approached her. Everything froze.

Ruthie stood down, still seething. She glared at Lisa for several seconds, shaking her head in rage. Everyone, including Amanda, stared silently as Ruthie cut through the parting crowd and stomped out the door. Amanda ran after her.

Luckily, no black robes were in sight. I could only guess why the marshals didn't cuff Ruthie and charge her with assault and felony threats. Can't lock up an old woman? Or were they afraid of the power radiating from her?

"Sorry, Lester. I had no idea she'd pull this." I paced toward the open doors and spotted Ruthie gesturing and shaking her fist as she spoke with Amanda in the outer lobby. Lester wiped his brow, forehead, and large bald head, threw up his hands and walked back to the clerks' bench, muttering.

People whispered to themselves as they pushed to get down the aisle and out of the courtroom. The newspaper illustrators drew furiously, and I could already imagine Ruthie's image staring out from the *Post* Metro Section.

A strong hand grabbed my shoulder. Rhondo. He motioned to a small anteroom that opened into the paneled wall beside the prosecutors' table. I followed him in, threw my briefcase on a chair, turned, and got into his face.

"Why'd you bring a murder charge against that pathetic man?" I pointed at Rhondo. "You're no damned fool and neither is Lisa."

"We had probable cause, man. Plus the powers that be are on top of me. Lisa, too. She's following orders and the FBI guys will snatch this away from me if I don't follow her lead."

"Orders to do what? You saw the witness report. The dead guy left with a blonde babe on his arm. Where did she go? Did he eat her before the chop job? And do you really think a street dude did a mob guy?"

"You know the drill, Kentucky. Clear probable cause."

"I heard you the first time, but who gives a rat's ass? It's still not likely, so tell me why."

"Why what, man?"

"Rhondo, look at the facts!"

"Here's the deal," Rhondo spoke, angry now. "Some guy got his neck sliced. The folks that pay me want it solved yesterday. The FBI is going to invade the case if we don't move pronto and they might invade it anyway. We got a right to want a resolution, man. We got a right! A right to—"

"To what? To help set up a fall guy?"

"Don't you say that." Rhondo glared at me.

"This is going nowhere, pal. I see your point, but I still don't buy Cleveland as a murderer." I picked up my briefcase and headed for the door, and then turned around. "Do you really think this guy is involved? Or don't you think at all, for Christ's sake?"

"Think, smink," he growled at me. "You and your goddamn

martyr complex can come talk to my eight year old daughter. She walks to school four blocks from that club every morning. Tell me to think? Those words will come back to haunt you!"

We stared at each other for a moment. The noise outside subsided, and I felt that Rhondo was about to tell me something important. He studied me for a moment, then continued.

"Lisa got the case under the normal Violent Crime Unit assignment system. Potomac Club is in her beat. They wanted to take her off because of you but Lisa pushed back hard. Margery Foxwell told Lisa not give you jack or she'd be trying misdemeanor assaults in the domestic branch for the next five years."

"And what would warrant our esteemed U.S. Attorney herself to deliver that dire threat?"

Rhondo studied me, musing over some unspoken fact.

"You'll probably get it in discovery."

"Get what?" I picked my bag up again.

Rhondo shrugged.

"Batiste's dirty."

"This ain't news, Einstein. Read today's paper."

"More than that, man. We know he was part of the Spilotro organization out of the Bronx."

"Doesn't matter if he's Al Capone's reincarnation! Cleveland's not in that league. Spilotro might still run drug imports out of the containers in New York Harbor, but Cleveland Barnes doesn't strike me as his D.C. connection."

"And that's where you're wrong."

"How?"

"I can't say, and you didn't get your lead from me. There are connections. There are. I'm not gonna lose my badge giving up grand jury stuff. File your discovery with Lisa and let her committee decide what to give you."

"Come on man." I said. "You got my interest now. Keep talking. You know I'd never quote you."

"What about if you're under oath on the stand? I'm not going to put either one of us in that position."

"I swear before God and country that whatever you tell me won't be repeated until and unless it could be wholly documented and attributed to a collateral source."

"Damn straight you won't, man. Cause you're not getting anything else. But I'll tell you one thing. With your guy we start with the assumption that everything is related. I mean this isn't six degrees of separation, pal. It's just one."

I studied his face, knowing that it would be futile to ask for more. But I didn't see the connection he did. Who was Cleveland separated from by one degree? Who was Benny related to?

"What about the FBI?" I jumped to another question. "This is an interstate case. Why haven't they asserted jurisdiction?"

"The case just started, man. They're busy chasing terrorists, but don't think the turf warriors in the field office aren't licking their chops and waiting for the right angle. Clear enough?"

"Nothing's clear. You haven't given me squat." But of course he had. Rhondo wouldn't bluff, not on this.

I had to find the one degree of separation before it ruined my case.

# CHAPTER 15

WE walked out of the anteroom. C-10 had emptied out. Rhondo and I had sort of cleared the air between us, though nothing was clear in this case.

"Can't you at least get me some discovery? Any heads-up from the crime-scene guy?"

"We don't have test results yet. The techs from 2D taped everything off including a few dozen customers' cars that are still there. Folks were extremely pissed off and tried to leave but we stopped them. All the cars are still there. Nothing moved. Then Byno Sanchez came in with the Mobile Crime crew and walked the grid in his Captain Video costume. Divided the whole parking lot into squares and picked up everything on it like some archaeological dig. The police chief took one look at the body and the scene and insisted they get the chief medical examiner out of bed and over there. The medical examiner came with his photographers and went over the body before they bagged his mitts, feet, and head and shipped it off to the freezer."

"Delightful." I checked my watch. Had to get to Georgetown.

See the parking lot.

"Whole damned scene almost turned into a disaster because all these white shirts from 300 Indiana came racing over to get in and take a look. Byno Sanchez exploded and threw them all out. I got two guys with sticks guarding the place now. Civilians still showing up, yelling to get their cars out of the lot. We should have given a breathalyzer to the whole bunch and parked them at the 2D jail."

"Do you have Byno's tape?"

Rhondo shrugged his shoulders and reached in his breast pocket.

"Here." He handed a microcassette to me. "That's my working copy, and I need it back. Have Cyndi go through the motions and serve a subpoena for a copy over at 300 Indiana. I got to run but you should also know that somebody shot out the overheads in the parking lot with a .22, apparently sometime after midnight. And there was no residue of powder on Barnes' hands."

"Glad to hear that, but how much residue comes off a .22 anyway?"

"Enough to tell. And there's a fair amount of oil."

"If they had a .22 why not just pop the guy's noodle and split? Why do the gruesome?"

"Because it's not just a murder, Stuart. It's a fashion statement."

"And Cleveland's no designer."

"That remains to be seen. Meanwhile, let's hope we don't have a new serial killer on our hands."

"I don't think we do, not in my corner. But thanks for the tape anyway. I'm going to the club now, Rhondo. Maybe we can get over to Chinatown and work out later. I think I'd like to toss you around the dojo a few times."

"Likewise," he said.

We pushed through the double doors into the hall. Soon the crowd would return.

"Enjoy the club." Rhondo said. "And enjoy the movie."

"What movie?" I stopped and looked back at Rhondo. He just kept walking past me.

"Don't worry, man. You'll find out soon enough."

# CHAPTER 16

WALKING out of the courthouse, I grabbed another piece of black licorice from my inside suit pocket, and bit off three inches. A half-dozen reporters and their camera crews fixed on Lisa. Scott Baldwin, a short black reporter from Channel 7, spotted me and in an instant held a microphone to my face.

"I'm with Stuart Clay, defense counsel." He spoke to the viewing audience, sporting his ever-ready news guy look. "Would you care to comment on the charges brought against Cleveland Barnes?"

More reporters drifted over.

"Thanks, Scott. Today, Mr. Cleveland Barnes was presented to the court for an initial hearing. The government asked for a hold as is its right in a case like this. That doesn't mean that Mr. Barnes is guilty. This case is highly circumstantial and I believe Mr. Barnes will be vindicated. He's just a guy from the streets."

"Isn't it true that they caught Mr. Barnes red footed?" A large gray haired reported called out the line that Lisa had probably just given. The group tittered and more reporters noticed us.

"Bloodied Ballys don't prove murder," I announced. This sound bite, counter to Lisa's, would hopefully become a headline or at least the blurb under my photograph.

"Comment on the murder itself?" The question came from Fred Collins, the *Post* reporter who had this morning's story. I paused for a second, studying Collins thick gray hair, beard, and wire frames. Had to talk to him, but not here.

"It looked to me like a message, Fred. Somebody sending somebody a message. That's my opinion. Given the discussion in your article this morning, you'd have to kind of ask, who would want to send this type of message? Who were the people that the decedent associated with? Not street folks, I assure you."

"Don't you think that—"

"Sorry, folks. I'll have another statement tomorrow." Didn't want to give them too much information. Better to spew a few quotable lines and leave.

I headed for the curb and waived down a cab.

I felt edgy, uncomfortable, eager to find something, prove something, grasp that canard of proof that made the difference. Where would it be? I slid into a rickety Caprice cabbed by a calm old gent. We did a U-turn west on Indiana Avenue, swung south on Sixth Street to Independence, and motored toward Georgetown. Digging in my briefcase, I retrieved the cellular phone, flipped it open, and dialed Cyndi. Her line rang as we drove parallel to the Mall, past tourist lines at the old red Smithsonian building. Scads of folks in shorts and sunglasses walked across the Mall and around the Washington Monument. We hit a traffic snag.

"Stuart," Cyndi answered.

"Need your help, Cyndi. You still on trial hold or what?"

"My case is going to be continued in about twenty minutes, but I got to change out of the court duds. I'll grab your car. Where am I meeting you?"

"Potomac Club."

"Twenty minutes, big boy. Then I'm all yours." She kissed into the phone and hung up.

I clipped the phone shut, warmed by Cyndi's intimate tone. I turned back to business.

I pulled out my crime scene microcassette and recorder, set up the machine to play and connected a small earphone. In a heavy Hispanic accent, Crime Scene Investigator Byno Sanchez detailed the discovery of a headless torso and Benny's head mounted on a parking meter. Byno talked for fifteen minutes and only changed his even tone when he screamed at some downtown desk detectives who started to step over the yellow tape so they could gander at the headless corpse. Such an invasion could lead to violence with this thorough man. He examined every inch of Benny's clothed anatomy and severed head. Then he collected, cataloged, and correlated every Coke can, condom wrapper, cigarette butt and every other item in the parking lot.

Most importantly, Byno found what appeared to be dried semen on the outside of Benny's trousers and found long blond hairs caught in Benny's zipper. He also found tire tracks driving over top of blood drippings left by the head when someone carried it over to the parking meter. Kind of impossible to believe that a person could drive out of the lot and not notice the head mounted by the parking lot exit.

I tried to imagine what had happened and flashed on a scene in my mind like a video clip. I watched a black SUV driving over the blood spatters, past the mounted head, and out of the lot. A petite blonde sat in the passenger seat. She wasn't strong enough to do the deed that had just been done. I saw strong male hands at the wheel of the car, but the face was shadowed. I clinched my eyes and pushed the image. Who was she? And who was the driver?

The images faded into grayness.

# CHAPTER 17

I GOT out of the cab and studied the front of the Potomac Club, tried to imagine big Benny walking out the door with a hot blonde on his arm. They would have walked to the right and then a quick right again into the parking lot. At that hour the lot would be very dark, especially since the overhead spotlights in the lot were shot out. Plus the club and lot were covered, under the Whitehurst Freeway at the spot where K turns into Water Street, a place confined on all sides. The Potomac River flowed on the left, and on the right a steep hill sloped up to the old C&O Canal. Cool black asphalt ran beneath my feet and overhead, the girders of the Whitehurst Freeway supported a cover of metal, concrete, and asphalt. It had a tucked-away feeling, a place where odd little shops and a few restaurants could thrive away from the buzz of business Washington. The Potomac Club fit right in, seeming more like something one would find on a side alley in the French Quarter of New Orleans than off K Street in the District of Columbia. None of these shops would thrive for long if people didn't feel safe to come here. I respected this economic truth, but it didn't help my case.

I felt the zone of the crime. Places like this have a bruised aftershock to them. Maybe that's just a psychological impression, but I think not. Somehow there is a real aura, a pain that hangs in the air like a ghost in the night waiting to wither away.

I walked over to the beginning of a narrow, cobbled street known as Cecil's Place and looked back at the scene just portrayed in Byno's monologue.

Three layers of yellow police tape framed the parking lot at the corner of Water Street and Cecil's Place like a big letter L. Centuries-old red brick walls formed the inner L boundary of the lot and bore a faded advertisement for Iron City Ale on one wall and Chesterfield Cigarettes on the other. At the curb a large handwritten placard warned that moving cars from the lot would result in criminal penalties.

A police cruiser idled at the corner of Cecil's Alley and another was parked close to the telltale parking meter. I flashed a wave at the lady in the passenger seat of the Cecil's Alley cruiser, a face I knew from the courthouse. About ten feet from the northeast corner of the lot, close to where the two walls met, I spotted a reddish-brown residue that I knew to be blood spurt and spray, less than a dozen hours old, staining the ground of broken shells and pebbles and spattering a poplar-white Mercedes-Benz S Class sedan in sickening contrast. Even stranger was the parking meter, capped with a clear plastic cover now red-brown stained and tied with yellow crime scene tape like a surreal lollipop from hell, jutting out into the sidewalk.

I studied the scene for several seconds, trying to get a sense of it, trying to see Benny walking out the door and then moving back into the lot. I studied the broken overhead lights at three spots along the east wall. Why would he go there, back into the corner? Why would Batiste have walked into the dark? Did the woman go with him? Who did he meet there? When Cleveland looked in and saw the shoes, what source lit the body?

The most plausible scenario seemed to help our case. Intoxicated Batiste is seen fondling and groping an attractive young woman in the club. She goes under the table for a while. They get up and leave. What would Benny want next and from whom? The answer seemed obvious.

A horn blasted. Cyndi drove my car around, a black 1961

Oldsmobile, four-door sedan. She pulled up beside me and then came to an abrupt halt half a block from the covered meter. Now in jeans and a tank top, she slid out, shook her long dark hair back behind her and flashed a smile. She reached back in to grab her camera bag. I tried to keep my mind on business.

"Ready to rock," Cyndi said.

I pointed into the lot at the blood spatter that sprayed over the white Benz.

"Yikes! Doesn't leave much to the imagination." She snapped photos as she spoke, taking dozens of shots portraying various perspectives in the lot. "How was the hearing? I assume her honor held Barnes?"

"She did, and Barnes didn't help the debate by holding out on me. He's a talker, but he didn't tell me about a cigarette lighter and some cash he'd helped himself to from our dead guy. Doesn't change the bottom line, but it muddies the water. Anyway, look at this. Here." I pointed to the nightclub door. "Dead man comes out of the club door with a lady. He or they turn right and then go back into the lot. Those overhead lights are already shot out so Batiste and whoever are going back into the dark. Best guess is that Batiste walked back there to kiss or whatever, but someone was waiting. Either she set him up or there's a second victim the police have yet to find. Either way, his semen and her hair were on the body's trousers."

"Lends new meaning to the term 'giving head,'" Cyndi said matter-of-factly.

"Wicked investigator!" I laughed and then shivered as I looked over a the blood-spattered white Mercedes. "By the way, just to liven things up, Cleveland's sister is one Ivyroot Malveaux, formerly of New Orleans. She put a hex on Lisa after the hearing. Ivyroot happens to be a voodoo priestess."

"Did it help any? I mean, with your pom-pom girl."

"Shut up about Lisa." I shook my head.

"What's Rhondo-mon saying about the parking lot?"

"He gave me Byno's crime scene recording, but we've got to push on the government to cough up the reports. There is at least a suspicious tire track. Somebody drove out of the lot over blood spatters and past the mounted head. It's kind of difficult to believe that they wouldn't have noticed given where that meter is located." I pointed at the covered parking meter situated by the exit drive from the lot.

"Does Rhondo think Barnes had a car tucked away?"

"Rhondo says things aren't as simple as they look, but I don't know what to make of that and he won't give me any details. Frankly, I could strangle him." In a hushed tone I explained to Cyndi the alleged tie between Benny, the Spilotro organization, and Cleveland. Cyndi shook her head.

"He must think Cleveland takes direction from somebody at odds with the Spilotro people. Or maybe from the blonde. But what is his basis for that belief?"

"Don't know," I said. "Bottom line is we've got to find the lady. If we get her, we probably find the truth."

We grew quiet and studied the lot as much as the situation permitted. But as we couldn't lawfully cross the yellow tape to get samples, we soon turned our attention to the Potomac Club. Before entering, Cyndi retrieved a three-by-two-inch thick microcassette recorder and positioned it in her cleavage. We'd used it several times before. The thing could pick up sound surprisingly well through clothing and proved to be extremely useful. The District of Columbia was a "single consent" jurisdiction and as long as one party knew of the recording, the practice was completely legal. Oddly enough, the law in Virginia and Maryland made clandestine recording a felony. I felt happy to be on the right side of the Potomac River, for these purposes, and to use the recorder. Lots of times witnesses disclose the most amazing things in the initial interview, give highly useful evidence, and then get amnesia after they see what being a witness in court entails. Can't say that I blame them, but I had a job to do and a guy to defend. I needed the recorder. My assistant's cleavage gave the device an opportune vantage point from which to function.

I opened the door for Cyndi, and we entered the club. A young hostess busily fixed her long black hair in a wall of gold-frosted mirror. This time of day the two dozen tables were vacant, and a long mahogany bar seated four early birds imbibing a liquid lunch. The absence of customers suited me fine. Waiting, I studied a wall-length mural, twenty-foot Rubenesque nudes cavorting with a satyr. Cyndi smiled at me, but glanced around restlessly. After a minute, our hostess ambled over.

"They're from a vaudeville house in San Francisco," she said, in no hurry to serve us.

"Must have cost a mint, Tamara." I read a name tag announcing her name and date of birth.

"Don't know," she said. "But they certainly keep the customers entertained while we're trolling for tables."

"Worth a toast or two," I ventured, "but right now we're here on business." I handed her a card. "The guy that got murdered in your parking lot last night, Benny Batiste. Anybody here who waited on him or was here when everything went down?"

Surprised, the woman snapped to attention.

"Don't mean to make you uncomfortable," I added. "Just looking for anyone who was here."

"Jennifer just got back. She had to crash out at home for a while. Poor thing. I thought you guys got all that from her last night, but I'll find her."

Tamara disappeared through double doors. It seemed like my role as a civilian defense attorney was lost on her, but I felt no compulsion to explain it. It could wait and, in any event, Jennifer quickly appeared. She wore a revealing black dress with wide white trim and gold buttons, all glitter and smiles. Didn't seem like a poor thing to me.

"You're not a cop. You must be the defense lawyer and investigator he told me about."

"He who? I'm Stuart Clay, a private attorney involved in the Batiste murder. This is my assistant, Cyndi Oh. I'd like to ask some questions about last night."

She motioned us to the bar.

"He who?" She said. "Roland Dewey, or something like that."

"You mean Rhondo Touhey? What time did he come here?"

"Dewey, Touhey, whatever. Talked to him at about 4:00 A.M. I have his card in back."

How did Rhondo know I was on the case before I did?

She accepted my card, but put it on the bar without a glance.

"Did you talk much to Batiste?"

"Yeah. Actually, I waited on him. Her, too. He was big. Well-dressed. Drank a hell of a lot. They were over there." She motioned to a table against the back wall. "Grey Goose martinis for him. The lady had a salty dog, grapefruit juice, and house vodka with salt on the rim."

"How'd they act?" I asked.

They were quiet, but…," Jennifer turned away.

"What?" Cyndi said.

"Oh, man!" Jennifer giggled nervously. "I already told this once. You really need to hear it?"

"We could subpoena you to the preliminary hearing and you can talk on the witness stand if you prefer," I said. Probably I would never do this, but it got her talking.

"Alright you bastard, it's like this." Jennifer took a deep breath and sat on a bar stool. "When I served his third or fourth martini—you know, leaned over to pour it out of the shaker—I stood beside them at the wall where nobody could see and damned if she wasn't under the table like it was nobody's business. Grinned at me, and I think she even got turned on by me seeing her there. I just poured the drink and left, and after a few minutes the both of them left."

"Did you tell anybody?"

"Not really. I mean, couples disappear into the bathrooms to snort cocaine and get it on all the time. Plus it was dark and loud, so I don't think anybody else noticed."

"What happened next?" Cyndi said.

"They left. There was goop all over the table cloth where he sat. I think she wiped him off with the cloth—pretty gross, but she left a really nice tip."

"Do you have the table cloth?"

"Roland Dewey took it."

"Naturally." I sighed. "Anything else about them?"

Now she laughed at me, and her left eyebrow gave a sly raise.

"Look, mister, she did him under the table. Other than that I couldn't tell you."

I smiled back. "What exactly did the woman look like?"

"She had a blonde cut, kind of like a longish flapper—attractive, five foot two or three, slender. Wore a black dress. Real nice. They were both very classy, cosmopolitan—like from New York or L.A. He was much harder looking than her."

"What about her? Did she seem tipsy?"

"Nope. Not a bit. Maybe she had two, maybe three drinks at the outside."

"Smoke cigarettes?"

"Both smoked like chimneys. And he had this amazing lighter. Even in the dark I could tell it looked like a museum piece."

"I guess it would be too much to expect that you might have

61

saved the cigarette butts."

"Oh, I didn't save them. Didn't get the chance. The ashtray hadn't been emptied, but Roland Dewey took them in big baggies."

"He's a good cop," I cursed to myself.

"Did Batiste and the woman leave together?"

"Definitely."

"How much time elapsed between when they left and when the police came into the club?"

"It couldn't have been more than twenty-five or thirty minutes before all hell broke loose outside and everything, like, went nuts. All these people here wanted to get in their cars and get out of Dodge City. The cops showed up and told everybody nothing could be moved because the parking lot was the scene of a murder. You should have seen all these bleary-eyed folks arguing with the cops!

"Actually, we were about to close for the night when the big guy and the blonde left. You know we hadn't even had a chance to clean up their table before some huge cop with a butch hair cut came running in here, yelling we shouldn't clean any more anything or empty the ashtrays until the crime scene search crew came through the restaurant. He was awfully nasty. I didn't want to say anything earlier to the other policeman but was that right? Seemed like he was bullying us."

"Barry Acres. He makes his rules up sometimes. In fact, he makes his own rules most of the time," I said. "But tell me, were the glasses and dishes that they'd used taken for prints?"

"Those were bussed out and washed immediately after the two walked out. We still had thirty or so people in the club and the kitchen was doing clean up."

"Table wiped?"

"Dewey took prints first. Had glue all over the surface and pulled it up in strips and laid them on some kind of flat boards that he brought with him."

"What else do you remember about Batiste and the woman? Anything. Any special movements or words?"

"She had a little bit of a Southern accent, like. That's about all I can think of. Except maybe the tape."

"The tape? What kind of tape?"

"Over the door." She pointed at a tiny movie camera mounted several feet above the inside wall of the Club's entrance. "The one that thing made."

# CHAPTER 18

FOR the next hour Cyndi and I watched a clip of Benny and the lady entering and leaving the Potomac Club. The Mobile Crime Unit had taken the original, but luckily the club had a backup copy.

Benny walked like a loaded thug. The blonde hanging on his side didn't exactly look like his niece from Wisconsin.

I imagined my line of defense: moll leads prey to mob hit. Not a bad defense. But what truths lurked in the wings? Could Rhondo prove Cleveland's ties to the same unsavory crowd that Benny worked for? Lisa would look for any way possible to get such evidence in at trial. I had to anticipate her moves, prepare the blocks.

We talked for another fifteen minutes with Jennifer, going over details again and again, discussing anything and everything about Benny and Madame X: from his unusual cigarette lighter and slob laugh to her muted Southern accent, demure manner, and not-so-demure behavior.

After a while, I sat back in my chair, took out my own note

pad, and let Cyndi run with the questioning. Our different styles worked well together. I shot from the hip in search of spice for the jury. Cyndi systematically pursued every crumb. That was a good thing. Cyndi asked for the name of every person Jennifer could name who'd been at the Potomac Club the night before. Forty possible witnesses. Then she asked to see any cards left by the officers detailed to the scene—a shortcut for the officer subpoena list. I liked this. Subpoenas directed toward each individual officer carried more oomph and put the government on notice that we were on the trail.

I listened to Jennifer and thought back to Byno's tape and the court documents. One problem shouted at me. On the one hand, I believed that Benny and the blonde parted ways outside the club like I believed that Adam left Eve's apple untouched and went to choir practice. Anybody who watched the tape would conclude that the two were headed to a lust-fest. I'd bet plenty of people noticed them, and that was the problem. Why would the blonde be so bold? The "mob hit theory" could work, but I had trouble imagining a professional killer dumb enough to attract this kind of attention to the prey. The blonde had been too obvious, bringing Benny to a public place, performing services in a place where they could be noticed. Her DNA traces would be all over the body and other physical evidence and would therefore be a matter of court record in this case. The traces could be easily contrasted with Cleveland's DNA. Also, if she touched Batiste's belt or trouser legs while doing the deed, her fingerprints could possibly be identified when the medical examiner did a fluorescent scan of the clothing or especially a leather belt. Her lip prints were probably on the cigarette butts. These items were just for starters.

Either the woman had no regard for the evidence she'd left behind or she was no professional killer. Maybe both. So who could she be?

I saw it again. The black SUV drove out of the lot by the head on the meter. The blonde gazed at me from the passenger window. Almost a kid. Who was driving?

Just a shadow.

Cyndi subpoenaed the videotape and the club manager Henry Rogers to the preliminary hearing. Henry promised to produce a copy of the tape for us later in the day and to come to court and testify if we needed him. I doubted that we would need him. D.C.

judges expected stipulations on such things to cut down on trial time, and they generally got them.

The videotape framed our case. Judge and jury would see the unknown woman walk out with Benny at 2:13 A.M., approximately seventeen minutes before the 911 call. I could hear myself repeating the golden one-liner that the prosecution couldn't stop. "Where did she go? Ladies and gentleman of the jury, wouldn't you like to know the answer to that one question?"

"Where did she go?"

# CHAPTER 19

"MAY I help you, sir," he said in a Caribbean lilt. I nodded to the valet, studying his gold trimmed red trench coat and black top hat.

"My friend and I were supposed to meet a fellow here today." I motioned to Cyndi. "Mr. Ben Batiste. Could you ring his room please?"

The concierge looked down and typed onto a computer screen then looked up.

"He would be behind you, sir."

Someone grabbed my right arm and I instinctively broke the hold and spun around into a block and punch position, then came eye to eye with a big, mad white guy. Barry Acres, the terror of the Second District.

"For Christ's sake, Acres!" I stepped away, but he followed and pointed a fat finger in my face.

"What are you calling that room for? It's a police stakeout, a controlled place tied to a crime scene. You're interfering with a murder investigation!" He ran his hand over his blonde butch cut.

"You ought to watch the touch thing."

"You ought to get a real job." Acres glowered at me. His reddish face sprouted blond bristle and his eyes squeezed into angry balls. "This is a homicide investigation, bucko, and I'm not discussing it with the likes of you. We don't need a turncoat Hardy Boy messing up the evidence. Get your discovery from Lisa Stein."

He stomped away.

Cyndi watched from the telephone table, saying nothing during my exchange with Officer Acres. Now she pointed to a nook in the lobby, and I followed her to an overstuffed red leather sofa.

"Why do you think Mr. Personality is staking the place out?" Cyndi asked.

"Probably the same reason we're checking it out. From what Rhondo says, and I don't think he's holding out, they don't know any more than we do about who might show up. I guess they might have found something in Benny's room too. Hit the hotel manager and the police with a subpoena for anything found there."

"Right. But what now?"

"Don't know." I surveyed the lobby. "Maybe I'll check the hotel watering hole. See if they drank there."

"I'll catch up." Cyndi pulled out a subpoena form with the clerk of the court's signature electronically entered. The "Stalingrad Defensive" was underway. I wanted every piece of data I could find.

While Cyndi completed the subpoena and found a manager, I ventured through frosted double doors on the east wing of the lobby and sat at the bar. Inside the bar people ate sandwiches and drank amidst a loud buzz of lunchtime conversation. I sat on a bar stool and placed my notebook on the stool beside me. I picked up a fistful of small crackers and motioned to a stocky, bearded bartender busily washing rail glasses.

"Hey guy." He nodded at me as he dried his hands on a long white apron and stroked his salt & pepper beard.

"Two diet Cokes. My partner will be here in a second."

"Two DCs it is."

I looked at his shirt and noticed the name "Cornelius" had been sewn above the pocket. He pulled out a dispenser hose from the bar and sprayed soda over glasses of ice. Though I'd planned to buy the drinks just to talk, I found myself picking up a Coke and downing it. Cyndi came through the doors moments later, handed me a signed subpoena form, and slid in beside me. I motioned to Cornelius and noticed an attractive waitress holding a tray of oversized burgers above her head. She served the food to businessmen seated across the room, arguing over the new stadium being built for the Washington Nationals as they drank dark beers from thick ceramic mugs.

"Listen, Cornelius." I moved forward over the edge of the bar and motioned. The bartender came over. "I'm working on a case involving the guy who got murdered last night. You probably heard about it because he was staying here at the Lathrop. Named Benny Batiste. He was about five foot ten inches, kind of a heavy, dark wavy hair, big drinker. Was last seen with a blonde in the Potomac Club, but we assume he left from the Lathrop before that yesterday. Any chance he might have come in here for a drink?"

"Call me Con." He gave a pained smile. "I'd like to help, but you've got to understand. My boss rents at the hotel's pleasure. If I start blabbing about the clientele and word got back, boss would boot me out of the joint, and I'd be blackballed at all the M Street bars."

"No, you wouldn't," I responded quickly. "If you have information you have to tell the police about it anyway. Your boss and the hotel would have to respect that."

He studied me from behind the bar, saying nothing. I pulled two twenties, folded them into a small square, and laid them on the bar. Con glanced at the frosted double doors quickly and then snapped up the money and jammed it in his front pocket.

"I didn't know the big guy," he said. "But they were both in here last night and the night before. He and the blonde. She's a high-class call girl. Two-grand-a-night kind. Works all over Northwest. Name's Mona Day."

"Have you told this to the police?"

"Hell, yes! I hope they catch the slime that slit the guy and fry him. It's kind of bad for business, you know?"

"When did you last see the two?"

"Like I said, last night. The night before, too. Last night, they just had two quick doubles, then they split."

"Do you think he knew her before?"

"Hard to say, man. A whore's a whore. A broad like that can be a total stranger and you'd never know it. She's a pro at working

68

strangers."

"How long have you seen her around?"

"I've been here a year and a half. Never saw her before five or six months ago. Showed up all at once and, believe me, you notice her. Since then, I've seen her four or five times, no more. Never with the same man. Don't even know who first told me her name, but she's been here with a bunch of different guys."

"How do you know the woman is a hooker?"

"How do I know? I've been a bartender for twenty-seven years. There's certain stuff that comes with the turf of being a career booze seller. You get to know how to spot a hooker and you get to know how to spot the well-dressed guy that will sit and drink the better part of a fifth of top shelf vodka at eight bucks a pop. Take my word for it. I know. Babe's a hooker. And the dead guy was a drunk."

"Would you be able to identify Mona's picture or help a sketch artist?"

"I could, but don't know if I would for you. That degree of cooperation could be bad for my image with the hotel management, if you know what I mean."

Which meant it would cost me more. I parted with another two twenty dollar bills.

"Did the cops do a photo spread?"

"Yeah man, forty photos. None of them was her. A maid service lady and I already spent time with their sketch artist."

"Which lady?"

"Sorry, pal. Your meter just ran out, and we got company."

# CHAPTER **20**

CON turned around, grabbed a clear-colored bottle off an upper shelf, and moved over to the sink to clean off the spout. Without looking up I picked up the Coke and tilted it back, then chewed a piece of ice and picked up another handful of crackers. Cyndi sniffed her drink, then sat it back down beside mine with a wince and shoved it toward me. I sipped it as Barry Acres pulled out the chair and sat down beside me.

"Don't you have an ambulance to chase? Better paying than that grease-ball stuff in the courthouse basement." Acres stared straight ahead.

"Not my gig, big guy. But you keep grabbing defense attorneys like you did out in the lobby and somebody is going to sue your ass off."

"Let them come. I barely touched you," he sneered and wagged his head for several seconds. "You just let them come. Corporation counsel will whip their asses." Acres grabbed my arm again and stared straight at me. "What the hell happened to you, Clay? You were a decent prosecutor and now look at you.

Representing crappola. What the hell happened?"

I studied Acres' beady eyes, wondering how he got through life with his nasty outlook. But I had to give the man his due. Though he was a crude, rude guy, Acres had asked the question that probably came to the mind of a lot of my friends. I didn't care—at least not too much. I threw back the rest of the diet Coke and studied Acres' blotchy white face.

"I haven't changed a bit, Acres. It's the same city and I'm the same guy. I can be on either side of the street. Both sides have their problems and their merits."

"Merits, schmerits. Who do you represent now? A smelly street bum who goes around cutting citizens' heads off."

"So you got it all figured out, right? Guilty as charged?"

"That's how I see it." He stared at me.

"You don't really think that, do you? You know as well as I do what's going on here." I stood up and started to walk away. Cyndi followed. At the brink of the doors, I turned around. "And anyway, thanks for the lead on the missing witness."

I pushed open the doors.

"What lead?" he called out. The officer didn't sound amused.

"Come on, Acres." I looked back. "If this is about a street person killing a tourist, why are you here?"

# CHAPTER 21

*BANG.* I fired off a goodbye at Acres, closed my thumb down on the index finger, then flicked my hand into a wave. He glared at me.

Within minutes, Cyndi and I were in driving up the small strip of Wisconsin Avenue from Bridge Street, and then turned left onto M Street, driving towards the Key Bridge and Virginia route back toward the Fourteenth Street Bridge and Judiciary Square.

M Street sweated sex. Georgetown students and D.C. townies swarmed the sidewalks, an ocean of nubile women with bulging T-shirts and tight round parts strutted in an urban legend ritual for the tanned young men ready to ride the fertile waves. Decked out in denim and khaki, basking in the glory of sun and American affluence, they were a sight to behold, a mating ritual going on among the aged facades that lined the streets of this college town. Slow traffic afforded an opportunity to study the soft parade and the sidewalk leading up to the Key Bridge.

"I'm coming back later," I said to Cyndi. "Cover all of M Street and go underneath the Key Bridge, then back to the

Potomac Club."

"I'm game, too," Cyndi replied.

"Good." Maybe we'd visit some afterward. I hadn't been home for two days. "We'll need to go after dark. My guess is that there are street witnesses who only came out at night. And we can search for Cleveland's roommates, bridge mates, whatever the devil they are, and hunt down the kids Cleveland saw playing soap buckets and dancing."

We idled in traffic, approaching the Key Bridge. An oversized American flag waved over a small park established in memory of the great man, Francis Scott Key, whose home once stood on this spot. Across, on the north side of M Street, stood Dixie Liquors, a Georgetown institution for generations of students, followed by a large Victorian structure named the Car Barn and a large parking lot beside it. In the movie the *Exorcist* a young priest took a possessing demon into himself, jumped out the window of a Prospect Street Victorian, and tumbled stairs that led down to this lot.

We drove under the flapping flag, past the lot and across the Potomac River via the Key Bridge. We agreed that Cyndi would drop me at the courthouse and go by the medical examiner's office, then subpoena a copy of the Byno Sanchez tape and any test results at the main police headquarters. As we drove, I plotted possibilities.

"With coaxing, I think Con could remember more," Cyndi said.

"Could be," I replied. "His memory responds well to twenty-dollar bills. Makes me wonder, but we should try him again, try to find the maid who saw Benny with the blonde. No matter what they say, I bet they're thinking the same thing we are: Where did she go? Where did she go? The more the government thinks about it the more ridiculous Cleveland's arrest is going to seem."

Or so I hoped.

We drove down Constitution Avenue into the District of Columbia. Traffic was clogged in both directions. Finally, the car arrived at Sixth Street. I heard a female's voice blasting into a megaphone and noticed a dozen TV trucks parked along the curb of Indiana Avenue.

Street protests had died down in this city, but something odd was underway in front of the courthouse. Even so, I recognized the blare and feedback of angry protests, distant but still familiar, the sound of 1969. Something had happened, and dozens of people ran or walked fast to the front of the courthouse.

Cyndi drove over to the curb on Sixth Street just past Constitution Avenue. The car windows shook from a blaring megaphone. "See you later." I looked at her reluctantly. She caressed my cheek and smiled. I leaned over and pulled her head to me with my right hand. I kissed her and held her close as she jumped with surprise. After a moment she relaxed and clutched my thigh.

"See you later, baby," I said, kissing both of her cheeks. "Maybe we can get a drink after we go out tonight."

"It's a date, big guy," she whispered.

I slid out of the car. Cyndi called after me, wishing me luck. Then she made a U-turn back to Pennsylvania Avenue and drove out of sight.

I walked up Sixth Street and over to the growing crowd into what the next day's *Post* labeled a "Voodoo Protest."

# CHAPTER 22

"WE will vindicate our rights." I recalled Ruthie's last statement in the cafeteria, and the violent rage that filled her face in the courtroom. I should have talked to her again, though it probably wouldn't have made a difference.

Over 300 people covered the sidewalk and part of the lawn. Tall television lamps stretched to the sky and pointed down, radiating heat into the humid July air. Ruthie presided, defiant in the midst of it all. She stood in front of a large wooden pole in a support platform placed upright and adjacent to the courthouse flagpole.

"We summon the root man of justice for Cleveland Barnes." Ruthie shouted at the building's face, her raspy deep voice shaking with anger. "We summon the spirit of the Loa, the ancient spirit who walks the earth, to this poteau-mitan, this ceremony. We are going to make a voodoo gris-gris, make a charm and cast a spell on this man." She pointed at the building. Reaching into her pocket, she pulled out her hand closed, flung a dark powder, and shook an oddly shaped gourd held in her other hand. Drums beaten by several old men made a three-beat rhythm, and Ruthie sang into the megaphone:

"Here's my gris-gris—on this house of justice!
I put this gris-gris—on the front steps, and
Make them shake—until they shutter,
Make them do the justice—for this man Cleveland Barnes,
And the Great Papa Legba—the great voodoo god
Papa Legba will come—for Cleveland Barnes,
Papa Legba come—for Cleveland Barnes."

Ruthie's voice seethed into the microphone and out across the crowd. Ruthie, Amanda, and several other ladies prayed for the arrival of Papa Legba—a voodoo spirit that I hadn't heard about since Elton John sang about him twenty-five years ago.

I counted fourteen ladies moving back and forth under both their wooden poles. They wore a rainbow of colors, from turquoise and bright yellow to green and red. Ruthie wore a scarlet dress with a matching scarf in her hair. Beside the female chanters were five older men. Three had skin-covered casks made into drums and long bones carved to strike the hide-covered tops. Two other graying gents shook large gourds filled with something to make them rattle and they all spun and danced in a big semicircle. They circled and shook their hips and knees, hands open above them, blocking all entrance to superior court.

No way could Ruthie have obtained a permit this fast, if at all, so the police had every right to break this crowd up. I saw several marshals watching, probably hoping this odd display and collection of sixty-somethings would peacefully disperse and take the gawking crowd with them. Ruthie danced in the middle of the crowd, circling around a metal box on the sidewalk in front of her. After several minutes she picked up a megaphone and pointed and shook her fist at the courthouse. With head up and arms wide open she shrieked words in a language I didn't recognize.

The concrete sidewalk burned in the July steam-bath, yet no one showed signs of tiring. The crowd grew by the minute, taking on a carnival tone as more news trucks arrived and cameramen roamed the scene. Courthouse marshals shook their heads in wonder and frustration. Two black vans full of police in riot gear pulled up across the street, by the Securities Exchange Commission building.

Sparky Nucose and a cameraman from Eyewitness News

came at me. I had to get away. Couldn't be identified with this spectacle. I abandoned my court plans and cut for the office. Too late. Shoving his gut through the crowd, red-haired, freckled Sparky poked a cordless microphone at me and flashed a grin full of yellow-stained choppers.

"Stuart Clay, counsel to Cleveland Barnes. We see before us a Voodoo ritual led by the defendant's sister, a Ms. Ivyroot Malveaux of Washington, D.C. What do you think of this development?"

"It's a free country, Sparky. This woman has a right to express herself." I studied the man's bulbous honker. "Of course, we didn't know this was going to happen, but it's certainly the First Amendment right of these people to protest the outrageous arrest and prosecution of Cleveland Barnes."

"Why do you say outrageous, counselor?"

"The facts speak for themselves. This case should never have been brought. Bloodied Ballys don't prove murder. Now I don't think I should comment more at this time."

I nodded to the eye of the camera, turned and walked away, eager to control press exposure with a single sound bite and keep my message simple. Save the substantive comments for reporters like Fred Collins who might give something in return. Also, I wanted to avoid the bane of defense lawyers in a high profile case—the certified letter from bar counsel regarding pretrial publicity. I'd suffered through two bar counsel complaints since hanging out my shingle. They were dismissed at an early stage, but they burned up valuable time. I had no time to spare.

I crossed over to the north side of Indiana Avenue. Ruthie spoke to the courthouse again, as if she were addressing a large head jutting up from the city block. Her voice became garbled. Distance. Needed distance.

Looking behind me, I saw a black Lincoln coming slowly down the street. New York tags. There were two white-haired guys with sunglasses in the front seat. Twins.

The car braked in front of me. I tried to speed up and maybe duck into the back door of the Public Defender's Office, but the oversized-white hairs had other plans. In a New York kind of way they made me an offer I couldn't refuse, but I didn't like bullies who made offers. When the uglier of the two made the mistake of grabbing my right arm, I swung the back of my right fist up and smashed it into his right eye socket and nose. Blood trickled down over his white shirt and black suit. The second twin rushed me, but I stopped him with a round house that caught his ear, and followed with a torso punch. The men blocked me on either side, both moving and looking for an opportunity to strike. Then the back window of the Lincoln slid down, and an ugly little man pointed a snub-nosed thirty eight pistol straight at me.

"Glad to meet you, Mr. Clay," he said. "Could we have a word?"

# CHAPTER 23

THE rodent pointed the gun at my head and motioned for me to open the door and get in the back seat. Tweedledee and Tweedledum licked their wounds and got in front. Windows slid up. An electronic lock clicked on all the doors. The Lincoln motored down D Street.

"I'm Mickey Jaworski," he said. I thought he looked more like Joe Pesci's balding father. He slid the gun into a carrier on the left door and turned back to me, smiling. "Sorry to meet you like this," Mickey chuckled, "but we really just wanted to have a quick word. You ought to do something about that temper of yours." He held out his right hand.

Reluctantly, I shook. Like squeezing a dead fish.

He made a shrill whistle at the driver. "Get a move-on boy. The man's office is around the corner at 603." He smiled at me again, flashing broken teeth beneath his drooping schnauzer, beady eyes, blotchy forehead, and thin gray fuzz.

"Sorry for the misunderstanding. We'll drop you off at the office. I just thought we should have a chance to talk before things go very far." He handed me a card announcing Milton S. "Mickey" Jaworski, Esq.

"What was it that we wanted to talk about?" I spoke politely, not to be too much of a wise guy, since he and his goombahs had me. I had no idea who this guy was.

"We want to talk about my friend and client, Benito Batiste." His eyebrows raised and the smile disappeared.

"So talk," I replied. Too bad Cyndi wasn't here to record. I waited.

"Your new client is accused of murdering Benny."

"I'm aware of that."

"My client was a man of honor."

A man of honor? Was this guy doing a Brando imitation? I stared at him, waiting to hear whatever he had to say, realizing that I could bail out and roll without too many scratches.

"I know you have a job to do. But my client left behind a loving widow and two wonderful kids." He flashed a maudlin gaze out the window down Seventh Street, affecting sudden interest in the Olson's Bookstore and Shakespeare Theatre behind us. I said nothing as the car turned left again and pulled in front of the Law Offices of Mitchell & Strong.

"How can I put this?" He raised his dead fish hands to gesture in the air and scrunched his face into a knot. "Let's just say that Benny's family would appreciate it if you didn't drag his good name through the mud on this. Right, boys?" Mickey called to the white-hairs. They nodded in assent and grumbled as they licked their wounds. I wondered what family we were discussing.

"I don't drag anyone through the mud, Mr. Jaworski. I just represent my client."

"Well, that's good, right, boys? You heard what he said, right, boys?"

Grunts.

The car stopped. They were going to let me go.

"Frankly, it would help if I knew why Mr. Batiste was in town," I said. "Maybe his death had something to do with whatever business he had."

"I don't think so, Mr. Clay." Mickey grimaced and waved a stubby index finger. "Benny came here to meet with an old associate who is beyond reproach."

"Who was it?"

"Attorney-client privilege, counselor." He smiled. "Now back to what you say about Benito and what you just did to the boys and me, for one moment, so we understand each other. You know and I know that sometimes you make your guy seem good by making some other guy seem bad. Like you might imply or infer that this other guy was involved in some illegal activities, right?" The smile disappeared. "And I'm telling you nicely, Mr. Clay, don't make that other guy Benny. Just don't do it, counselor, cause if you do there will be hell to pay. The felony assault and threat charges for what you just did to my assistants, and the death threat my boys just heard you make to me, and my firm's bar counsel complaint against you—those will be the least of your worries. You will never be safe again. Capische?"

His black eyes flashed coldly, and I locked onto them, all pretense removed. Message delivered. Seconds ticked on the Lincoln's console.

No use wasting my breath here. Nothing could be proven but the physical injury to the white hair, the thirty-eight would never be found, and the white-haired guys would no doubt testify about my unprovoked attack. And if things ever came to a crunch, these three and whoever sent them here would kill me in a hot second and forget about it by feeding time.

I smiled knowingly and nodded. The staring contest ended.

"And anyway," Mickey brightened unnaturally, "what's in these court cases for you guys? Not much, right?" Transformed, he launched into banter about low fees—the favorite small talk of many lawyers.

"I don't go hungry." I cracked a smile, thinking that this scum ball should get disbarred for what he'd just done.

"Tell you what, Clay," Mickey continued. "Give me your card. We got some transactional-type business here in Washington. We could use a local contact."

We who? Why had Benny and this guy really come to Washington? I reached in and grabbed a card, hoping Jaworski might incriminate himself on a voice message.

"Call me any time. Hope to hear from you soon, Mr. J."

"Mr. J?" He laughed. "Hey, I like that. You could hear from me real soon." He kept laughing. "Because I know where you live. Fact is, I discussed my concerns with a Mr. Haskell Eaton of your firm this morning and mentioned the possibility of some business to him." His grin tightened. "Haskell seemed very interested, if you know what I mean."

Haskell Eaton? I reached for the door. If that bean-counter managing partner had compromised my case, I'd rip his face off.

"Well, that is great," I said. "Listen, I have to run. It's been a pleasure." A real bowl of cherries.

About as much fun as a hangnail.

The driver sprang the electronic, and I got out of the car.

# CHAPTER 24

"BLOODIED Ballys don't prove murder."

My face crowded the television screen as I walked through the lobby of Mitchell & Strong. Two well-dressed men looked up with raised brows from the waiting room sofa. Jo Ann motioned from the receptionist desk and handed me a collection of message slips. I headed down the hall, unlocked and quickly shut my office door behind me, and dropped onto the sofa. This nine-hour-old case felt more like nine years, and it just kept coming at me.

The red light on my private line blinked. I smacked the replay button.

"Mr. Clay, I'm Adrian Sewell," the silky voice said. "We're impressed with you, and Mom wants me to offer our services."

What services? I'd have to call him back. The written messages from the receptionist all related to U.S. versus Cleveland Barnes. Six were from reporters, including one from Fred Collins. I'd talk to Fred, but not the rest. Another call came from Lisa Stein about the upcoming court date, and a call from Rhondo asked that I stop "jerking the chain" of Barry Acres.

Before I could settle in to return calls, my inner-office line buzzed. Jo Ann informed me that Managing Partner Haskell Eaton requested my presence in the main conference room.

Haskell never requested meetings with me. I knew he'd howled about Jack Payne's decision to offer me an of-counsel position, but we'd only conferred by email—once about my use of firm services at odd hours and, more recently, he wrote me to express appreciation after I rescued the teenage son of a notable D.C. businessman arrested for mooning a policeman. Now Haskell wanted to see me face to face?

Life has many truisms. If you haven't learned this one yet, I'll tell you flat out: Never trust a man named Haskell. Always be on guard. The Beaver knew it. I knew it. This always was and always will be so.

Even so, a request for a meeting from the managing partner had to be complied with—if I wanted to stay at the firm.

As I headed toward the conference room, I passed a Charlotte Flemming, a junior associate specializing in Mergers and Acquisitions. Flashing her fawn eyes, the beautiful brunette acknowledged me with an admiring sort of look. Since becoming a trial lawyer, I'd noticed that media attention seemed to elevate my standing with women, even ones like Charlotte, who could probably be my daughter. So I surmised my new case and its hoopla had been observed and discussed on the Mitchell & Strong gossip circuit. Nice, but of no real import, especially since thoughts of being in the same space with Haskell hit my stomach like salt peter for the soul.

I knocked on the door.

"Come in, Stuart," Haskell called in a friendly sort of way. Out of character. People like Haskell don't do things in a friendly sort of anything. Kind of like having a vampire invite you to a late-night cocktail party.

I opened the door, smelled lemon oil, took in the huge mahogany conference table and army of overstuffed green leather chairs. Two blue-suited men sat side-by-side. Haskell sort of looked like a mean version of Ed Sullivan. The other man, Percy Diel, was a tall skinny fellow with short dark hair and a college-kid face. He reminded me of a young Anthony Perkins.

"Hello, Stuart!" Haskell grinned. A scary sight, like a mortician stifling gas. Percy shifted uncomfortably in his chair, shoving back and crossing one long leg over the other, then brushing wavy dark hair off his forehead. On first impression, I'd have wondered if Percy inhaled a few scotches at the Capitol Grill before popping into the meeting. He'd been this way the few times I'd been in the elevator up next to him, kind of detached and off kilter, but never a booze smell.

"Stuart, this is Parcival Diel." Haskell motioned over. "He's one of the partners at Mitchell & Strong. I'm not sure you've met."

"Right." I reached over and shook hands. Percy didn't stand up. "Don't think we've been formally introduced, Parcival, but I certainly know who you are."

"Likewise. Call me Percy."

Percy Diel was the son of Morton Diel, District of Columbia icon-at-large, a developer, businessman, and community leader responsible for bringing professional hockey, professional baseball, home rule, and a new convention center to the District of Columbia. When other businesses nearly abandoned the district during the decades after the riots, Morton Diel doubled and tripled his efforts to restore and even improve his beloved hometown, and those efforts paid off. The greatness of Morton Diel made his son all the more of an enigma at the firm. This beanpole of a man didn't look like an heir to anyone's throne.

"We know you're under pressure," Haskell wheezed. "That's why we're here." He looked out the window, seeming to study the National Archives' façade of pillars and classical figures. "You know, Stuart. We at Mitchell & Strong are about business, but we're also about seeing that the poor are properly represented. That's why Jack Payne brought you onboard."

"Right." No reason to let on that I knew that Haskell and Jack had a shouting match at the partner meeting where Jack proposed that they hire one of those "sleazy courthouse defense attorneys" into the firm. I smiled at Haskell.

"Jack called in from Los Angeles, Stuart. I guess he discussed your appointment with someone over in the superior court." I wondered if Haskell had ever even been there. "Bottom line is that you'll have firm resources backing you up on this one. The court approved Percy to assist you as second chair. The city's edgy and wants resolution, but nobody needs a scapegoat."

"Right." I wondered if "the city" had confided this fact to

Haskell. Percy glanced at me, nodded towards Haskell, and rolled his eyes. Haskell missed the gesture.

"I'm with the program, Haskell." I cut through. "It's a gruesome murder and there's some folks making noise in front of superior court, but we have to be reasonable."

"That's right. And we have to think of that street man, unable to defend himself."

"My father called this morning and he's pissed," Percy declared, ignoring Haskell's rendition of St. Francis. "He was very explicit about the case involving Cleveland Barnes and wants me to personally help out on this one. Wants to show Diel family commitment to equal treatment, but, frankly gentlemen, we all know the other story, too.

"Nobody needs another spring of '68! My father represents over six billion of capitol investment in the new Judiciary Square and new Gallery Place, and we don't want another damn riot!"

"That's not going to happen," I said. But his logic made good business sense, and I had no problem with it. The House of Diel represented big money in the urban rebirth, and I didn't want to see it burn either. And at least this guy didn't mince words. "But Percy, do you have any criminal law experience?" I struggled to keep the edge off my question.

"Yes," Percy said. "For the Public Defender's Service in Prince Georges County. I was out there for two years in Upper Marlboro."

"See, Stuart? We've thought it through and everyone has already okayed this," Haskell said. "And it's not a bad idea. You have exposure here and you know it." He dug at me, mortician's smile still intact.

"I've been around the block, fellows." I stared flatly at Haskell and then at Percy. "We all know I don't really have a choice, and I don't object anyway, okay? So let's move on."

They looked at me, surprised. I sighed and sat back, not showing a thing. Over and over, I repeated Talleyrand's words in my head: 'The art of strategy is to foresee the inevitable and expedite its occurrence.'

"That's good," Haskell chortled one time too many. "Let's move on."

# CHAPTER 25

"IN fact, I can use the help, Haskell," I lied. Percy grinned. Did he read my thoughts?

"Another thing, Stuart," Haskell said. "If this works out, Jack and Percy here want you to do some work over on the commercial side in a few cases growing out of the Diel mall project. Percy has handled himself very well, but he's going to be swamped soon. A senior level person with a litigation background."

"Well, that's fine, but I just remembered something," I said. Not that I forgot having a pistol shoved at me. "This doesn't have anything to do with a guy named Jaworski, does it? He claimed to have talked to you this morning."

"Oh, him." Haskell waved peevishly. "Hell, no, come on Clay. We know what he is. They talk about him at the New York office all the time. One of those sleazy criminal defense law—" Haskell caught himself and stopped. The mortician reddened.

Silence. I raised my eyebrows at Haskell and opened both hands to the sky. But none of this mattered.

"Welcome to the case, Percy." I stood and reached over, shook his hand again. He still didn't stand up. "Ever done a homicide trial?"

"Well, no." Percy suddenly seemed interested in his Blackberry. "Mostly drug cases. Stolen cars. That sort of thing."

"I'm sure you'll be a great help." And I'd make sure he didn't get in the way.

We talked for several minutes, agreed to meet and create a list of projects later in the evening. That would give me a chance to figure out how to use Percy to an advantage without cramping my style. Percy did the "my father this, my father that" routine. This kept Haskell salivating, gesturing with interest. Made me want to scream, but I didn't. In my old age I have learned to suppress such displays of emotion. Just barely.

I itched to get back to my office. Lots of paperwork had to go out before I met Cyndi and returned to Georgetown. The only saving grace was that Percy's blathering on about his family ties ultimately shut Haskell up. He turned a practiced eye on Percy, content to listen now that I'd agreed to Percy's entry into the Barnes case.

Minutes later I excused myself and made it to the hallway. Had pleadings to draft and letters to write to prepare for Cleveland Barnes' next hearing, I said. They understood or said they did. Pacing down the corridor, I ticked off the types of motions I had to file: suppress, disclose, compel. Good stuff, but the interruptions weren't over.

Jo Ann's voice sounded over the front desk page.

"Stuart Clay to the front desk immediately. Stuart Clay to the front desk immediately."

Was it a subpoena or a U.S. Marshal sent by an irate judge? Turned out to be neither.

# CHAPTER 26

HIS tie cost more than my suit, no doubt. Red and green silk, woven in a subtle pattern, matched to a taupe shirt and olive suit, all tailored for the tall thin black man who shook my hand. No wonder Jo Ann called me.

"Adrian Sewell." He squeezed my hand.

"I remember you." I led him into a conference cube and closed the door.

"Didn't know if you would." Adrian sat down. "We never spoke, and it must have been at least three years ago."

"I mentioned that to your mother today when I met her at the courthouse." I studied his face. "Actually, it was about two weeks before I got a job offer to come here. You were in the character file for the trial, but we never got past motions."

"Yeah, you did right by Abdul. Works in P.G. County and no trouble since that verdict."

"Dismissal," I said. "There was no verdict. We won the motion to dismiss. And he works for you now?"

"Sewell Grocers." Adrian smiled.

Abdul Orleans had been arrested and charged in the shooting death of another teenager in an alley off of Alabama Avenue, Southeast Washington, D.C.—in one of the most troubled sections of the city. Our defense rested on challenging a faulty eyewitness identification by a young librarian who saw the killing through the back door of her row house. Though the case looked very difficult going in, we won a three day motions hearing. The librarian turned out to be an awful witness on the stand and other people came forward to vouch for my client.

Abdul's family had paid me $15,000 dollars in cash. His mother said there was a wealthy aunt in South Carolina. The whole thing became a headache because I had to report the cash payment to the Internal Revenue Service and the District of Columbia taxation authorities, and then put the money in a safe deposit box for a year while they decided whether it was possible "proceeds of a crime." The government finally passed on the money without ever even coming over to my bank and inspecting it or doing anything else, as far as I could see.

Adrian assured me that Abdul was on the straight and narrow.

"The way it works with the community team kids is this, man." Adrian sat down and put his elbows on the table. "Lots of kids work for us. Or we place them. In decent jobs. Part of the league effort. Good for the business." He gestured a lot with his right hand, popping a finger open with each statement until the hand was wide open.

"And now you're here for Cleveland Barnes?"

"Damn straight, man. Cleveland's my godfather. Ruthie and Cleveland were our neighbors for years growing up. Always around on the holidays. Everybody loved Cleveland, wanted to help him." Adrian frowned. "I'm saying, the man had troubles in his head. The guy's just kind of out there in lala land."

"When is the last time you've seen him?"

"Long time, man. Like, I'm busy, especially since my pops passed last year. I run a business, want to build it into something else, plus work with the basketball team. But Cleveland is somebody that my mother loves, and Ruthie is her sister now." Adrian looked down at his open hand. "I can't let them down."

We discussed the case for several minutes. The man seemed genuinely concerned for Cleveland. He respected my need not to divulge details of the case, but offered to help.

"Tell me what you need and we'll help," he said. "You need a retainer to get you out of the court-appointed thing and pay you like a private lawyer?"

My pulse quickened.

"I sure don't mind being paid." To put it mildly. "But we need to wait until after the preliminary hearing. Since the case began as court-appointed, we'll need to file notice with the court that the case is out of the CJA system. I'm concerned that could get out into the media and hurt us. So let's wait."

"You got it, man. But I want Cleveland taken care of."

"You aren't alone," I said. And I'd started to wonder about just that.

# CHAPTER **27**

"YOUR investigator ran in, said she was double-parked, and tossed this to me." Jo Ann motioned at a large manila envelope.

I took the envelope, tore it open, and eyed a subpoena return wrapped around a videotape with the handwritten inscription: Byno Sanchez, crime scene video. I walked with Adrian over to the elevator. He gave me a translucent business card with his cellular and twenty-four hour pager number on it. We shook hands and parted.

Returning to my office, I bolted the door, switched the telephones to voicemail, and sat down to get to work. I needed a chance to think. Percy and I planned to meet around five. Had to keep everyone away until then.

Over the next sixty minutes I spun out six emergency motions for the defense in U.S. versus Cleveland Barnes. A motion to dismiss for illegal stop (what's so suspicious about pushing cans down the street?); a motion to suppress physical evidence (they were just shoes that he had found and there was no basis to conduct any further search); a motion to suppress statements

(statements of religious beliefs to the police were irrelevant and the Miranda Warning was poorly documented); a motion to disclose all evidence relied on pursuant to U.S. versus Rosser (contained a three-page bill of particulars stating the sorts of evidence I needed and had a legal right to, and especially focusing on evidence of grand jury investigations involving Benny Batiste and third-party witnesses); a motion to disclose all exculpatory material (like maybe the Organized Crime Task Force reports discussing Benny!); and a motion to conduct a forensic evaluation of Cleveland Barnes without the delay of a commitment to St. Elizabeth's Hospital (Cleveland wouldn't like it, but I had to CYA for an ineffective assistance of counsel challenge if there was an insanity defense that could be raised).

I wrote a long, self-serving letter to Lisa Stein. It recited every aspect of the case and spelled out in mind-numbing detail what I thought the government was claiming and what they had to disclose to the defense in light of those claims.

My files from earlier cases included the legal arguments, in support of most of these arguments, and I just had to fill in a few blanks. I had prepared a collection of "canned motions" that were ready to fire. One way or the other I'd tease out the information that Rhondo felt duty bound not to disclose. Then I'd deal with it.

Even if I lost every single motion, we would still win the motions war. We had a right to ask that hearings be held on all motions before the jury was sworn. To oppose my motions, the government would be forced to put on evidence, release documents, and present live witnesses. This would be a tremendous boon to the defense as we tried to sniff out and diffuse land mines. Plus there was a lot of symbolic value in pelting the prosecution with a stack of motions.

I faxed, e-mailed, and mailed all the pleadings to Lisa Stein and put multiple packages out for a messenger to take next door and file in the night depository at the superior court lobby. Then I buzzed Cyndi Oh and left a message to confirm our 7:30 trip back to Georgetown, to ask if she'd snagged an autopsy report, and to tell her how fine she looked in court.

As I readied my stack of court documents, I sang an old Garth Brooks song to myself. A little hokey to be sure, but it perked up my sleep-deprived soul and reminded me that the case rested on the client, the client's needs, the facts, and the law. Those things counted. Haskell didn't—or so I told myself.

By the time Percy and I met at in the small conference room at five, I felt organized and ready to delegate some backup work to him.

"Here are the PD reports from the officer in charge, copies of the court docs, and some canned motions just filed." I handed him the stack. "Maybe you could bug the medical examiner's office for the autopsy report. Double-check the records over at 300 Indiana to make sure there aren't additional police reports. Get a law clerk working on cutting and pasting press coverage and getting videotapes of all the news on the case. Sometimes they find out stuff or spin it in a way that we don't think about. That's how I found out about Batiste's mob ties. Compile a list of all the witnesses, documents, physical evidence, and related evidence in the case. "

"Aren't those things that an investigator would normally do?"

"No, man. I'd do them now if I had the time. That's where the key to the case might be. Don't know how they do it in P.G. County, but I don't trust an investigator on fundamental facts— and mine's a Yale brat. I head my own investigation. Work with me, follow my rules." I stared Percy straight in the eye, making my point.

"What else?" He deadpanned.

"Just read this stuff. And look at the article from today in the *Post*. I'm kind of wondering about Fred Collins, the crime beat guy. He had a real fix on who Batiste was and on the government's case. Sort of leaves me wondering what else he knows."

"Did you want me to call him?"

"God no! I'm the mouth. Plan to call Fred later anyway. We belong to the same karate school. No offense, but I control the press statements in this case."

"Fine," Percy said, a little sullenly.

I thought of the card Fred had handed me in front of the courthouse. Had to call him soon.

"You got enough until tomorrow, Percy. Maybe we can talk in the early afternoon." I stood up, eager to get back to my office and prepare to go to back to Georgetown.

Percy started to get up and then he sort of lost his balance and caught himself on the table, like a drunk falling down.

"You okay?" I leaned over to brace him. Smelled deeply. Nothing.

"Just a little faint sometimes." He gave a hollow laugh. "Need some vitamin B12 or soy bean milk."

"Try a mud bath," I quipped uneasily.

We shook hands. Percy picked up the stack of pleadings and headed out the door. I watched him leave carefully, and reached a conclusion based on knowledge gleaned from hundreds of criminal cases, evaluation of witnesses, and helping troubled clients. One way or the other, this well-dressed, well-groomed, connected lawyer was one stoned puppy.

# CHAPTER **28**

FRED Collins answered his cell on the first ring.

"Hello, Stuart," he said quietly. "I've been waiting for you for hours. Seems like you have a major league case on your hands."

"You can say that again." I leaned back on my couch, watched the screen saver logo bounce around the sides of my computer. "I haven't had two minutes since you handed me your card."

"So what's new?" He said it quietly and waited, like a shrink or some other trained listener.

"Nothing for attribution, Fred."

"You got it."

"Okay. I had a strange little man pull a pistol on me earlier. After all the nights I've spent tracking witnesses in the streets of D.C., and it's some damned lawyer that threatens me with a snub-nosed thirty-eight. Think I'll move to Sheboygan."

"The bratwurst capitol? Isn't it cold up there?"

"Right. Out in god's country, away from the mob. Now tell me how you got all that stuff on Batiste." I lay back on the couch and closed my eyes.

"Confidential man. What've you found out?"

"Come on, Fred. Is your source connected to the parties? I'm asking because if he or she is, you might want to watch yourself."

"Can't say, Stuart. And I'll guard you the same way."

"Between you and Rhondo, I could use a few friends with a little less integrity—and a little more mouth."

"No you couldn't. Now come on, Stuart. Have you found out anything else on the mob angle?"

"Nothing you won't find easily." I couldn't disclose what Rhondo had told me. "The guy who held a gun to me is Batiste's lawyer, a slime-bucket named Mickey Jaworski. He and his peons squeezed me on D Street today."

"I know who Jaworski is. He's an urban legend in the Big Apple. Has his own retained publicist and counsel for the bar complaints. What else?"

"From my point of view, this case is about the lady who left the club with Benny. Find out who she is and Cleveland walks. Did you get the probable cause papers from the court jacket?"

"No, man, and I'm not happy about it. That Magistrate judge took the file to chambers and the records people over at main police headquarters can't cough up the PD reports."

"Can't or won't?" I looked up at the clock over my file cabinet. Had to get dressed soon and go meet Cyndi downstairs.

"Same difference for me, and I never know what the real deal is. I just write stories."

"Well, I can help you out with the PD reports and all of that. Still got the same fax as on your card?" I eyed the facsimile number at the *Washington Post* offices, walked over to my briefcase and pulled out the PD reports. Easy to do, and a small price for continued cooperation.

"Please send them ASAP. I'm on deadline."

"I'll shoot stuff over to you—the GS on probable cause and some of the PD reports. It tracks what Lisa said in C-10 at presentment. They left the club at 2:17 A.M. and Benny's parking meter violation was discovered about thirteen minutes later. Plus today I got a videtape from over the club door that shows our dead guy groping his date's gluteus maximus as they walked out. I don't think they smooched and went their separate ways until the ice cream social on Sunday. I'll bet she set him up."

"Thanks, Marion. Where's the videotape? How can I get a copy?"

"You'll see it, man. I only have one copy and I need to guard it."

"If you loan it to me I'll have it back by six A.M. Promise."

"You owe me, kinsman," I said. But I trusted Fred to bring the tape back as he said he would. "It'll be with the bald-headed night attendant who monitors the lobby at 603 north building. My buddy William. But get it back to me. You say by tomorrow morning?"

"Right. Any leads on who the woman is?"

"Can't say yet," I lied. "What have you got for me?"

"You'll read about it. Can't say yet."

"Is that fair? Look what I'm giving you?"

"It's fair and you know it, Stuart. We both have obligations. I hold back on you because I have to. You're doing the same, and I'm not calling your bluff. I'm telling you honestly what I can and can't do. So come on man, cut it out."

"Listen, I've got to return a call to Bridgette Ginadio, too."

"So what?"

"So maybe before I call her you and I can agree that if you'll share what you're finding out about Batiste I'll agree to give you first shot at anything that breaks the case open?"

The line went silent for several seconds.

"You think something will short circuit the prosecution," Fred asked?

"Better than 50 percent chance. Something or somebody will get short circuited."

"Why?"

"Because." I considered my words carefully. "My best guess based on all of the evidence is that the murder is incidental to a war between criminal enterprises. Cleveland has no significance in this conflict." I formed the defense theory as I stated it to Fred, rolled it around in my mind, and thought about it. Sounded good to me.

"No significance?" Fred replied. "What if he's an insignificant player in a criminal enterprise? Isn't that a legitimate question?"

"I suppose it is," I replied. "But I don't see that either. Do you have any reason to think differently?"

"Not really. My source seems to think that Cleveland has nothing to do with the murder.

"Any chance I could talk to the source?"

"I'll ask, but I doubt it. Let's talk again later. I'm expecting another call tonight."

"If you don't get me here, try my cell. Cyndi and I are going to Bridge Street."

"Right. Spar tomorrow?"

"If there's time, sure. I love beating up reporters."

"Later, dude." The line went dead.

I faxed Fred the GS statement of probable cause and various other police department documents, then picked up the horn and called Bridgette Ginadio at Court TV. We'd been in the same law school class back in Rhode Island. Her father was a Rhode Island Supreme Court Justice who'd resigned under a cloud, a good guy as far as I could see, guilty of nothing more than knowing guys from the old neighborhood. No one ever proved that he did anything wrong, but in the rapid evolution of Providence and high-tech New England, some friendships proved deadly.

Bridgette and I agreed I would read a prepared statement the next morning at 11:30 at the C Street entrance to the D.C. Superior Court, the proverbial back door. I could only hope that Ruthie and her spell casters would stay around front so I could do my job.

# CHAPTER 29

"EVERYBODY deserves a lawyer. Everybody." Mickey sneered out from the Google report on my computer screen. In page after page the sneering man posed over his captioned mantra. I agreed with him, of course, but coming from Mickey it seemed vulgar, like a snide excuse to protect wrongdoing rather than a noble principle raised against a despotic British crown.

Benny made Mickey look wholesome. A series in the *New York Times* referred to his alleged Spilotro organization ties and claimed that the Seabreeze trucking business operated as a profitless shell. In a letter to the editor, the Law Office of Mickey Jaworski disputed claims of Batiste's mob involvements, and listed several actual clients served by the company.

I couldn't simply conclude that Seabreeze was a non-business shell. But it didn't matter. Mickey was just a whitewash man. Benny might as well have had a tattoo that said "mob thug" stamped across his forehead.

Lots of shameless hoods like Benny are protected by bar licensed rats who talk high principle and constitutional justice, give to charities, appear at bar functions, and snicker all the way to their safety deposit boxes. Many take their lump sums in cash, don't report that income to the IRS. Everybody knows it, yet the world goes on.

My problem happened to be a more discrete one. Assuming Seabreeze was a pretext for Benny's other business, why did he really come to Washington, D.C. and who had Benny come to see? Did local players whack Benny because he'd tried to muscle them? Or had they wanted to change something in the business against the wishes of New York?

I didn't know the answer to these questions. Even so, these were straightforward problems and, notwithstanding Mickey's threats, I'd find straightforward answers. Mickey meant business but I still abided by a simple code. It said I should provide rigorous representation within the bounds of the law. It didn't say rigorous representation until a wise guy muscled me. Couldn't change that, not in this world. If doing the right thing, the pure thing, brought danger, I'd do what I needed to do to—what my union-leader father did over forty years before. He put a gun to the forehead of a small town bigot who led a mob to pelt my one year old sister and I with rocks.

I thought of Mickey holding the gun on me briefly and couldn't get past it. My gun was lawfully and properly registered to an old farmhouse address out in Fageyville, Maryland—a village outside Frederick where I rented a room and sometimes escaped to. D.C. had the toughest gun control laws in the United States, and possessing this weapon could lead to felony charges against me. Too bad.

I took the metal box out of the bottom file cabinet, opened it and took out the Berretta Cheetah and its magazine.

As I dressed, I studied a face on the wall over the walnut desk. Various framed mementos and other items hung there. Beside all the diplomas and court certificates, I saw my model, Tameka, the nineteen-year-old black girl who'd choked to death on a garden hose because she tried to do the right thing and stand up against a murderer. Thus does this world treat purity.

I locked the magazine into my Beretta, and put it down on my desk.

The phone rang and I picked it up. Without introduction or small talk, Cyndi launched into summarizing her afternoon.

Notwithstanding her best efforts, the autopsy report wouldn't be available until the next day, but the chief medical examiner David Sahi had offered a preliminary opinion: "Benny Batiste died due to decapitation."

Cursing to myself, I removed my suit and shirt and hung them on the door hook, then pulled out black jeans and a black long-sleeved shirt and black sneakers out of the file cabinet's bottom drawer. The ME's report just about summarized the state of our intelligence to date.

What did I really need to know? That seemed simple: who was the blonde that left with Benny? We'd gotten no closer, but now that the day shift had departed for the suburbs, the real investigation could begin.

I put on the black clothes, reached in the bottom file drawer again and grabbed a bag containing a night camera, tape recorder, and night vision goggles. I jammed the gun under my waistband and pulled the shirt over top, then stowed the rest in a small arm bag. Pausing one more time, I considered the need to carry a gun, and the risk that it might result in a criminal conviction and suspension from the bar. No matter. I'd be a fool to go under the Key Bridge at night without protection. I was no fool.

# CHAPTER 30

CYNDI looked like one of painter Paul Gauguin's fruit bearing islanders dressed in black spandex. She didn't have chopped kiwi, but, instead, a meatball sub loaded with peppers and Tabasco from the sandwich shop that replaced the FOP bar, across from the courthouse. I took the food and followed her to the Oldsmobile double-parked in the Indiana Avenue entrance to the 603 north building. The sedan sped out to Independence Avenue, motored on and turned onto the Fourteenth Street Bridge. I ate the sub and drank my twenty-something coffee of the day.

We discussed voodoo gods, Mickey Jaworski, the white hairs, Percy Diel, Adrian Sewell, and more. As one in the know on such things, Cyndi educated me about Papa Legba, a Voodoo "Iwa," or spirit, who possesses mortals and performs fantastic feats. She told me a "gris-gris" is like a voodoo mass, and that Ruthie had cast a spell or placed a curse on the courthouse. We circled around on the Virginia side toward Georgetown.

Washington's rush hour ran its course, taking workers off to Northern Virginia, Bethesda, Greenbelt, and other places, away from the hot, tired city. As the sun set, some of the new urban dwellers went to the bright spots—to the Verizon Arena, the new movie complex at Gallery Place, and the one at Union Station. Elsewhere, the street people replaced departing commuters. They wandered out and begged. Kids peddled poison. Hookers strutted their stuff, flicking their skilled, agile tongues to passing motorists.

Three helicopters chattered through twilight, transferring unseen power brokers from National Airport to a helipad in the northwest quadrant. Car lights pierced the humid exhaust as the sun disappeared, slicing through the growing darkness and putrid steam. Tired workers went to their hovels, to what peace they'd carved out, to the spouse and kids, an old episode of *Everybody Loves Raymond*, the newest whatever. Still others took to the streets and the cocktail circuit. The powerful and busy shuttled off to the right dinner, the right cocktail appearance at the National Press Club, the right delivery of product from New York or Miami.

Looping into Rosslyn, we swung onto the ramp up the Key Bridge, resting at a stop light on the Virginia side. A disheveled man in an overcoat and toboggan cap ambled through the July heat up to Cyndi's window. His long blond beard was discolored with dirt and he carried an oversized soda cup and a sign reading "Vietnam Vet. Please help." Cyndi rolled the window down two inches. "Time to seed the crop," she muttered, waving the man over to the Oldsmobile. He leaned against the Oldsmobile door and peeked in the window.

"I'm Cyndi and this is Stuart. We're looking for guys named Zebra, Duckie, Snapper, and Shark."

"Whoop-di-doo, Bambi Chen. You need another man, I got it for you now." He flashed a grizzled sneer. I caught a strong whiff of sweat and feces. Nonplussed, Cyndi slid a dollar bill into his two filthy long-nailed fingers, snatched before she could even let go.

"I'm an investigator," she said. "We're looking for guys who live by the bridge—Zebra, Duckie, Snapper, and Shark? Ring any bells?"

"Come on, lady. I got love for you."

"Not about that." She slid a second bill and both our business cards through the window. "Anybody finds those guys for me, you tell them there's lots more where that came from. Call anytime, okay?"

He stood up and studied one of the cards then stared at us and saluted as we pulled away on the changed light. We pulled onto the massive six-lane bridge. It was dark now, but with both shores combined I'd guess the underside of the Key Bridge and the Whitehurst Freeway Bridge would be the size of a football field. I wondered what hid underneath.

At the other side we waited at another light, then pulled across M Street into a parking lot, paid twelve dollars and got a receipt, then parked at the back right-hand section of the lot close to the long narrow staircase up to Prospect Street.

As I opened the door, a barefoot Latino kid sped past our car like a bat out of hell. I was about to walk over and get a better look at him when I saw trouble coming. I slid back into the car and punched the lock.

"Duck quick. Look away."

"From what?" Cyndi put her left hand over to shade her forehead, and I pulled her head down across my legs. She mock-bit my thigh and laughed. Seconds later, Jaworski's white-hairs rushed off the stairway and streaked past like two hounds after a fox.

The kid raced over M Street through a cacophony of blaring horns and darted into the Key Park and down toward the Potomac. One of the men tripped and punched a car roof, and then the two of them continued in hot pursuit.

My stomach turned as I realized that all three were headed under the bridge.

# CHAPTER 31

EVER been under a bridge at night? This is not something covered in law school education. Even so, cases are won because of facts gathered in such places.

I got out of the Olds, grabbed my night bag, moved the gun so that it was secured in the small of my back, and joined Cyndi. We walked out of the lot and past a massive Victorian structure on the north side of M Street, and then crossed over toward the Francis Scott Key Park. To the left of us, lights shined on a strip of students and city people going to bars, restaurants and boutiques in the M Street corridor, spanning east from where we walked all the way to Farragut West. We journeyed onto a path leading from the back of the park to the bank of the Potomac River.

Thirty feet from the Potomac, another path veered off to the right and split, heading to jogging paths under the Whitehurst Freeway Bridge and the Key Bridge. Maybe people camped under both.

As we walked to the bridge, we came upon two men standing close to an overhead lamp, drinking from paper bags. Reaching into my waistband, I cupped the gun inside my right hand, then slipped it in my front pocket.

One man was tall and black with a stripe of white discoloration across the right side of his face. The other was a stout, short white guy sprouting an enormous gray beard. They were engrossed in conversation and unconcerned by our presence. As we approached, I again smelled the sour sweat odor. I grinned at both the men.

"Did you see the kid and those white-haired guys that just ran by us? Where'd they go?"

The taller man grinned back at me, pointed under the bridge, and grunted.

"Under there. Could be anywhere."

I reached out to shake his hand and leave a card in it.

"Name's Stuart Clay, and this is investigator Cyndi Oh. We represent Cleveland Barnes. He says he lives up under the bridge, that you'd remember him because he has a TV set that he lets other people watch."

I spoke to the tall man, trying to include both. The short man sneered at me.

"What's your name?" I addressed the tall fellow.

"What?" He squinted as he took a long draw on the bagged bottle.

"What do they call you?" I smiled.

"Zebra. This is Snapper." He pointed to the short man, who eyed me suspiciously.

"Cleveland said you're his friend," Cyndi ventured.

Zebra looked at his hands. "I know a guy named Cleve that hangs out down here. Brought a big-ass TV down and connected it to the power and satellite at the boathouse. What do y'all have to do with him? What are you doing here?"

"Cleveland's arrested for murder. Last night. I'm his lawyer and he said you'd help. He also mentioned Duckie and Shark. It would really help us, man. Can you tell me about Cleveland?"

"I don't know what he does," Zebra waffled, looking at Snapper then looking away. "I mind my own business and he minds his. People down here don't mess with the other guy's stuff."

"He ever caused you problems?"

"No problems." Zebra fumbled for a battered red cigarette

pack in his pocket. He shook out a bent unfiltered Pall Mall, then slid a battered matchbook from under the cellophane wrap, lit the cigarette, and pulled tobacco off his lip as he blew smoke. "When exactly did Cleve get locked up?"

"Last night about three A.M. The murder happened a few blocks from the Potomac Club about two-thirty in the morning. Cleveland thought that you might be able to help us find witnesses for him. Folks who know the streets and live down here."

"What about a few kids playing on plastic buckets and dancing?" Cyndi added. "Or a woman named Tiffannie out in front of the club?" She squeezed on her shirt pocket turning on the small recorder.

"How did that happen to Cleveland?" Zebra frowned. "I just saw him last night!"

"What time?" Cyndi asked.

"Was about…"

"Who do you represent?" Snapper growled at me and motioned at Zebra to stop talking. "You the DA?"

I suppressed my irritation. "Like I said, we represent Cleveland Barnes. If he's your friend, you should help us. Where did you last see him?"

"On Bridge Street, hustling." Zebra looked uncertainly at his companion, then took a long pull on his beer.

"Do you remember what time you saw him?"

"Don't know exactly." Zebra rubbed his chin. He paused. "Let me get this straight now. You want to talk to us?"

"We're trying to help Cleveland," Cyndi replied. "We want to talk to you, see where Cleveland lives, meet the people he calls New Columbians."

Zebra's eyebrows shot up, and his red lips pinched amidst the sprouting white stubble.

"Snapper and I, we're done with these beers, but we're still kind of thirsty. You want to talk to us and meet people, well—"

"Got you, man." I jumped on the chance. "Let's hit the package store."

"Now you're talking." Zebra barked a laugh and motioned for us to follow.

I'd given up alcohol several years before, having seen too many trial lawyers go down the tubes from booze. But I understood the value of ninety-proof witness fees. Smoothing my hand over the outside of my pocket, I made sure that I'd remembered my roll of bills—something I expected to be needing tonight.

We walked back up the hill to M Street and Dixie Liquors. Cyndi said nothing, but made a "V" sign with her right hand when the two weren't looking. Victory, but thin, as booze always proved to be a limited entry. Still, I hoped the alcohol would attract others and loosen their tongues.

In short order we were across M Street watching Zebra fish a fifth of Napoleon brandy and a case of Guinness chasers off the shelf. Snapper grabbed three packs of Newports. I paid the large unshaven man in the Plexiglas cashier's box in twenties, took a receipt, and wondered if this could ever be listed on the expense report. Certainly, not on a CJA voucher.

We walked back through the park, past the huge American flag still flapping in the July breeze, and back down the hill to the path veering off beneath the bridge. Snapper waddled like an obese, upright lizard. I decided to make sure he never got behind me. My instincts screamed in protest as I followed him to the edge of the light under the bridge. I patted the pistol in my pocket.

"What about the woman named Tiffannie?" I returned to the earlier inquiry as we passed the site of our earlier conversation and approached the part of the path that led under the bridge. Zebra looked over at Snapper, questioning as he ripped the paper off and twisted the cap off a Guinness.

"We ain't your tour guides, mister," Snapper said. "Maybe you should wait."

"Oh, come on, Snap." Zebra took a draw off his Guinness. "Cut the bullshit. This man is trying to help out Cleve, and he bought us the best liquor we've had since the delivery truck turned over," Zebra turned to me. "Mister, the lady's Tiffannie Squires. She's a high yellow, built like a brick house, blonde hair rolling down her back. Not ashamed to let anybody buy a ride."

"Alright," I said, impressed with both his description and sudden animation.

"She work around here most nights?"

"On the weekend. Make it worth my time, and I'll try and find where she is now. I will. I promise." Zebra held up three fingers clasped on either side, the sign of the Boy Scout's oath.

"Sure thing. A 100 bucks to find her," Cyndi said. "Does she know Cleveland well?"

"Oh, yeah." Zebra continued. "Everybody have to know Cleveland because—"

"Come on, man!" Snapper hissed. "You have got to wait."

"Wait for what?" Cyndi called back to Snapper, stepping into his face. I studied the glazed leer in Snapper's bulging lizard eyes.

"What about a guy named Shark?" I continued. "Cleveland sent a message for him."

"He's around, man." Snapper sneered at me.

"We're only trying to help Cleveland," I replied, "so maybe you could lose the attitude."

Snapper jumped in front of me and brushed his left hand around to his back pocket. I looked for a weapon and jammed a hand on my gun's grip.

"Listen to me, courthouse lawyer," Snapper hissed. "You'll find Shark if Shark wants you to find him. And don't you mess with the Bridge People, else you be fish food! Understand?"

"Sure, pal!" I growled back at him. "I'll be sure to tell Cleveland how helpful you've been!" We stood nose to nose in silence. Seconds passed.

Nothing like being dressed down by a guy named Snapper.

# CHAPTER 31

"ALRIGHT, let's get this crap over with," Snapper barked. "Give me some of that damned brandy. All this jawboning with his highness Mr. Courthouse Lawyer has made me thirsty." He grabbed the bottle out of Cyndi's hand, twist-ripped the cap off and took a long swig. "All right. Let's go see who'll talk. Probably nobody." Snapper stomped off.

Zebra shrugged at us and followed Snapper underneath the Key Bridge. Darkness surrounded us as we followed. I could not imagine how anyone navigated under here. I put on my night-vision goggles, took Cyndi's hand, and we walked over on the smooth ground. My eyes scanned the area for rats, and I wondered about the kid running away from Jaworski's thugs.

I spotted a tall chain link fence against the base of the bridge. It seemed covered with some dark fabric or perhaps metal strips. Behind it, in the area leading up to the base of the bridge, a glow peeked over the top. Zebra walked over to one of the anchor poles for the fence, lifted the chain length mesh up, and swung a four-foot portion out like a hidden door. We all walked inside and he placed the fence back in its regular position. Inside this area I saw an outline of several people sitting around a propane lantern. As we moved closer I saw several bed rolls and a small tent against the other side of the fenced-in area. Soon we could see, in here, so I took off the night goggles. As we drew closer in, the area brightened and I heard quiet talk and laughter. Snapper announced that he would look for Shark, then walked back to the tent and disappeared.

A ragged couple kissed and groped on a nearby sleeping bag, but no one seemed to notice or care. Cyndi and I exchanged glances in the half-light and she let my hand loose and ran her nails across the small of my back. Zebra motioned at us to join the group.

Cyndi sat the bottle on a sideways box and Zebra placed the case of beer beside it. We began this oddest of cocktail parties.

A frail man hobbled over to the box and introduced himself as Duckie and, in turn, pointed at a middle age man with him. Beside him sat a Latin or Middle Eastern fellow who seemed taken with his young female friend. Duckie handed both of them bottles of Guinness.

A few more silent ones appeared: a thin white woman with a recently shaved head and a gaunt frame covered by a filthy old pair of mechanics coveralls. Another large man in bib overalls just smiled and said nothing before he guzzled from the brandy bottle.

Ill at ease, I kept my right hand in my pocket. Then I noticed Snapper come out of the tent. Light shined briefly inside the tent and seconds later a tall, barebacked man emerged. He had straight black hair that ran to his stomach. I took it this must be Shark.

"Get out," he hissed at me in a heavy Hispanic accent. "You've no damned business down here. Get out!"

"But I'm Cleveland's lawyer."

"What part of 'get out' before I kick your ass don't you understand?" He rushed at me and pulled out a gun before I could get mine. I threw a heel, kicked, and knocked him back. A shot blasted upward. Everyone ran off into the shadows.

I heard the bullet ricochet on the bridge's underbelly and saw the man raise his gun at me. Before he could take aim I did a second kick at the gun, and the weapon flew off into the darkness. I tried to pull out my Berretta, but he somersaulted and jumped to his feet with one movement, then came at me with a roundhouse kick aimed at my Adam's Apple, a death blow.

I blocked the kick with my left forearm, but the force of his foot felt like a jackhammer and struck the side of my face. I feared he'd broken bones, and noticed that he wore ninja boots. Ignoring the blood trickle from my nostrils, I twisted away and drove a flat fist into his gut.

I heard the man grunt as he fell over, but he rolled away quickly and jumped up again, now running back to the area where his gun had fallen.

"Freeze it, Jack," Cyndi shouted, pointing a small, dark pistol at the man. She stepped out of the shadows. "Cool your heels and we're gone. You stay away from the bang-bang."

"Get the fuck out, schoolgirl!" he growled.

I pulled out my Berretta, flicked off the safety clip, and took aim at his head, backing away slowly.

"We're gone now, pal." I said. We backed into the dark. I readjusted my goggles and saw the man picking up his pistol. "You come after us and I'll plug you!" I shouted.

He stayed on the other side of the camp sight in the dark, but started moving down to the covered fence.

"I said stay," I fired a shot several feet in front of him. He froze, then hit the ground in a roll and flattened.

Reaching the edge of the fence, we pulled it open and slipped out, then readjusted from the outside, and ran from under the bridge, up the path, and into the tree-covered area of the Francis Scott Key Park. We ran into the trees by the park.

"Nothing like a friendly drink," I gasped.

"The creep was on the verge of killing us both right there," she panted, pulling me farther into a covered area.

"And why would he do that?"

"Because— I don't know. But I know one thing: I've seen that schmuck's face in a post office. He's on the top-ten most wanted list, I swear to God."

I thought of the pistol pointing at me.

"You sure?"

"Come on." She pulled me. "We'll track down the face tomorrow, but we need to be out of here." We crossed back into the Key Park, walked across M Street, and got into the car.

Moments later we pulled out and turned left onto M Street, a world away from underneath the bridge. Georgetown students ambled down the sidewalk in pairs and groups, enjoying the laid-back night. They had no idea of the lurking danger.

"Wonder what he's doing down there?" Cyndi checked the rearview mirror.

"No idea," I said. "But you can bet he won't be there tomorrow. The guy is paranoid, maybe with good reason if you're right."

"We'll find out. Got to get back down there."

I phoned my backup investigator, Chester Morgan, gave him the man's description, and asked him to stake the north side of the Key Bridge for the night. Didn't even know if he'd get my message, but I didn't see anything else we could do.

While I discussed the assignment with Chester, Cyndi turned onto Frederick's Alley, south of M Street and slid up by a dark metered space on a street. I flipped the phone shut, took Cyndi's hand and squeezed it.

"Just a second." She checked in the rearview mirror again. "Shark or whoever he is could be the murderer. Shouldn't we call Rhondo?"

"No can do. Might backfire. Remember, that's where Cleveland lives. What if that guy killed Batiste and Cleveland helped him? We don't know. Plus you saw those people. If we send cops in there, we'll never get any help."

"Guess you're right."

I studied her in the street light, relaxing for the first time since our flight from the nether-world

"Didn't know you packed a weapon, Madam. Not that I'm complaining."

"Need to know basis, Stuart. Just like you." She glanced down and laughed. "And is that a pistol in your pocket, or are you just glad to see me?"

"Both." I turned away. "And since you brought it up, I think we need some time at the firing range." I leaned over and kissed her lips, then stopped for a second. I kissed her again, slowly, taking her into my arms. My hands slid underneath her shirt and down the back of her spandex pants.

"Not bad for a karate kid." I groped her skin.

"Kid my ass." She pulled me to her before I could say a word.

Minutes later we came up for air. "Cyndi, my love." I rubbed her lips with my index finger. She grabbed my wrist and smiled at me as she flicked the side of my index finger with the point of her tongue. "We have got to focus."

"Now there's a joke," she said. "Seems to me like there's quite a focal point here."

"Damn it girl, you're making me confused," I said, not liking this a bit. Opportunity delayed can mean opportunity lost. "Please let's revisit this later. I'll make you a double scotch with a shot of Drambuie, and I promise not to let Snapper drink from either bottle."

"How about you?"

"Not for me. I plan to be driving," I winked. "Now come on, we've got to go look for the sidewalk tap dancers."

Cyndi grinned as she sat up, pinched me, then hugged me to her. She smelled sweet, moist and musky, like violets and dainty sweat—if sweat can be dainty. I closed my eyes and felt her kisses on my forehead, nose, cheeks, and neck. She nibbled my left ear lobe.

"It will wait until later," she whispered in my ear. "Just make good and sure you don't get that sweet ass of yours shot up."

# CHAPTER 33

CYNDI pulled the key from the ignition, and we got out of the Oldsmobile. I inspected the perimeter, grateful we'd been spared an audience. I needed to think. In the back of my head I could hear the cross-examination of Cyndi regarding her relationship with me.

We left the car and walked down the hill to Bridge Street and Cecil's Place. A cool breeze caressed us as we passed under the Whitehurst to the street below. The zone beneath the parkway was even more self-enclosed at night.

This place stood apart, still another separate world. Fluorescent lights shown on weathered brick walls, cast shades of half-light, evoked the brooding whispers, sighs, and sadness of fifteen generations. The unseen. The force of history. They seemed to be whispering —out in the reverie, the ghosts around us, mumbling over groups of students who laughed and talked, unaware of the brooding like all fresh life, unaware of those who have passed and who watch us and whisper. I felt their souls among us as much as I felt the pavement beneath my feet.

A few couples made out in darkened storefronts and on benches by the Potomac. More paused around a sidewalk. Three kids performed on the sidewalk by the Potomac Club.

They were probably fourteen at the most, all three at least as tall as I with half the weight. Two of them pounded cadence on soap-bucket tops in sync with a saxophone blowing out of the club. Our intrepid tapper cut a swath across the sidewalk and pavement, sometimes leaping onto a bench and dancing across it, then flying back down to the crowd's applause. The kid was good. Savione Glouver without the press hype. I guessed he'd come from some project in Southeast, or somewhere like it, where nobody notices if three boys stay out all night. He didn't even have real tap shoes—instead, tennis shoes with cleats nailed on. What he lacked in costume was abundantly replaced in style. This was also true for the guys keeping time.

Dollars and change went into an old bowler on the sidewalk and, after several minutes, our dancer took a break. One drummer threw him a towel, which he rubbed over his drenched face and arms, then pulled open a garbage bag, took out a fresh T-shirt.

The crowd dispersed while the three counted their earnings, then Cyndi and I stepped closer. I dropped a ten-spot in the hat.

"I'm Stuart Clay, a lawyer on last night's murder. Any of you guys know a fellow named Cleveland Barnes? He was out here pushing a cart last night."

They shook their heads. "Never heard of him," the dancer spoke. The dancer had put on his clean T-shirt. His name was Le'Roy. Another kid with a shaved head was named Rascal. His fellow pounder went by Neiman.

"What about a lady named Tiffannie Squires? She was here too, looking for dates." Dates with a wad of greenbacks.

They all grinned.

"We know Tiffannie. She works the street all summer long out here."

"Works?"

"You know." Neiman studied his shoes.

"Where can I find her now?"

They broke out laughing, glancing at each other. What was the joke that went with my punch line? Rascal spoke again.

"She gives shows." He looked over at the club.

"She's a stripper?" Cyndi asked.

117

"Not exactly, ma'am," Rascal began to speak then stopped.

I motioned to the edge of the parking lot. He had something to say. Not in front of Cyndi.

# CHAPTER 34

"TIFFANNIE gives shows," he blurted.

"Heard you the first time, man. You mean lap dances?"

"No man. Shows. At the porno shops." Rascal looked away again.

"Help me out," I replied. We'd exhausted my repertoire on the subject. Another five-spot wetted his blabber.

"She gives private shows. In booths with glass dividers. You slip her five bucks, and she rubs herself and moans for you, you know, while the guy does whatever."

"A busy girl, to be sure," I said. "Where does she do this at?"

"She's all over town. I'm not sure where she is now, but she's at the bookstores."

"How do you give shows in a bookstore?" Not speaking of a literary event at Borders.

He sighed and looked at me.

"Alright, dude. Here it is. The porno bookstores have peepshow things, dig?" He looked me straight in the eye.

"Sure. Peepshow booths where you sit in the dark in a locked booth and watch coin operated movies." The porno shops and peepshow booths were a product of the '70s and could be found in any major city. There were a few dozen in Washington, and they were frequently cursed as an indicator of urban blight.

"That's it, man."

"What's that got to do with Tiffannie?"

"Well, there's another kind of booth, too. Sort of like the peepshow, but bigger. Like it's a booth with a glass window in the middle of it with a curtain. Dude goes in one side and locks the door and broad goes in the other side and locks the door. Nobody can touch nobody, and no one but the broad and the dude can see each other. Dudes slip money through a hole in the glass and sits while the broad pulls back the curtain and gets naked and do stuff for him, you know."

It occurred to me that this violated nothing in the District of Columbia criminal code. No touching, and who could ever see? The case wouldn't last through the motions hearing.

"Any idea which shop she's at?" I fingered my final fiver, vaguely aware that it could be a very costly night.

"I don't know, man. Bunch of them around town." Rascal eyed the bill.

"So she's an independent contractor?" Over his head, but I needed a laugh in the face of all this slime and couldn't help myself.

"What?"

"Never mind, guy." I gave him the fiver. "Fifty bucks for whoever finds her."

"We will find her, man. I will find her." He held up his right thumb to seal the promise and I motioned to Cyndi as we walked back over.

"These are worth forty-five dollars from the finance officer on the fifth floor of the D.C. Superior Court." Cyndi handed out the subpoenas for the preliminary hearing. "You have to show up at superior court for the hearing on the date at 9:30, and then we'll give you a witness fee form at the end of the proceedings."

"You want me to testify?" Nieman looked confused.

"Maybe. Maybe not. But we do want the ability to put you on the stand without having to hunt you down if your testimony is needed. And I don't mean to be heavy-handed with you, but the court will send out a Marshal to arrest you on a warrant if you don't show up as required by this document." She pointed at the subpoena.

"We'll be there, lady. Now we got to earn our living." Rascal stuffed the subpoena in his hip pocket and started back to the sidewalk.

The bucket drumbeat resumed as we left the scene.

We walked around the outside of the club for a few minutes. The police had released the lot from impound, new lights shined on the Potomac Club parking lot, and a fresh coat of paint glistened on the west wall. I discussed Rascal's report with Cyndi and we decided to visit peepshow houses the next day.

We went to my place. My apartment is on the third floor above an espresso bar at the corner of Seventh and H Streets, NW, in Chinatown. It's convenient to the Metro, near lots of good restaurants and the karate school. I loved it, the price was low, and I had a right of first refusal when the gentrification crowd turned the building condo—as I'm sure they would.

I disengaged three cylinder locks and swung the door open. Cyndi followed me in and stood quietly as I relocked the place and re-engaged the alarm. I turned around and hugged her to me for what seemed like an awfully long time, looking at her soft face and long black hair in the half light shining in from outside, smelling that sweet, moist smell.

"I'm staying the night," she informed me.

"Far be it from me to protest." I touched her cheek with my hand, stared into those dark eyes.

"You know you are well preserved," Cyndi mused. "A little heavy, but I like you." She ran the tip of her right index finger over my cheeks and nose. "You just need an extreme makeover."

"An extreme what?"

"You figure it out," she said, looking at me intently.

"Dangerous thing to say." Especially if you're one of Gaugin's fruit-bearing nymphs, magically taken from the South Pacific and put down in Washington, D.C. with a black Irishman.

"Why don't you shut up and make me that drink."

I went into my studio's kitchenette and poured Drambuie liqueur and Johnnie Walker Red over ice cubes in a cocktail shaker, stirred the elixir and poured it into her cocktail glass. I toasted with my drink of choice, Diet Dr. Pepper. Punching the CD player, the sound of Luther Vandross played in the background. Cyndi took a sip of the thick sweetness, then put it on the studio room's coffee table and clung to me again in a long fragrant kiss. She giggled softly as we awkwardly pulled off our black clothing and guns, tossing clothes into a corner and guns away, in a locked desk. I pulled out my sofa into a queen-sized bed, and we quickly finished getting naked and lay down in the half-light, looking at each other, tasting, reveling in this thing that we'd started.

I caressed and kissed Cyndi all over, marveling at her beauty, her sculpted hips, breasts, loins, and shaved parts, the way she fit together like a masterpiece. She was incredibly muscular yet there was nothing about her that was not utterly and completely feminine.

I smelled her delicious skin and hair as the night passed. Caught in an odd continuum, I felt dizzy at the perfection of her beautiful body and my own raging arousal. We did it again and again and after each time we came together I closed my eyes and pretended to sleep. Then I opened my eyes and pretended to wake. We rose and fell in the nether world that lovers know. A place where souls are free and insatiable and consequences are remote and forgotten.

As the night passed, I gazed at the light framing the pulled curtain and thanked the powers of life for letting me have this experience, a time etched in stone for all the days that I would suck in air.

It was a magical, a memorable night, a lyrical night, a night where poetry was flesh and conflict joined in the balance of loving bodies, a night where there was no pain or sorrow and all was well, a night when my body felt immortal and the amazing creature beside me seemed like someone I'd known forever, a night when there was no shame, only pleasure, only eros and Drambuie and Johnnie Walker Red and Diet Dr. Pepper, blessing us as the apostles of pleasure.

Remembering this night helped me cope with the hell that followed.

# CHAPTER 35

PROGRESS buzzed in a cacophony outside my window. Trucks backed up as their safety beepers chimed. People in orange helmets barked questions and answers over the roar of machinery. Jackhammers blasted, girders cabled through the air, positioned by crane to the huge muscled arms reaching from below.

The reality of their labor was clean and pure. Bangs, whistles, clatters, all beautiful, bustling, full of life. The old and decrepit blasted away, carted away. The façade glowed, a beautiful thing, now uncovered. They'd seen the angel in the old Gallery Place and carved until they set it free. Now the rest of us saw it, too. Behind the freshly blasted façades a huge hole opened, chiseled and scooped. Inside it, they built a big new thing, day by day. A renaissance, day by day.

My Washington, D.C., my New Columbia, my city by a hill to the glory of achievement, largely wrought by the business genius of Morton Diel. He'd opened the center on Seventh Street like Prometheus, stealing light from the gods and beckoning the fearful back into the capital city with a huge new sports stadium. Slowly but surely, businesses came back, new structures were built, residential projects planned, restaurants opened.

The sight of the Chinatown project seemed breathtaking, spiritual, my personal Diego Rivera mural. I'd spent two years watching it unfold. Right across the street from my corner apartment, this new vision exploded into view, taking the facades of an old block and transforming, reaching out, to a brave new world.

Cyndi had slipped away before dawn. Thoughts of her left an indelible lightness upon my spirit. Finishing the fourth cup of coffee from my home brewer, I pulled the window shade closed, then turned attention to the choice of clothing. Having slept in a little, I'd bathed and shaved carefully, then called the courtroom where I was due at nine to inform them that I'd be a little late because of another case. That seemed fair to me in view of the facts. I'd worked past midnight on another case, during which time somebody had pointed a gun at me. I claimed a brief time out. Given the front page of the *Post*, which carried my image and a discussion of Cleveland Barnes and Benny, I hoped the black robe presiding in the morning preliminary hearing courtroom would read through the lines and not make an issue of my late arrival.

I dressed carefully today because Bridgette Ginadio would interview me for Court TV and people from Orange County to Nashua would be watching a lawyer in Washington, D.C.—and that would be me.

A *Post* photographer snapped a shot of my brooding face around the time I was ducking out from Sparky Nucose's microphone. Nice of them to picture me over statements that weren't my own. Somebody, some "confidential source," did Cleveland's bidding quite nicely. That must have been who Fred Collins had planned to speak to last night. A voicemail from Fred told me about the article, but I'd missed it the night before. All that I'd shared with Fred, and all the articles I'd read on Google the day before, had been accessed by the reporter. But there was more. Somebody had gone to a lot of trouble to detail Benny's mob baggage for the press. "Confidential source" told the reporter that Benny had been under investigation by grand juries in the Southern District of New York and three other federal jurisdictions. Benny had been tied to more than a dozen violent murders, smuggling and distribution of cocaine imported through

Miami, and a host of related crimes. All of this was news to me. Who knew? Who told? Why?

The newspaper article seemed somewhat odd. "Confidential source" had an agenda. It helped my case. But where did it come from?

And so my day began.

Turning up the volume on my computer's screen saver, a dancing judge who yelled "hi-dee-hi-dee-ho," I locked up and romped down two flights. I ducked out the door by the espresso bar before you could say Jimminie Cricket. But instead of an insect, I saw something worse.

Mickey Jaworski sneered up at me from the back seat of his Lincoln.

# CHAPTER 36

"WE didn't much like that story on my good friend, Mr. Clay."
God knows how long he'd been sitting there. The Dum brothers,
Tweedledum and Tweedledummer, were back in the Lincoln,
returned from their aerobic escapade beneath the bridge.

"That was a bum rap, Mickey. I declined comment, and those
weren't my words. What else do you want?" He didn't scare me.
At least not here.

"But what about the confidential source, counselor?" He
seethed. "Are you the source?" He looked at the white hairs. "You
want I should ask my assistants for help in this bibliographical
inquiry? You think I wouldn't, pal? Got some news for you." He
angrily jabbed his dead fish pinkie in my direction.

"Don't strain yourself with too many syllables, Mickey. I
don't talk to reporters." I lied. "End of discussion. You want to
help me deal with your enemies, then tell me who they are."

"We don't have any enemies."

I bit my lip, then spoke. "I didn't talk to the press. Got no idea
who did talk to the press. Don't know who you're wrestling with,

but it isn't me." I debated whether to ask who the brothers were chasing and why, but dismissed the idea. I didn't want Mickey to know what I knew, scant as that was.

Mickey frowned and shook his head. It would be a cold day in ratland before he gave me any leads.

"You want a ride to court, counselor?" Suddenly Mickey became my colleague again.

"Don't think so." Maybe in my next lifetime.

"Well." He paused. "Maybe you aren't squealing." Mickey's eyes narrowed and stared at me. "But I tell you what. You think I don't see things that I see. I'm around, pal. You talk to them guys by the bridge. You tell them. Payback is a bitch. You tell them Mickey Jaworski said so!"

He pointed at me, and his lips pinched into a righteous pink sphincter. The electric window slowly came up over his pouting face. The Lincoln pulled away.

Mickey assumed I knew things I didn't know. Why? What could I infer? A beef between Benny and somebody resulted in Benny's murder, then prompted Jaworski to come to town. Somehow, the brothers' presence in Georgetown related and maybe prompted the man with the long hair to come after us. Had to find out who that was today if, as Cyndi said, his face was in the post office.

I could also infer that Fred's source was the other side, the somebody. They wanted to cast doubt on Benny's character. Maybe even help Cleveland. Who could that be?

Juggling thoughts, I walked over to the Gallery Place Metro, past the Chinatown arches over H Street, through the massive construction site, and down the escalator to the Red Line.

One stop later I was at Judiciary Square. Riding the Fourth Street escalator up, I watched the City Hall building come into view on my left. Off in the distance, to the right, I heard the microphones blaring. More demonstrations in front of the D.C. Superior Court. But the voice wasn't Ruthie's.

I recognized the silver tongue of Happ Duncan, former mayor of the District of Columbia, sent to the big house for smoking crack. Happy D had sucked up the smoke that sucked up civilization until my old boss shut down his parade. Back from the federal pen, he grabbed a city council seat from the part of town where conviction was a badge of honor. Slowly but surely Happ plotted his return to power, and he was coming back like the charismatic leader that he was. I crossed over toward Paradise and heard Happ's voice boom: "Papa Legba come for Cleveland Barnes!"

# CHAPTER 37

THE French surrealist Marcel Duchamp remarked that any man who couldn't imagine a jockey riding a racehorse through a tomato was an idiot. Apropros to this, I often tried to keep my mind limber by imagining impossible things. But nothing prepared me for this.

"Now people wonder why I'm here." Dressed in a dark blue business suit, white shirt, and red tie, Happ stared at the audience. The crowd quieted.

"I'm here because this is where the people need me." He gestured to a group of chanters.

"This is the expression of the oppressed." He motioned to Ruthie, the multi-colored pole behind her, and the crowd of forty women and men now presently fixed in a low pitch background chant.

"The slaves of Africa embraced this religion as they were savagely carted away to the Caribbean and the Americas." He gestured out Indiana Avenue. I followed his arm, gazed out past the Bob Hope Building.

"The poor of Louisiana embraced this religion as they tolerated the unspeakable bigotry after the Civil War." He turned around and pointed at the courthouse, directly south behind him.

"Like most great religions, voodoo is a cry for justice in a city that has turned away." Both arms were up in fists. "This is a cry for justice in a city hijacked by a Congress that doesn't care! And I'm here to tell you that Happ Duncan doesn't turn away. Happ Duncan is here for you. So we are here to make a gris-gris for Cleveland Barnes!"

He raised his hands in a Nixon-like "V" sign to acknowledge roaring applause.

Happ held hands with Ruthie and Amanda. They started a new round of chanting. The crowd roared. They loved Happ. I saw why. Gofers from the "Happy D for D.C. Committee" rushed around. They distributed handbills and bumper stickers. Grinning reporters and camera nerds captured the roaring street theater. All well and good. I had to get away, though. I needed to preserve my message for the blurb.

The marshal at the door took one look at the camera crew pursuing me and gestured madly, urging me to get inside. Passed in, I stared through the glass walls at my pursuers.

I needed to talk to Ruthie. Didn't dare risk photos linking me with her. Didn't want somebody complaining to Bar Counsel, accusing me of trying to influence potential jurors. In a city where destroying opponents is a sport, this not only could happen—you could almost bank on it. Bet on the certified letter.

I worked my way through the crowd to the preliminary hearing courtrooms along the south wall of the first floor. Pausing outside courtroom 115, I left Cyndi a message. Had to meet Ruthie ASAP and I wanted to know if she had a name for the guy under the bridge. We'd planned to see Cleveland after my hearing. Maybe Ruthie next.

Peeking into the courtroom, I spotted a full house in the midst of calendar call. Judge Paul Miller sat at the helm, tweaking unprepared government and defense lawyers with impunity, complaining of absent attorneys and parties. He issued bench warrants like party invitations, whacking the lectern with his hammer to hush the bustling masses.

Courtroom clerk Steve Sykes spotted me and grinned. He made a telephone-to-ear motion. I went to the anteroom and picked up a telephone. "Not to worry, Mr. Clay. The body has been lost," he said.

Too bad for my client, Duane Howard, as he was the *body* probably taken to a wrong location somewhere, to the wrong courtroom or mistakenly taken back to jail. I entered the courtroom and settled into the far right front bench. I powered my laptop.

Defending my preliminary hearing this morning, U.S. versus Duane Howard, could be done by most anyone because the government's case had fallen apart and everyone knew it. Duane was falsely charged with rape. A twenty-two-year–old Howard undergraduate named Melody Johnson met Dwayne at a Fourteenth Street club. Passions ignited, they stole away back to Melody's dorm. Unfortunately, Melody's roommate returned to discover Duane atop fair Melody. The embarrassed undergraduate blathered out a story of assault. Buck naked Duane headed down the fire escape, only to be chased, cornered, and cuffed.

In the hours after, I'd sought out Melody. She gave me a videotaped statement admitting that she had invited Duane to her room, thought his shaved head and tattoo were cool, that they agreed to do what they did. Half a dozen witnesses from the club corroborated her videotaped statement.

The prosecutor on the case must have been swamped. In any event, he didn't return my calls. With no alternative, I filed a copy of the videotape, sworn affidavits of witnesses, and a motion to dismiss. Also a motion to seal. I liked Melody. She did the right thing in the end. I respected her for it and stipulated in my motion to close the whole unfortunate record of the whole event to public scrutiny.

Of course, the government could object to my videotape on foundation grounds. But they wouldn't. Nobody had time for this foolishness. So I didn't worry about Duane. Cleveland Barnes was another story.

While the marshals tracked down Duane, I took the waiting time to outline the case of United States versus Cleveland Barnes. Time to guild the lily. I started to type.

The prosecutor had to convince the jury that a lily was indeed a lily. I had to convince them it might be another flower. Anything would do: a geranium, a marigold, even a petunia. The key to this process is to look, look, look. Look at the obvious until it is not obvious at all. Look until your eyes water and your goldfish are complaining. Look at what you know till it tells you something you don't know.

I had plenty to sort out from the past thirty hours. Everyone had to be listed on a grid.

Column A was Cleveland Barnes. Beneath Cleveland I placed Ruthie, Amanda Sewell, Adrian, the Capital City Voodoo Society, and Happ Duncan.

Benny topped Column B. Beneath him I placed Mickey, the white-haired dum brothers , and the Spilotro organization. Mona Day topped Column C. Though I knew little about her, she was pivotal to understanding what had happened to Benny.

Column D included all the street witnesses: Zebra, Snapper, Shark, and the rest of the bridge people, drummers Rascal, Neiman, and Le'Roy, and the witness who had thus far eluded me—Tiffannie Squires.

Various witnesses came under Column E: Jennifer, who served Benny and Mona Day at the club, Cornelius who did the same at the Lathrop, and a chambermaid who we hadn't talked to yet.

Column F included the known quantities in the justice system: my ex-fiancé, Assistant U.S. Attorney Lisa Stein, Rhondo Touhey and his partner Jesus Martin, Barry Acres from 2D, Cyndi Oh, Haskell Eaton, and Percy Diel.

If past experience was any guide I'd already met all the people needed to win acquittal for my client. But how did they fit together? Where was the code that would solve this rubik's cube?

Mysteries bear a certain likeness to one another. Be I Sam Spade, Archie McNally, Harry Bosch, or Miss Marple, the task is the same. How to figure out the obvious?

I saved the document around 11:17 A.M. They found the body. Steve called U.S. versus Duane Howard and the marshals hoisted Duane out from behind the courtroom. Assistant U.S. Attorney Rundle Beers announced "nolle prosequi" to the court— which means there would be no prosecution. The judge explained to Duane that he was free to go. The orange-suited man screamed. He hugged me.

Duane's reaction was understandable, but still struck me as part of the odd world of the criminal lawyer. Some days you worked yourself half into the ground and lost the case. Everybody sneered, and you felt like a loser. Other days victory fell in your lap. Everybody thought you were brilliant. But all you did was point out something obvious.

Either way, the winner got the spoils.

# CHAPTER 38

"COUNSELOR."

Adrian Sewell grinned. Today he wore a white linen suit and silk black shirt with no collar. "Slumming again, Adrian?" I shook his hand.

"Nah, man." He laughed. "Just over meeting with Quinton Myers. He sends his regards."

"Good councilman. How do you know him?" Myers was the chair of the committee on the judiciary.

"Basketball stuff. Community stuff."

"So you sold him tickets to the Kiwanis pancake breakfast?" I studied Adrian's face.

The grin disappeared. "I talked to Quinton about Cleveland." Voice lowered. "Raised my concerns about what the police and prosecutor are doing. We're pushing for an investigation on this one. I want the Inspector General and the IAD to look at the police actions in the case. They're putting some Mafia guy's hit onto Cleveland. That isn't right."

"IG and Internal Affairs? Might help. Might generate some

useful paper." I felt uncomfortable. As an experienced criminal lawyer I knew that what the defense referred to as the *Vendetta defense* is generally not popular with juries unless the evidence is very, very clear. Juries saw right through it. Even so, vendettas existed—though I had not seen one here.

"Just trying to help." Adrian spoke softly. "Let's brain storm about other ways to run the ball. Ratchet up the tension on the government guys."

"Okay." I nodded. "I'll see Cleveland in a few minutes but why don't you meet me at Ruthie's house this afternoon about four P.M.?"

"That's great, man." He shook my hand again. "See you there. Got to run. Got to see the chief judge."

He disappeared up the escalator.

The chief judge?

"Adrian, hold up." I got on the escalator behind him, heading up to the second floor. "Does your business with the chief judge in any way involve Cleveland? I mean I—"

"Hell no, man." The smile faded. "You know Mulroy wouldn't cut me slack. We're talking about the league and sponsoring some anti-drug ads."

"Okay." I backed off. "I had to ask."

"Right," he glared at me.

We reached the second floor, shook hands again. Adrian headed for the east corridor. I watched him move away. My gut raged.

# CHAPTER **39**

AT 11:32 A.M., I stepped out the back door of the courthouse to Bridgette Ginadio and her waiting camera crew. I had nothing prepared, but I had a good idea about what I wanted to say.

Bridgette squinted at me for half a second, and then turned to the camera's eye.

"Hello, Bob," she spoke. "This is Bridgette Ginadio live at the Washington, D.C. Superior Court where a shocked city yesterday watched as a street person, Cleveland Barnes, was presented on charges of murder and robbery involving the brutal beheading of New York trucking executive Benito Batiste. With me is defense counsel Stuart Clay at the south entrance to the D.C. Superior Court. Attorney Clay, can you comment on the status of this case."

"Thanks, Bridgette." I looked at her. "Cleveland Barnes is a homeless person who lived until yesterday under a bridge in the District of Columbia. He doesn't have a single conviction for any violent crime. The guy doesn't even have a misdemeanor assault conviction!

"Any citizen reading the file in this case will see that before midnight yesterday the defense filed motions with the court based on the background of the decedent. The decedent, Bridgette. Who was the decedent? The facts clearly demonstrate that there are legitimate questions regarding the activities of this decedent. The public record already discloses that he had organized crime ties and was the subject of ongoing grand jury probes in the eastern district of New York and other federal jurisdictions. Given these circumstances, we expect to develop and show reasonable doubt that the decedent's death was caused by any act of Mr. Barnes. Thank you."

"But wasn't your client arrested with Mr. Batiste's property?"

"Ballys don't prove murder," I said, dropping the word "bloody" from my sound byte.

"But they do prove contact with the decedent," Bridgette shot back.

"Not necessarily."

"But Mr. Barnes stated in court that—"

"Bridgette, I'd urge you and your colleagues in the television and newspaper business to get a verbatim transcript of yesterday's hearing and read it to the public. It is too bad they won't let in cameras here. The record shows that Mr. Barnes is a homeless guy that forages the streets. The fact that he may have, and I stress may have, picked up some shoes left in an open area doesn't make him a murderer."

"But surely it's suspicious."

"Suspicion and guilt are two different animals, Bridgette. And as you know, Ballys—"

"Don't prove murder. Yes, we heard that one, Mr. Clay." Bridgette squinted again, then shifted gears. "Attorney Stuart Clay, what's next for the defense?"

"Because of the unusual nature of this case the court has appointed a second counsel, attorney Parcival Diel of Mitchell & Strong. We're making an intensive effort to prepare for the preliminary hearing by conducting research into the relevant facts, obtaining all government reports, and interviewing witnesses."

"Isn't it true that the key witness, the woman who left the club with Mr. Batiste, has disappeared. Any leads on where she is?"

"The facts show that Mr. Batiste left the club with the young woman at—"

"Just this morning," she cut me off, "the Washington MPD released a photograph of the missing witness that Mr. Clay is referring to."

The camera followed her as she stepped aside and pointed to a photograph mounted on a white board, propped on an easel behind her. It looked like MPD had gotten a still shot made off the Potomac Club's videotape and enhanced it. She continued.

"Anyone with information leading to the identification and location of this individual please call the MPD hotline listed on your screen. This is Bridgette Ginadio with Court TV. Back to you, Bob."

I nodded at Bridgette and hurried off down C Street. Cyndi would be waiting. Hoped she had some good information for me. I pushed past vooduns, a montage of clambering reporters, camera geeks. Ruthie and Happy D were nowhere to be seen. Amanda barked through the handheld microphone.

Cyndi idled in my Oldsmobile at the corner of Sixth Street and Indiana Avenue. Rhondo appeared out of the crowd.

"Get your prozac today, man?" he said.

"Very funny." I motioned at the chanters. "Look at this jazz."

"It'll get stranger."

We'd been made by the cameras. Both of us deadpanned and walked straight ahead.

"What do you mean stranger? What?"

"You've got to stop sending all those love letters to Lisa. She had to get another lawyer to handle the paper."

"Those were motions, my friend. And my love interest is sitting in that car if you want to know."

"You dog!" Rhondo looked at Cyndi and whistled.

"Actually I got a second lawyer, too. If you can believe it, Jack's got Morton Diel's son entered as co-counsel."

"Great. Now you guys are really going beat up on us."

"Nothing personal."

"You got it, man. But it's what it is."

"And what is it? When are you going to tell me your big secret?"

"Let's talk later, Kentucky. You think this is about representing some poor street guy that's been wrongly accused. But you're dead wrong. You're just dead wrong."

He slapped me on the back and walked quickly away, then rapped the Oldsmobile' hood twice, waived to Cyndi, and crossed over to a double-parked cruiser. As he drove away I wondered. How long? How long until my brother spilled the beans?

# CHAPTER **40**

"SMILE. We're on candid camera." I motioned at the reporters filming us and I slid into the car.

"Cheese," she replied, pulling away from the curb and heading down Indiana Avenue. "I have a lot to report on and we got to scoot. Otherwise, we could do something in the back seat and wave to the cameras."

"Very funny." I watched Sparkie Nucose and his cameraman scrutinizing us from the curb in front of the courthouse and flashed a "V" for victory sign.

"First of all, the guy under the bridge is in the post office. His name is Carlos Moldano, the brother of the former president of Mexico."

"What? That makes no sense whatsoever."

"I should have said the scandalized former president of Mexico. The brother's corruption drove him out of office. Moldano is wanted in the U.S. and Mexico for everything from murder and conspiracy to drug trafficking. He's a conduit for smugglers from all over Central America."

"So what's he doing under the Key Bridge? Is he a New Columbian too?"

"Beats the hell out of me," Cyndi said. "But to your point, you can bet he's not waiting for the coming of New Columbia unless it's a shipment of new Columbian cocaine. I'll bet the hair is a wig and he's down there doing something or meeting with someone."

"With Benny?"

"Maybe. Maybe Benny is competition." Cyndi maneuvered around a cruiser double-parked in front of police headquarters with its emergency lights flashing.

"That could make sense." I thought of Jaworski's thugs chasing the Hispanic kid under the bridge. "A lot of sense. Could this tie in to Rhondo's secret?" Not about a pair of shoes, he said. What about a war of the mob against the Mexicans? "The problem is that Cleveland lives under that bridge."

"So we keep all this under our hats. Right, I know. So let's move on."

"What else?" The lady had obviously been busy.

"You have some fan mail from a flounder." As we turned into the I-395 tunnel under the Labor Department, Cyndi grabbed a thick document from the back seat and handed it to me. I opened it. The autopsy report, which began as follows: "Received is the un-embalmed, symmetrically developed, well-nourished, and well-hydrated body of an adult white male appearing to approximately match his given age of fifty-four years..."

The report droned on about various aspects of Benny's remains, his weight, beginnings of cirrhosis, and a 1793 Carolus III silver dollar found in his throat. I flipped through pages ten through fifteen of the report, a section devoted to the grim business of the internal examination of poor Benny. The ME gave copious details of the "Y incision" performed on the headless torso and detailed the condition of all of Benny's innards. The internal exam was, as they say, unremarkable.

The description of the laser examination of Benny's clothes simply confirmed what we'd inferred about Benny's final hours. Numerous long blonde hairs and dried semen were found on the front of his trousers. Shell and rock residue removed from coat and trousers for testing. Inspection of black leather belt reveals ten different fingerprints on various parts of the belt. All prints copied for comparison with NCIC files.

"So did you read the whole thing?" I looked over at Cyndi as drove the sedan through the dense traffic of 395.

"Sure did. Every line of it twice. Pretty gruesome, huh?"

"Yeah. But what's it worth? We knew Mona had given Benny a going away present on her knees. Too late to suggest that he join AA. What do you make of the silver dollar?"

"Same as the beheading. We got a grandiose killer on our hands. This is his or her idea of a crime fashion statement."

"I got a feeling it's a he." Didn't feel like a woman's crime, though I knew I could be wrong.

"I agree. The man or group wants to be noticed, wants to be feared, wants to cultivate some sort of mystique."

"Why?"

"That's the million dollar question," Cyndi said. "Do you think the guy under the bridge knew the answer?"

"Damn right I do." I lapsed into thought and Cyndi said nothing more. What did Rhondo know? I had the dull feeling that I was being gamed by my own client while the other team knew the score.

Cyndi's eyes never left the road. After several minutes, she swung onto 295 and bee-lined for a service exit off to the Robert F. Kennedy Stadium parking lot. We navigated through a bumpy pass and arrived at the D.C. Jail complex.

Cyndi slid into the lone vacant spot in the crowded lot and turned off the machine. For a moment we just sat, looking forward. I wanted to kiss her, but I didn't.

"I'm sure the autopsy report stimulated your appetite, so here." She reached into the back seat and pulled a shopping bag onto the console. It held hot & sour soup, moo goo gai pan—a shredded chicken wrapped in a soft shell, Hunan shrimp with broccoli and extra peppers, sodas, and a few huge plastic bibs.

Cyndi kept the car running, cranked up the air conditioning, and punched the CD button on the dash. Al Green's "Love and Happiness" filled the air as we plunged our plastic forks into the food. We didn't talk, didn't feel a need to. In short order we demolished everything edible.

I liked a few hours in jail. Going to jail can be relaxing for a defense attorney. Moments and even hours spent waiting for a client in a Plexiglas and iron interview cubicle can sometimes be very restful. Nobody can bother you once you're in, no courtroom clerk can summon you back to represent fugitive clients picked up on bench warrants, nagging people can't gain access as cell phones and beepers are not allowed. It's a good place to get thinking done, to organize a case, even to catch up on billing.

Today I especially looked forward to a long, uninterrupted talk with Cleveland. But unfortunately my cell phone chimed before we could get out of the car. Flipping it open I spotted Mitchell & Strong's number on the caller ID.

"Stuart Clay." I held the phone to my right ear, tapped Cyndi's thigh, and rolled my eyes. She pulled out a notebook and started jotting something.

"Stuart, its Haskell back at the firm. I'm on conference call with Percy."

"How are we doing?" Percy inquired impatiently.

"We're doing great, Percy. Sorry I wasn't able to hook up with you this morning, but things got too rushed. Let's meet this afternoon."

"Well, what about this stuff in the *Post*?" Percy whined into the phone. "Sounds like this Batiste man was a real mobster. Can't we use that?"

"You're right on the money, Percy. I was aware of everything in that article before I saw the article." Well most everything. "We'll use that information at the appropriate—"

"Well, when is the appropriate time?" Percy interrupted impatiently.

"At the preliminary hearing."

"Why don't you file a motion now?"

"Because that would be bad strategy." And stupid too. "The motion wouldn't be considered until the preliminary hearing and filing it now would give the government more of an introduction to defense strategy than we want."

Haskell jumped in. "Now let's not misunderstand each other. I think that--"

"No misunderstanding, Haskell. You guys just don't assume I don't know how to do my job. I'm glad you're on the case, Percy, but I do know what I'm doing."

"Well, let's talk about that case." Percy turned terse. Maybe Caesar Caligula wanted to appoint his horse as lead counsel!

"We can talk to a point, Percy. I'm at the jail. I have to go in and get Cleveland to sign a document agreeing to your entry as co-

counsel before I can discuss much that isn't on the public record. It's a formality, but I've got to do it."

"Now let's not misunderstand each other!" Haskell quivered.

"No, let's not." I bit my lip.

We agreed that I would keep Percy posted on the progress of the case. I wouldn't. Not without Cleveland's blessing. And besides that, I didn't want to tell them anything new, not about last night, the details of the autopsy, or about case developments. Nobody was going to be trusted until I determined who was who. Not Haskell. Not Percy. Not Cyndi. Nobody.

I snapped my phone shut and gazed out the window, shaking my head.

"Having fun, Stuart?" Cyndi grinned at me.

"Just yucking it up. How about you?"

"Trying to ignore all your chatter while I review the case plan. Forget about whatever Bozo you were chatting up for a second. You know we have got to nail the witnesses today. It's slipping away from us, but it's still here. It's right under our noses but we're missing it. I smell it. This is the day, dude. I hope this Cleveland Barnes guy isn't gaming you."

"That makes two of us." After forty-eight hours, our chances on witnesses dropped markedly.

We got out of the car. I shoved the paper cartons and cups into an overfilled receptacle on the broken sidewalk.

Before passing through the thick glass doors into the jail, I left a voice message for Jack Payne. I hoped to have Jack's support. Unfortunately, he had to answer to a lot of people. I feared the bottom line was simple, too simple. If Percy got mad, Percy might get Morton Diel to say a word, any word, to Jack. If the firm's largest client complained about me, my arrangement with the firm would be toast. But I couldn't help it. My skills at firm politics were poor to nonexistent. Even so, I would jealously protect that which enabled the voodoo that I do.

# CHAPTER 41

WE pulled the barred glass doors open and trudged onto the tattered linoleum floor of the jail lobby. Normally, the public siphoned through metal detectors and past a thick iron door that opened and shut with blasting electronic locks. Not today. Some manner of backup had seized the jail, shut down movement in its tracks. I beheld more than a hundred folks mulling about, bored and uncomfortable, gabbing and shaking their heads. The overwhelming majority of these were poor folks, many of whom looked like they had the weight of the world on their shoulders. Teenage mothers with two or three toddlers coming to see pop on a Tuesday afternoon. Friends paying a social call or reporting on profit and loss statements for the week. Massively overweight middle-age mothers and grandmothers still wheezing from their long walk from the subway exit several blocks away. All here, a congealed mass of humanity with its hopes, fears, aspirations, and resignations, all trying to do their best. Looking at these people I was struck by how hard it must be for them. I don't pray often, but I said a prayer for them.

More than a dozen marshals stood restlessly behind a thick glass window. Usually charged with conducting a massive visitor intake operation. Now they stood semi-idle, talking to people in the lobby or making telephone calls. Either somebody had gotten hurt or the count of prisoners didn't add up. A quick inquiry at the speakerphone confirmed my suspicion. The count did not reconcile by three bodies. No one could enter or leave until the count matched the previous records.

Several times a day the jail conducts a count of all prisoners and, when this happens, all bodies are frozen in place until all inmates are accounted for. Today the eleven A.M. count had turned into a warden's nightmare. From what I could tell, no one believed that an escape had occurred. A body got lost, just like the Marshall Service and transport team had lost my client Duane Howard earlier in the day. Happened all the time.

Lucky for me, attorneys and investigators could enter the jail while the count and recount took place. We would in all likelihood be stuck waiting outside the attorney interview cells with some of the prisoners who'd been in the process of returning to their cellblocks when the count began.

Cyndi and I raked our pockets for anything that would set off the metal detector. We walked through the detector. We cleared and walked a few steps and through a thick metal door that buzzed loudly as the electric lock released. Inside, a short squat marshal checked through both our briefcases and cleared us to take the elevator to the second floor interview block.

The second floor elevator opened up into a dark hall that led to an area outside the interview block. Stepping into the hall I started to walk forward when I heard an agitated voice declare: "I am a disciple of Mabutek from the people of Amalek, come to proclaim the New Columbia!"

Motioning Cyndi to wait, I peeked around the corner into the lobby.

Cleveland held court in the center of a half dozen young men, a senior statesman of the orange-suited crowd. Obviously, he enjoyed whatever role he'd taken on and his appearance and invective had improved considerably with only a day of jailhouse nutrition and sobriety.

A few young men seemed quite interested. A few smirked. All listened.

144

Part of me wanted to rush in and tell him not to say a word in a group where a jailhouse fink might find something to bargain with. But I stood still and out of sight, hoping to hear the *full* version of Cleveland's rap. Raising an index finger to my lips, I winked at Cyndi. We held back, out of sight.

# CHAPTER 42

"IF you want to embrace our ancestors, my dudes, believe in Mabutek," Cleveland preached. "In the early years of this country, the Amaleks were here. In 1835 we lived here. Free blacks and Indians living here, special type persons. They had their own sort of spirit and free ways. Then the mechanics burned them out in a riot that started in Lafayette Square."

"How come we never heard of them?" A whiney soft voice.

"Who you think writes history?" Cleveland scratched his beard.

"So?" A short, thin man with a scar face spoke. "What's that got to do with anything?"

"So you think they are going to tell you about something that makes the powerful look stupid? You think they're going to admit to stealing businesses and jobs away from other men?"

"Why not?" Another voice. Older, with a lisp. "People wrote about slavery."

"That's not a secret," Cleveland said.

"How many people were there?" Another voice. A *high yellow* man with no teeth.

"Probably two hundred. For a long time people kept their distance, but hired them to do jobs and stuff, even hired them in places like Georgetown because Amaleks worked hard. But after the riot, things changed. 1835 ended everything."

"What happened then?"

"Francis Scott Key, the guy that wrote the Star Spangled Banner, tried to hang an innocent man. He was the lawyer for the city then. And there was a big riot and they came after us. The free black men were driven out of business. I remember. I was there."

"What do you mean?" another asked.

"I mean I was there. The Amaleks settled land over by where Sixth and Seventh Streets now run into Pennsylvania Avenue. They called it Georgia."

1835 in Georgia? Where the National Archives building now stood.

"Some men wanted it to build houses and stores. Mr. Snow had his eating house right there. We built it up fair and square but the mechanics wanted it. So one night a mob came and burned it down. It was hell. Babies and women were burned."

"But I never read about this."

"Are you deaf? I just got done saying that people aren't going to write about stuff that makes them look bad."

"But that isn't true, man. Plenty of things are written."

"It is true!" Cleveland screamed. "I was there!"

"What?" a sullen voice asked.

"I tell you the Amaleks are bringing New Columbia for our people on the exact spot of the fire. The rays still come out there."

"How?"

"Mabutek will show us. The spirit is still there. It's the old Amalek rays, the old force. You can't hide the fire."

"Man, you're making me shiver up my spine!" The whiney voice laughed. "Dude, you a trip! Maybe you should go on Oprah."

"You a rapping man," another chimed in. "Ghosts of old slaves and Indians!! I never heard of anything like what you talking 'bout."

"Not slaves, man, not slaves. Free men. Like you can be too if you turn to Mabutek. "

Cyndi and I exchanged glances, shaking our heads.

The jail was full of proselytizers, daily visitors who came to spread the word, and Cleveland had his own brand. Hard to see this as anything bearing on the case.

"You're joaning on us because we're jailhouse," a new voice accused.

"Not Joaning man. I'm declaring the righteous truth. Just wait and see what happen the next ten years. I am a New Columbian. We New Columbians come back to claim our home, the land taken from the Amaleks. You'll see. In the world of the rays, a thousand years is a hiccup, boy. This is just the closing of a circle. It began a long time ago. Most the others don't know who we are, what we are, but they will see our power and that's what the man understands. Power."

"So how many people believe this?"

"A lot of people do," Cleveland retorted. "A lot of people."

A raspy overhead speaker cracked out: "The Count is clear at 1:46 P.M. Count cleared at 1:46 P.M."

Down the hall an electronic lock blasted and a thick metal door swung open. Resounding thuds and squeaks came down the hallway toward us. I spotted the thick boots as they tromped down the walkway. They were connected to a massive whale of a marshal. He came to a halt by Cyndi and me. A little head poked out of his large body and I watched his thin lips flutter up and down.

"Count is clear, gentlemen!" he declared in a high-pitched voice. "You all get into the hall. Cleveland Barnes, wait for your company. You have a legal visit."

The marshal tromped away. We'd been made, so I walked around the corner.

# CHAPTER 43

THE inmates took one look at us and clamped up. Younger inmates stared away. Cleveland stood up. He still had on handcuffs and loose shackles on his thighs and calves.

"You don't waste any time." He smiled.

"What do you mean?"

Cleveland nodded to Cyndi as she introduced herself. He turned his head back to me.

"I hear you went under the bridge last night and got into it with Shark. Don't take Shark too seriously."

How would he have known this? "Remember what I said at court about talking in front of other people, Cleveland?"

"I don't care, Snick. Later, dudes." No one responded

We walked into the interview hall, found a cubicle, and went inside. The enclosure separated us from other orange suits by a half wall of gray metal and a second half of Plexiglas.

"We need your help," I said. "You've got to stop holding back on me. When I talked to you in the bullpen yesterday you didn't say anything about getting caught with the dead guy's lighter and the money. That really messed us up in court. I have to be able to prepare. I need to know what you know. Come on and help yourself. It seems like you have more access to the witnesses than I do."

Cleveland said nothing.

"Tell us about the people from Mexico. Tell us about Shark," Cyndi said. "Do you really know him?" She pulled out her notebook, opened it up, and put it on the table.

Cleveland looked off into space, hypnotized, caught himself, then threw up his hands and laughed. "I don't really know him that well. He showed up about three months ago. I don't know where he sleeps. The man said he believes in Amalek. Told me so. He has a tent under the bridge but he doesn't stay there. He and Snapper use it."

"Have you ever seen him there with a woman? A blonde?"

"Nope."

"How about with a younger man. Maybe a Latino man?"

"You mean a Spanish?"

"Right."

"Yeah, couple times. But I don't know who that is."

Cyndi persisted with little questions, eking information out of Cleveland by dribs and drabs. When all was said it became clear that Shark had shown up out of nowhere, that Snapper marshaled his tent, and that Cleveland had no idea who Shark was. Not very helpful.

"You know he pulled a gun on Stuart last night?" Cyndi said.

"Yes, I know," Cleveland sighed. "Look, I already told him that wasn't right! And he, he said, he said he was sorry, and promised not to do it again." Cleveland grinned and scratched himself.

Sorry and promised not to do it again?

"This isn't the Mickey Mouse show," I said. "A guy pulling a gun is serious business."

Cleveland studied his hands, smiling to himself like we'd just shared a good joke. My words flew right by him.

"How did you talk to Shark? Who let you make a telephone call?" Cyndi said.

"Been here a hundred times, mam. Got some real good friends working here." He grinned.

"And they let you use a telephone?" Cyndi looked through the thick glass at two massive marshals talking in the marshal's cubicle nearby.

"Right."

"And you called Shark?" Cyndi continued.

"I called his cell phone."

"Why?" I asked. And why didn't Cleveland give me the number?

"To check on things," Cleveland sighed again. "I had to call somebody and Shark is the only one that picked up."

"And you think Shark's your friend?" I watched for Cleveland's reaction.

"Oh, yeah! Listen. He wasn't going to shoot you. He's trying to protect me, Snick. The man just didn't know you and so he wasn't going to trust you."

"So how do I do my job? You knew I was going down there. Isn't there anything you could have told me that might have helped? "

Cleveland squirmed. I drew back. Confrontation wouldn't work here. Had to try another way.

"Lets move on, Cleveland." Cyndi raised her eyes at me. "What did Shark say when you spoke with him? Does he understand the situation that you're in?"

"Shark says there's some funny looking guys chasing people and shooting the air last night. Says there is noise down there all night and people screaming off away."

"Okay. Listen, Cleveland," I said. "This isn't getting us anywhere. I need you to try and remember everything you can about Shark and we'll talk again next time. But we need to shift into what we do know. We've got to cover a lot of ground here because a lot has happened in a short time. So let's walk through it."

We talked. Cleveland got squirmier. Cleveland didn't want to give up his friends. Too bad. He'd have to learn that in the world of criminal defense, friendship is a fungible commodity.

In the minutes that followed, we went over all of the details of the case. I discussed Percy's entrance as co-counsel on Cleveland's behalf, then drafted a hastily written note signed by Cleveland indicating his agreement. I tried to educate Cleveland on the government's perspective and to better understand how Cleveland had viewed things. Also I wanted him to feel comfortable with Cyndi.

We pressed Cleveland as hard as he could be pressed. I went over each of the five categories of witnesses and other actors that I'd mapped out and tried to get Cleveland's take on all of the people involved.

Cleveland couldn't remember when he had last seen Ruthie or Adrian. Not recently, he claimed. By all appearances, the street world had taken him over. Cleveland had contact with Ruthie only when he got into some kind of trouble. Category B was Benny, Mickey Jaworski & the Tweedledum, and their New York connections. The only relationship with Benny was confined to a choice of shoes, a lighter, and some money that changed hands— and feet—over to Cleveland. I had no evidence of any other contact. Still, I couldn't ignore some relationship that Rhondo had claimed—though I saw no evidence of it. Aside from the arrest by Barry Acres and interrogation by Rhondo and Zeus, Cleveland had little relationship to anyone in the law enforcement and legal group that comprised Column C. Column D involved the big hostess at the Potomac Club, Jennifer, the woman who waited on Benny and Mona, Cornelius the bartender, and all the people at the club and the hotel, and Samantha Myers, the woman who discovered Benny's head on the parking meter. I had no facts to connect Cleveland to any of these people, but a few facts did stand out. Cleveland got arrested wearing a top hat. When I'd gone through the government's evidence report with Cleveland I found that the top hat's inside label listed the name and address of the Lathrop Hotel, the hotel where Benny stayed. Cleveland told me he'd taken the top hat out of the hotel trash several weeks ago.

Finally, we considered the last two categories, E and F. Cleveland again claimed that Tiffannie Squires could account for his presence at the time of the murder, that she was with him when he spotted the head and the body. Certainly we had to find Tiffannie as a potential witness. Still, this seemed odd. Mind you, the oldest profession was a diverse one with several classes of service providers. Even so, Mona Day had also been identified as a hooker. The fact that both of my missing witnesses were prostitutes struck me as significant. Tiffannie Squires could potentially be a cohort of the crucial key witness, Mona Day. Either way, Tiffannie and Mona were the keys. Tiffannie might very well provide Cleveland with an alibi. Obviously, suspicion could be cast upon Mona.

Like it or not, Tiffannie and Mona might be my best fact witnesses. Prostitutes might not be the most upstanding citizens but I didn't get to pick witnesses from central casting. A defense attorney, especially a street lawyer, must proceed like Samson of the Old Testament, who picked up the jawbone of a donkey and destroyed a thousand Philistines. Lots of times the evidentiary jawbone has to suffice. There is nothing else to work with. And I believed that Tiffannie and Mona would point me in the direction of other admissible evidence, to other facts and events, as yet unknown, that could prove the case.

Cleveland, Cyndi, and I talked for over an hour and a half. I made some headway. Cyndi took detailed notes on Cleveland's route of can collection the night of the murder. She quizzed Cleveland about each of the bridge people. I concluded that Cleveland didn't even know the people under the bridge. He and the others coexisted in a psychic half light, strangers to each other in a shared reality. They clung to a subterranean world the way the oppressed poor and sick cling to flawed ideas the world over. They huddled from a distance not of geography but of mind.

I studied the marshals through the window. They were ten feet away—as much as a minute away—separated by two electronic doors. This was a dangerous place, sometimes worse than the streets. Incarceration amplified class and race frustration. In a crowded elevator a few weeks back, a young man wearing a stocking cap over decided with no provocation to berate me as a "cracker m.f." The other five people in that car said nothing. Maybe preoccupied with their own troubles. Still I didn't know if I would leave unscathed or if caphead would try to plant a plastic shank in my gut. That's the way of the jailhouse.

Adrian Sewell walked into the outer area and waved to us.

"See that man walking toward us?" I spoke without even thinking.

"That's Adrian," Cleveland said. Cyndi and Cleveland watched the man as he spoke briefly to the guard and then came toward our booth.

"As your attorney, I instruct you not to discuss what we have talked about with this man."

# CHAPTER 44

"HE'S my Godson!" Cleveland moaned.

"Too bad. Talk to him about Godson things. I don't know what his gig is and we can't afford to trust anyone. You talk to him about this case, you find yourself another lawyer."

"Come on, Snick. That boy is family. I've known him since he was a twig."

"He's no boy. He's Adrian Sewell and he has his own take on you. I don't understand it. You have to cooperate. My way or the highway."

Cleveland frowned. Adrian sauntered toward our interview booth like a late arriving lunch guest. The fluorescent lights cast a purplish glow across his suit. Our cubicle door was still shut and I spoke quickly, smiling through the glass at Adrian and repeating my instructions to Cleveland. Cleveland said he understood. I didn't believe him.

Adrian opened the door and walked in.

"My man!" He leaned across the table and shook Cleveland's manacled paw.

Cleveland nodded deferentially and smiled.

"Called ahead and had you moved." Adrian grinned.

"How'd you do that? Does the warden play on your basketball team?" I studied Adrian's face.

"Ask me no questions, I'll tell you no lies. See, I've lived in this city all my life. I always know someone that is willing to help out."

"Fine. Since you're in the neighborhood, it would be real Godson-ly of you to go next door and use your connections at the medical examiner's office. Ask them about providing the complete set of photographs and lab results that went with the Batiste autopsy. We got a preliminary draft, but there is a larger file."

"Right," Adrian said. "Anything else?"

"I'll tell you if I think of anything. Are you still coming to Ruthie's?"

"I'll be at Ruthie's after a while. Want to catch up with my man here." He motioned toward Cleveland.

"Cleveland, let's talk about your friend Adrian for a second while we're all here together."

I motioned for Adrian to sit.

"Adrian wants to pay your legal fees and the costs of any expert witnesses that you might need at trial. If we did that, I'd have withdrawn the case from the court-appointed counsel system."

"You mean you would be a private lawyer then?"

"Right. That means that your legal bill wouldn't be paid by the court. It would be paid by Adrian and his business. The good part for you is that you will have greater freedom to choose things that can help you win at trial, like special people who can testify about things that can help you."

"Like what?"

"Do you know what an expert witness is?"

"Not really."

And so it went. For several minutes I parsed through the process, making sure that Cleveland understood what Adrian had proposed. Cleveland understood the issues well enough to make a reasoned decision. He consented to Adrian's proposal and I drew up still another handwritten document and three party contract in which Cleveland agreed to have Adrian pay his fees and Adrian agreed to pay all costs including an hourly rate to myself and

Percy Diel for work on the case. I'd have a formal document prepared. This would do for now.

Cyndi and I stood up to leave, shaking hands with Cleveland and Adrian. I wanted to stay and make sure Cleveland didn't start talking about the case, but there was no time. We agreed that, assuming the court found probable cause at the preliminary hearing, I would file papers to take the case out of CJA finance. In a world where money talks and everyone else walks, this was the right choice whatever my suspicions about Adrian.

I turned around at the room's doorway, and stared at Cleveland. "Remember my instructions, Cleveland. This place is full of snitches. Watch what you say."

Cyndi and I left the interview room and approached the elevator down. Looking back, I noticed Adrian and Cleveland engaged in a lively conversation.

We departed through the jail's now-vacant lobby and headed for the Oldsmobile. Retrieving my cell phone, I found the message light flashing. Jack Payne had returned my call and urged me to stay cool and persist, whatever that meant.

I needed to act better. Called Percy to smooth things over. Unavailable. I went to voicemail and left a conciliatory message informing him that Cleveland consented to his appointment and we should set up breakfast tomorrow to go over the case.

Cyndi pulled the car out of the jail parking lot and turned right, headed for the southeast corridor. An MPD cruiser swung out behind us and engaged its lights. A loudspeaker voice barked at us. "Pull over!"

# CHAPTER 45

THE sedan drove beside me and I read the words "Chief of Police" painted in bold letters on the side. Two large cops sat in the front seat. The back windows were dark. The window on the right hand back door motored down to reveal a bull dog of a man sitting in the back seat. He stuck his arm out the window and motioned for me to come over.

The constables in the front seat didn't have white hair and weren't Tweedles. These were the good guys, but the sight of flashing squad car lights still made uncomfortable. I had to relax. Radio blasts shot through the air. As I approached the right rear door opened. I got in and came face-to-face with the chief of police.

"Mr. Clay." He nodded. "I've got a big problem and I want you to help me."

"Hello, Chief." I offered my hand and he shook it.

"Like I said, Mr. Clay. I have a big problem." He stared off into space and I waited.

Chief Spike Armstrong resembled an African-American version of J. Edgar Hoover. He wasn't black so much as red-yellow with a million brown freckles and straight black hair that waxed straight back over his head. He didn't talk so much as whisper, like the man he was, up to his nose in conflicts and trying to preserve his strength for a greater battle. He sat poised for the long battle, always immaculately kept, contained, but somehow bursting with a sort of intelligent rage.

"We have only got money for so many police in this city and right now I got seventy cops in riot gear at superior court prepared to control two hundred citizens, not including forty reporters. Now that isn't right, Mr. Clay. These geezers shouldn't be allowed to tie up the resources of our city with their voodoo protest."

"I didn't start the bruhaha, chief."

"Mr. Clay, I know you wouldn't do that. But you have got to help me out here. We've got these old farts doing their voodoo-shmoodoo for the cameras. And now the Takoma Park City Council has passed a *Resolution of Cultural Solidarity with Cleveland Barnes.* A resolution of cultural solidarity, counselor. What the hell does that mean? In fact, I don't know, don't have a clue, but do you know what that result will be? What this resolution of cultural solidarity will cause?"

"You're the man, chief. Tell me. What will the resolution cause?"

"It will cause every goofball, never-say-die sixties holdover and their younger wannabe kids to take the Redline or the minivan to Judiciary Square and show up on the steps of my courthouse. This is suddenly their cause!"

He raised his right hand, pointed at me and continued.

"Counselor, I cannot afford it and the mayor cannot afford it. We got bigger fish to fry." The red-yellow beneath his dark brown spots was turning red, a sight to behold.

"We got this nasty little guy leading Congress." He gritted his teeth and hissed in a terse shout. "He wants to dissolve my city and make it a federal zone. My city. Your client's friends are handing him his opportunity to do just that!"

He put his pointing finger down and stopped, checking himself.

An officer in the front passenger seat looked back at the chief, then turned off the blabbing radio transmitter and ratcheted the air conditioning way, way up. Everyone looked straight ahead. Nobody spoke. Aside from the air conditioning sound all noise halted inside the car. The reddening in the chief's face peaked and started to recede back to yellow.

Two older women waddled by, trekking from the subway to the jail. A dark green prison bus packed with prisoners moseyed toward the electronic gates and maximum security docking. Cyndi idled behind us. The space around us seemed to swell, to take on a bigger dimension and, to tell the truth, I didn't know what was going on. Spike Armstrong and I were suddenly like two kids on the playground in a staring contest.

"What do you want me to do about it, Chief? I didn't have anything to do with this but you know I respect you and you know I'll help."

"That goes without saying, Mr. Clay. But thank you. Do you know an elderly female by the name of Ruth Malveaux?"

The whisper was back. He fixed me in his bull dog stare.

"She's Cleveland's sister. I've met with her once."

"A word to the wise, Mr. Clay. She's Cleveland's sister like I'm his uncle Charley. "

"What do you mean? Cleveland and several other people claim they are related."

"I don't need to get into that. All I ask is that you talk to Ms. Malveaux," he hissed. "Just do that for me, would you? That's all I'm asking. We don't need a riot on the courthouse steps."

"I will do that, but please clarify your statement."

"What statement would that be?" His eyes squinted into narrow slits as he studied me.

"Do you have a basis upon which to assert that Cleveland is not Ruthie's brother?" If Ruthie somehow masqueraded as a relative I absolutely had to know it.

He shook his head.

"Just blowing steam, counselor. I'm a tired cop with a thankless job to do. Now would you please help me out?"

"I'll do it. I'll talk to her." The Chief's color now appeared as it had when I'd first sat beside him. I looked back at Cyndi.

"You and I are both busy, so I'll let you go," he said. "Good to see you again." His right arm shot out like a spring loaded ham. I shook it and opened the door and turned back to the chief.

"I'll do what I can, but I repeat for the record: I had no part in setting up the demonstrations."

"Nobody thinks you did, Mr. Clay. Responsible people have to take care of problems that they didn't cause in this world, right?"

I got out of the car.

# CHAPTER **46**

CYNDI'S face fixed on me from behind the wheel of the Oldsmobile. I slid in beside her and squeezed her hand.

"We have got to get this AC tuned up, my dear. The Chief's coach is much cooler."

"Still going to Ruthie's?"

"Yes. Guess the courthouse antics are getting on Spike's nerves. He wants me to lean on the old girl."

"Ruthie? Will you?"

"Sure. I don't really like what she is doing, either. It could cut against us in the long run. But I can't control her. It's a free country and, truth be told, she has a point. I understand Spike's position, but I got a job of my own."

"How's that job doing?" Cyndi said.

"We're doing fine. We're definitely doing fine, and I don't mind the company."

She squeezed my leg as we pulled out of the parking lot and motored down East Capitol Street, past dozens of turn-of-the-century row houses, home to successive waves of immigrants.

Lined with covered front porches and chain-link fences, the yards had become frayed around the edges. Groups of restless young men crowded streets and playgrounds, stared up as we drove by. Small huddles were starting to form around street corners and in front of liquor stores. Tiny children with no hint of adult supervision walked on cracked sidewalks past the soaped windows of vacant storefronts, puffed with confidence and swagger, small and innocent yet hardened. A toothless old man staggered and fell on a stoop, bent and listless in the thick July air.

My mind wandered. It must have been the same for earlier groups in America. How many CEOs rose from streets like this and gave people hope by building their empires, starting their factories, their casinos, their professional athletic teams? The people who began life with nothing were often the ones who best appreciated both the need to take risks to get anywhere and the inherent uncertainty of life. These hungry ones stoked the great engines of free enterprise and progress and the masses went up with them. Staring out across a littered school yard and row of public houses, I wondered. Was a Henry Ford out there? Was one of these dirty-faced street kids destined to rise up and push the envelope? Truth is, I believed so. These poor people I saw around me were no different from the ones that loaded off crowded ships at Ellis Island almost a century before. They had the hopes, dreams, and the juice.

Heartened by my thoughts, I pushed aside my musings and reviewed a tick list of things to do. First, I called Adrian's cell phone and left a voice message thanking him for helping on Cleveland's case. I suggested that we meet separately after talking with Ruthie to discuss ways that he could be involved in and contribute to the Barnes defense team. As I clipped the phone shut it erupted with an incoming call. The name "Rhondo" flashed on my caller ID panel.

"Ready to drop the charges, Rhondo?"

"Not quite, my man. But you can tell me something. How well you know Mickey Jaworski?"

"You first." Several seconds passed. I didn't mind discussing the Bronx rat but I wanted something in return.

"What does that mean?"

"Rhondo, you already told me that Batiste was a poster child for the organized crime enforcement guys in the southern district of New York. Don't tell me you guys don't know who Batiste's lawyer is."

"I didn't say that. I asked what do you know?"

"And I said you first."

"I know he's Batiste's lawyer, man. Question is, have you seen him about here? If so, what has he been up to?"

"May have caught a glance of him around the courthouse," I laughed. "Between you and me, he pulled a gun on me yesterday, engaged in actions that would show probable cause for kidnap, and intimated that he might break my kneecaps if I played the mob card on Benny's reputation in proceedings for Cleveland."

"You don't want to press charges?"

"I'm a big boy, Rhondo. I'd press charges if I thought it would help Cleveland—but I think it would just be a distraction. Anyway, the guy doesn't scare me."

"So you aren't taking his advice"

"How well do you know me, Rhondo? What do you think?"

"I think this: a creep named Mickey Jaworski filed a Freedom of Information Act request with the police department and sent a big nasty letter with it. Says he's going to sue the police for malicious character defamation and civil rights violations on behalf of the estate of Benny Batiste. Got no idea what he's blabbering about. Who the hell does this guy think he is?"

"Look, Rhondo, I could tell you more about Mickey Jaworski if you could tell me more about Benny Batiste."

"I told you what I knew yesterday. Help me out, here."

"No, dude. I'm sure you can see the plain truth. Mickey is a consigliore. Like Robert Duval in the Godfather, except much, much uglier."

"I know that. But where exactly did you see him? When did he get to town? What exactly has he said to you?"

"Off the record?"

"Yeah. Swear."

"He's been here since at least yesterday afternoon, I met him on D Street yesterday and he gave a message—implied that using Benny's background as part of my defense would be bad for my health. Same message again this morning outside my apartment. And last night I saw his two goons chasing a Latino kid in Georgetown."

"Did he say anything about who Benny was here to see?"

"Nope."

"Talk turkey, Stuart. Anything about who his and Benny's buddies are in a turf war with? Anything at all?"

"Nope." I couldn't mention Benny's comments about paying back the guys under the bridge. This could conceivably be used to implicate Cleveland who was, after all, a guy that lived under that bridge.

"Does your client know anything about Jaworski?"

"I can't answer that. Maybe at some point we could do a debriefing at the Triple Nickel basement if there is a reduced plea in the works— like to one count of recycle bin theft."

"I'll relay that to Lisa. Don't hold your breath. But thanks for the information. It fits."

"Fits what?"

"Talk to you later, Stuart." The line went dead.

# CHAPTER 47

FITS what? I thought.

I repeated the question to myself, grateful that Rhondo did give me something—after all. I'd guessed that the police and prosecutors were trying to unravel the same conflict that I had stumbled into. Rhondo's statement supported that guess. This helped Cleveland because the bigger this other conflict got the more opportunities I had to find either fodder for the defense at trial or an alternative way to end the case without a trial.

I didn't see this case ending in a plea. Even so, the door had to be left open. Many times I'd gone full steam ahead preparing for trial only to find that my client had information that the government wanted. In such cases, debriefings were held at the Triple Nickel, 555 Fourth Street, N.W., headquarters of the U.S. Attorney for the District of Columbia. Defendant cooperation interviews took place in small cubicles of an underground interview facility housed in a third sub-basement of the building where prisoners and defendants generally entered and exited without being observed by the public. Many criminal defense lawyers think that cooperating defendants are a travesty and that it is the job of the defense lawyer to wage war on the prosecution without compromise. This is naïve. Such lawyers do their clients a disservice in the name of defense purism. The way I see it, my job is to get my guy out and off any way I can.

We drove into Southeast, D.C. headed for Ruthie's house. I knew this part of town, but not 46th Place where Ruthie lived. The Oldsmobile traveled over the place where H Street turned into Benning Road and passed the shrimp boat, a white restaurant crowned with a thirty-foot long inedible crustacean on its roof. We motored on, by several roadside barbecue stands set up on public sidewalks and vacant lots. People looked happy. Crowds of folk tended the grills and stood around, eating and laying down small bills and change and taking dibs on sizzling chicken parts and spare ribs. They huddled and laughed as smoke swirled up in the steamy afternoon sky, scenting the air we breathed with charcoal and barbecue sauce.

We drove past a line of parked cars with continuous weaving automatic bullet holes, sprayed like hell's graffiti in the past few hours, into the other Washington, with drug stores and small groceries framed in iron-barred windows, with trash-filled vacant lots and an occasional abandoned car, with off-brand gas stations where you pay first in cash to a man behind bulletproof glass.

Turning right, the Oldsmobile traveled up G street S.E., a winding little uphill road. It had a bastion of tattered brick housing projects, boarded and broken windows, lawns turned to dust and rubble, kids and old men every where, hanging out, marking time. As we went up I saw the U.S. Capitol dome off in the distance, across the Anacostia River. It jutted out like a white thing in the far off sky, a half moon at midday reflecting light from another world.

We followed the road until it dipped back down again. Then we came upon 46th Place.

The cul-de-sac had half a dozen wooden Victorian structures interspersed with two older looking brick housing projects. The wooden houses predated the brick row projects by fifty years or more and hearkened to a time when Frederick Douglas lived and held court in his Southeast home. The Victorian structures were in various stages of disrepair, but they all had beautiful trim work and banisters. Among these modest dwellings was 6226 46th Place.

It sat on the bluff overlooking much of Southeast D.C. and abutted a housing project on its left side. Ruthie's house showed its age but had recently been painted. It had creamy gray wood siding with red trim, a six foot high black high wrought iron fence, and a well-kept middle sixties black Cadillac in the driveway.

I asked Cyndi to turn on the microcassette. She looked at me a little surprised, but said nothing, reached up with her right hand, and pushed a button through her shirt pocket. We parked on the road in front of the gray house and walked up to the gate. I pushed, but it was locked. After I rang a small white buzzer a baritone voice sounded from a small box mounted on the fence.

"May I help you?" The baritone said.

"Stuart Clay to see Ms. Malveaux."

"Yes, Mr. Clay. But who's that with you?"

"My investigator. Ms. Oh."

"All right. Come on to the left side."

The gate buzzed and I opened it. Cyndi shut it behind us and I heard the electronic lock click. As we walked I noticed that the house and grounds had been retrofitted with various security measures. The lower level and first floor windows were all barred and small cameras hung above all the doors. The back and side yards had three rows of barbed wire strung above the top of the fences. A barred door on the left side of the house opened up and a large bald man walked over the brick sidewalk.

"I'm LaWayne, folks. Nice to meet you. I'll take you in," he smiled.

"Stuart Clay. Beautiful house. Much trouble with break-ins here?"

"Don't live here myself, but Ruthie is okay. She takes precautions." As he turned, the outline of a pistol pressed against the beige shirt draping his trousers. "People know not to mess with her."

"You sure can't take it for granted."

"We don't take anything for granted round here. You can sure bet on that." He patted the gun's bulge.

# CHAPTER 48

CYNDI and I followed LaWayne into a tidy side hall. We paused while he twisted the padlock bolts and tapped a code to disengage and then rearm the door alarm. Following him up the stairs, we entered an orderly kitchen smelling of chicory coffee that I recognized from my trips to the French Quarter of New Orleans, and the smell of freshly cooked bread. We passed through into a dining room and front foyer. On the left side of the foyer was a parlor with dark violet drapes pulled closed and an old chandelier refitted with electric sockets. I followed the half light down the dark walls to an octagonal oak table where Ruthie and Amanda sat, drinking coffee and eating bread rolled in powdered sugar. They both looked exhausted.

"Ladies, how are you?" I smiled at them and sat down. Cyndi sat beside me, nodding, but saying nothing.

"Hello, Lawyer Clay," Ruthie said. "Who is this pretty girl? Have some coffee. How's Cleveland?"

I poured Cyndi and myself coffee, and took a roll.

"This is my investigator, Cyndi Oh. Cleveland's better off than he was yesterday. I think he dried out some, got rest, and ate the prison food. We visited with Cleveland and Adrian dropped by."

"Lawyer Clay. When are we going get Cleavie out of there?" Amanda erupted. "That jail is a rat hole. That is no place for a human! What did Adrian say about it?"

I studied their faces in the half-light.

"Adrian is going to help us. Getting Cleveland out is another matter. You were at the hearing. Did you see anything I missed?"

"You were doing what you can, lawyer," Ruthie said. "But that Judge and prosecutor woman were full of themselves. I don't know how you stand it."

"Standing things comes with the territory. I don't think the Magistrate Judge had much choice about what she did even if she was abrupt. She's obligated to follow the bail statute."

"I don't understand." Ruthie frowned. "The man has no history of violence and a good explanation for how he had the shoes. Are we missing something? What else does the evidence show? Who are the witnesses?"

They wanted questions answered, but the purpose of the meeting was for them to educate me, not vice versa. Even so, I didn't want to anger them.

"Thanks to my investigator here, I think the case is on good footing. We've found several witnesses and have a solid defense. Cleveland has given us some leads and we have found others. The crime scene search and the autopsy suggest that the lady who left the club should be considered the chief suspect, not Cleveland. That's how we see it."

"What are you going to tell the jury?" Ruthie spoke plainly, intelligently as she braided her hair around her index finger again, looking off into barred window and the siding of the house next door.

"I'll try to show that Batiste, the guy that got murdered, was a mobster probably murdered by mobsters. Cleveland just wandered in and took shoes and other stuff that he thought were free for the taking." I had no problem telling her the obvious.

"We agree with that, lawyer Clay," Amanda responded, "but do we have any witnesses for Cleveland?"

"Actually, there is a missing witness. The guy that got murdered, Batiste, left the nightclub with a woman."

"What is her name?"

"I don't know," I lied. "Cyndi is trying to get a lead on that." I looked at Cyndi and she nodded. No need to name Mona Day.

"Who else?" Ruthie dropped her braid and stared straight at me. I shivered again, her eyes like a physical force thumping on my breastbone.

"Cleveland identified a woman named Tiffannie who was out there when he was by the club."

"Have you found her?"

"No, but we're looking." Time to turn this around. "But I need help from you. Do you know any of Cleveland's friends from around the Key Bridge?"

"Mercy, no." Ruthie shuddered.

"Ever heard of a man known as Shark?"

"No, sir." she spoke again.

"Do you know about Cleveland's 'New Columbian' movement?"

Ruthie rolled her eyes and huffed.

"I've heard all about this, lawyer Clay. I've told that boy that he needs to stop this and understand the old time religion. He just won't listen. I don't know where that man thought up that nonsense!"

"Old time religion?" I thought back to the courthouse spectacle.

"That's what it is, lawyer. I can show you books and historical accounts for the rituals we follow. But Cleveland? He sees something when he is drunk and decides to call it a spirit."

I shifted the conversation to other issues in the case and we talked for another twenty minutes. Cyndi had several questions and Ruthie and Amanda answered them all. Schools and dates for Cleveland. Hospitalization records. Case worker names. Subjective impressions. What did Amanda and Ruthie do at Sewell Produce? What did Cleveland do there? Chronology of the families and their ties, back to the sixties. Questions about Wendell Sewell.

They answered everything, giving more detailed answers than before. Ruthie worked with Amanda at Sewell Produce and had a thriving after-hours business telling fortunes, making potions, and conducting séances. Sewell Produce had distribution points all over Southeast D.C. and Prince George's County. After Wendell Sewell's death months before, Adrian stepped up as the new person running the business.

The visit yielded little new information, but Amanda and Ruth seemed happier by the time we finished. As I closed my notebook and got ready to leave, the discussion turned back to my case preparation. They wanted every detail. I shared what was on the public record and mentioned Spike Armstrong's worries.

"They want to save money on policemen?" Ruthie growled. "Then let my brother out of that hell pit."

"Don't think it will be that simple, Ruthie."

"Me neither. So that chief of police better settle in for a long, hot summer. I already told you. We will vindicate our—"

"Rights. I understand. I think they got the message."

We had to get back to the office and then to Georgetown. Adrian didn't show. I wondered what Cleveland talked about in my absence. Unfortunately, I had little trouble imagining him confiding in Adrian.

Ruthie and I agreed to meet again the next day at 4:30P.M., providing my court schedule didn't preempt planning. I planned to bring both Percy and Cyndi with me and to press for Adrian's presence. The public part of the case would be reviewed bullet by bullet, but I had to hold back some of the other things. I'd get the firm to draft up formal documents for Cleveland and Adrian to sign and work up a motion to remove the case from the CJA finance program and a second entry of appearance as privately paid counsel. Everything could be filed with the court if the preliminary went the way I thought it probably would.

It seems peculiar looking back. These were my definite plans. I fully expected to perform on each one of them. Not one of these things ever happened.

# CHAPTER **49**

RUTHIE'S house was a cellular dead zone, probably from all of the rows of barbed wire on the side and back yard fence, the thick iron bars, and security devices. Whatever the reason, my cell phone beeped and blinked, announcing nine new messages as we headed back down to Benning Road. I held the phone to my right ear.

"The time is 4:17 P.M." The voicemail system spoke.

"Dude, its Adrian. Just got done with Cleveland and think it'll help you more if I go over to see the med examiner guys next door. I'll let you know."

"The time is 4:27 P.M."

"Hello, Stuart. Percy here. I appreciate your telephone message and I'm just very relieved that we'll be able to see this thing through together. Let's just keep Haskell out of the picture from now on. We have a lot of mutual interests and he seems to rub you the wrong way and I think it—"

"The time is 4:28 P.M."

"Percy again! Damn these phones!! I'll be short and sweet, Stu. Your call was a good thing. Please call me so we can review some materials that I've put together. I've read everything and started putting together the defense murder book per our discussion last night. Also, I do want to go out with you to talk with the witnesses. Please call me."

"The time is 4:43 P.M."

"Stuart. It's Haskell back at the firm. I don't know what you said to Percy, but whatever you did you should just keep doing, big fellow. You know, the Diels have at least a dozen major business projects in this town and if you cultivate this relationship it could be very, very good for you and very, very good for Mitchell & Strong. Call me."

"The time is 4:56 P.M."

"Lawyer Clay. This is Lester in Courtroom C-10. One of your clients, a Ms. Luwanda Martinique, has been re-arrested on murder one. Where are you, man? Stand-in counsel had to take the case for presentment and the judge was miffed at you, man. Defendant is held without bond and a preliminary hearing is set for July 31 at 9:30 before Judge Wilkerson. You might want to write her a letter explaining your absence. We have got to be able to get you in here when a serious case like this comes down on your clients. Judge Reilly also issued a bench warrant for violating release conditions and set a hearing for the same day on the old case."

"The time is 5:22 P.M."

"Lawyer Clay. It's Rascal from down by the Club. I can tell you where Tiffannie is, but we have got to meet up so I can get the money you promised. I haven't got a telephone, so I'll call you back."

"The time is 5:33 P.M."

"Adrian again, dude. Listen, they'll have the final report tomorrow. I asked them if there was anything special they found and my little mole girl said they found a burn mark on the back of the guy's neck. Looks like the guy got downed with a stun gun before someone did the nasty thing. Also, the blade struck him at least six times and the spinal cord was cut with a different type of blade. See you later."

"The time is 5:43 P.M."

"Rascal again, man. I'll call you again soon."

"The time is 5:57 P.M."

"Rascal."

"End of messages."

We passed the shrimp boat heading west, back toward downtown. The eastern exposure of the large shrimp was spray painted with greetings from C-Boy of Anacostia. A few guys had set up another big grill in the westerly traffic direction and were selling cooked ribs to passing cars. They called and motioned at the smoking grill, trying to sell their meats to the passing traffic. I was pretty hungry, so we stopped and I bought some. They turned out to be delicious Southern ribs cooked better than what I'd had in local restaurants.

I licked the oil from my finger and started to write furiously, noting all my messages on the inside of the manila file jacket and considering the importance of each.

First, Adrian was right. He did help me more by speeding up release of the autopsy report although most of the snippets he discovered were old news. The stun gun was news; maybe Benny wasn't as drunk as everyone said when he left the club. But I already knew the killer had given Benny multiple whacks with the ax or whatever had been used. What I really wanted was the forensic reports returns analyzing the hair, the dried fluids, the other various forensic samples, and the follow-up on the fingerprints off the belt.

Percy still sounded like Norman Bates from *Psycho*, but so what? I'd rather have him on my team than against it. I wasn't frothing at the thought of Haskell's plan for me to do shopping mall negotiations. Even so, I might need a gentler, softer law practice as the years went by.

Lester, the court room clerk, had some nerve. Why didn't I appear for a hearing that I had no notice of for an alleged crime that just happened? I wasn't going to lose too much sleep over that one.

That left Rascal. He called three times. Great, especially since Adrian was going to cover the finder's fee. Please call again, I prayed. Please call again.

Cyndi drove past the point where Benning Road turned back into H Street, back to the Capital dome and points northwest.

I dialed Percy's personal line and he picked up on the first ring.

"Stuart." He sounded excited.

"Co-counsel. What's shaking?" Percy sounded up.

"The video from the club came back from that Detective Touhey. I've just been watching the thing over and over, studying the club and also listening to the crime scene guy's tape. This is one hell of a case we got here."

"You bet."

"Well, do you realize that Benny left the club with that woman at 2:17 and that Georgetown student came running in the club yelling about the murder around 2:30?"

"I do. That's one of the things that will work for us." This was all old news, but at least the guy was diligent.

"And the crime scene guy makes it sound like Benny got off sexually right before the murder?"

"Right." More old news.

"Do we have any idea who the woman was? Seems like she's the key to it all."

"Right." I had to decide whether to tell him about the name. I started to lie, but stopped myself. "The woman's name is Mona Day. Her street name, anyway. I'm hoping one of the prints off the dead guy's belt is hers and we can get a match off the National Crime Index Computer, you know, the NCIC, or the FBI data base."

"I see. Any other leads on her?"

"No, man, but I'm looking."

"Anything I can do?"

"Yes. Go online and get everything you can find on the Web about Benny Batiste, Seabreeze trucking, a New York lawyer named Mickey Jaworski, and anything regarding the Spilotro Family. I did some research last night, but it's the tip of the iceberg. We can't trust this task to a paralegal because it is too important and I don't want to risk a leak. It's you, me, and Cyndi Oh working the case. She's my investigator and I'll introduce you to her tomorrow."

"Yes, I saw her with you over by the court before. She should lose that rusty looking Oldsmobile."

"It's for going into the field without attracting too much attention." I winced at the slight to my vintage car. "Anyway, if you could do that work-up and we can talk tomorrow morning. You're definitely on the right track. At least I think so."

"Okay. Well, good luck with looking for witnesses."

"Later, dude." I hung up.

My cell phone rang and I spotted a 202 area code number that I didn't recognize. Flipping open the device, I answered.

"Stuart Clay."

"I want those fifty smackers and a bottle of Napoleon brandy, man."

"Got a cold, Rascal?"

"Who is Rascal? It's Zebra, man. I found Tiffannie Squires, so come and get the information while it's hot!"

# CHAPTER 50

CYNDI motored onto the Whitehurst Parkway, over top of our crime scene, up to the red light at M Street. Across from us the Dixie Liquors neon signs flashed Rolling Rock and Miller and the Great God Budweiser. To the left was the parking lot where Cyndi and I had parked the night before. This is also where the Tweedledums dashed off the stairs the night before, and where Zebra sat waiting for us now.

The traffic light changed and Cyndi slid across to the back right corner of the lot. Zebra stood up from the bottom stair, rubbed his grizzle and winked at Cyndi.

"Sorry 'bout that excitement last night. Shark has a short fuse."

"He's not like the rest of you guys." I stated the obvious. "Is he around now?"

"No, man. He doesn't really stay there that much. Plus when he's there I hear him chattering on some weird looking phone in Spanish."

"I thought he was an Indian. Do you know where he's from?"

"Indian schmindian," he scoffed. "That man is Mexican. Now let's get that brandy. I don't have all day." Zebra strutted toward Dixie Liquors.

"Has Shark told you exactly where he's from?" Cyndi caught up to Zebra while I lagged behind, trying to contain my annoyance.

"The man doesn't say squat. He and Snapper are both nasty. Both of them left after you were there, and that is fine with me. I just don't need it, Mr. Stuart." He turned around and addressed me. "How about we say seventy-five bucks and the bottle? It was real hard finding that girl and I'm very thirsty."

"Sure thing, Zebra," I said, biting my tongue. We'd probably pay the whole bunch before the case was over, but such is life. Certainly, Rascal would surface to claim his just reward. I had to keep their good will. There were more witnesses to be found and I needed help.

The sun had started to go down again and I had no urge to repeat the Dixie Liquor "interview circuit," especially when I could find an eyewitness and focus on pursuing that specific person.

"Here, Zebra." I pulled out a wad of bills folded and held by a gold Tiffany clip. I fingered five twenties and handed them to the man.

"Will that do it? We need to leave and find Tiffannie."

Zebra grinned. "Sure, man. Tiffannie is working at Peepers, corner of 9th and F Street Northwest."

Cyndi jotted down the address.

"She there tonight?" Cyndi asked.

"I'm sure. Talked to her myself not three hours ago."

"We're done for now." I shook Zebra's hand. "Please keep in touch. There will be more work and you can help."

Zebra looked at his pay and beamed.

"Any time, lawyer Clay. Any time."

We returned to the car and headed back in the direction of Judiciary Square. Almost eight P.M. and nearly dark. While Cyndi drove, I completed a subpoena for Ms. Tiffannie Squires to the preliminary hearing set in the matter of U.S. versus Cleveland Barnes. Unless I was mistaken, Peepers was on the edge of Gallery Place around the corner from the National Portrait Gallery.

I fished the recorder out of my brief case and spoke into it, testing it for operation and then making a record of the date, time, and purpose for the entry.

We located Peepers and found a parking space across from its entrance on 9th street. I had Cyndi set up a watch from the back of the Oldsmobile, which had the advantage of a comfortable seat positioned back behind darkened windows.

Peepers sat on the edge of a pedestrian mall where G Street was closed off and lots of park benches were installed. An ill-informed social planner must have thought this would promote "community." In fact, this setup gave the street people and prostitutes a place from which to panhandle and vend flesh.

I lifted the trunk of the Oldsmobile and fished for a hooded raincoat, then put it on. Cyndi sat with her back to me, pulled out her own microcassette recorder and set up operations. I slammed the Oldsmobile's trunk shut, then leaned into the car and kissed Cyndi goodbye. Pulling up the raincoat's hood, I walked across the street to the flashing neon lights of Peeper's Video Parlor.

I studied the odd scene in front of the southern entrance to the Smithsonian Portrait Gallery. Girls and boys with overdone mascara lounged in strange repose, primed for an evening of selling favors to whoever drove up. I saw a few potential clients trolling around in their cars. They looked like older men from suburban Virginia and Maryland, escaped from the world of well-trimmed lawns for whatever respite their night on the town afforded. The cars drove slowly by the park benches, obviously checking out the supply of available flesh. Police cars idled blocks away, but for whatever reason, this did not seem to halt the wheels of the flesh commerce now grinding before my eyes.

Pulling my hood up closer, I focused on the door leading into the flashing parlor at the edge of the mall. An overhead bell clanged as I pushed it open and entered the world of Peepers.

# CHAPTER 51

SHOVING the hood of my raincoat back, I glanced at the large man sitting by the cash register. He had bad skin and hair plugs. A rottweiler slept by his feet. An overhead closed circuit TV showed four shots from various angles within the porno store and four more on the outside.

The cashier nodded at me. I spotted racks containing dozens of magazine covers showing attractive naked women doing every conceivable sexual act. They featured "college girls," "kinky grammas," "horny housewives," "nurses at work," and more. Being a porn star was apparently an equal opportunity avocation as the magazines purveyed the explicit sexual congress of attractive couples, the elderly, the obese, and even a one-legged brunette captured as she embraced a gleeful dwarf. They had magazines devoted to cheeks, to jugs, to black, Asian, Latin, and blonde girls, to the heterosexual, the homosexual, and the bisexual and the over sixty. These covers were sealed in clear cellophane inviting the voyeur to purchase and partake of the erotic photographs promised within. Racks of videos and CDs also promised to show hours of joyous erotomania in every conceivable form.

Beyond the magazine display were a variety of sexual aids, oils, black leather masks, and silver-studded, black leather collars, then an array of organic substances promising to enhance, prolong, and enlarge, sustain, and titillate. There were big vibrators, little vibrators, pink, black, white, and dayglo purple vibrators, two-headed buzzing dildos with a string of beads attached, life sized blow-up dolls with indentations sporting "real hair" at the appropriate vinyl aperture, blow-up men made to resemble the porn star Johnnie Holmes equipped with a long, thick rubber body part. Another rack of magazines, further into the store, displayed more specialized pursuits and associational activities: leather bondage, leather bondage for big girls, rubber suits, foot worshippers, an undefined fetish simply referred to as "water sports," *Metro D.C. Swingers Anonymous*, *Platos Not In Retreat of the Greater Chesapeake Basin, Inc.*, and the *Swappers Liberation League of North America*.

Past the magazine and movie racks and the toy department were two darkly lit corridors going fifteen feet back to the east wall of the shop. The left corridor contained a dozen peep shows—narrow booths on both sides with locking doors— where viewers put tokens in a box to watch movies starring attractive nude models pictured in a lit display case. A window advertised movies with titles like *Jackie and the Bean Stock* or *Tailgunner Joe*, available for two minutes at a time for the price of a twenty-five cent token.

The right hand corridor had four larger booths and signage inviting the observer to watch a live show. This is where I had to go. My destination.

I noticed half a dozen other men mulling in the magazine section like overgrown toddlers that got into mommy's underwear drawer. I pushed past them and walked into the corridor of live shows.

The booths had no advertisements to explain what was within so I simply started with door number one. I knocked and then rubbed my knuckles against my shirt, hoping to brush away migrating cooties. Inside a female called out a "come on in baby" invitation to me.

Stepping into the booth, I closed and locked the door and waited as a dim red light came on. The booth was divided in half by a Plexiglas divider. The other side of the Plexiglas was covered by a black curtain.

"You have to slide five dollars through the slot. And pick up the phone." A woman spoke through a nickel sized peephole. I clumsily pulled out my small wad of folded bills, withdrew a rumpled fiver and slid it through, then picked up a black telephone resting on a flat holder with no buttons.

"That will get you five minutes, babe," the voice purred through the telephone receiver as the curtain drew back from the window, controlled by an unseen mechanical device. I beheld a curvaceous platinum blonde with blood red lips, reclining, spread eagled in a stuffed arm chair. She held the phone in her left hand. The lady wore a black military cap, a black leather garter belt with stainless steel spikes, stockings, stiletto heels, and nothing else. A vinyl zipper bag reflected the outline of something long and cylindrical and a half used bottle of Johnson's baby oil sat on a small table beside her. She winked and licked a long nail on her right middle finger.

"Nice suit, big guy. Why don't you show me your friend and tell me what you want to see me do."

Smiling, she narrowed her black-lined eyes and puckered, then licked her long-nailed middle finger again and ran it down in a light scratch over her chin and neck, and across herself. She arched her back and stuck her tongue out at me in a pout.

"Hurry up, baby. I want to see what you got," she said.

I thought of the audio recorder taping this entire matter. Glad there was no video. How to proceed?

"You're beautiful," I replied, "but I'm in the mood for someone a little darker. Anybody in the joint can help me out?" I slipped a second fiver through the slot. She cut her act short and grabbed the bill, then looked up at me.

"You sure, baby? I can ride the rabbit like no girl you ever seen."

"Yeah, I'm sure you're just one hell of a rabbit rider. But just not now. I need someone darker."

"Come back when you're ready for me. You should go see Tiffannie in Booth 4. Tell her Isis sent you. Hey, would you like to see us do an act together? I bet that she'd dig it."

"Thanks. Some other time. Enjoy your evening. Don't work too hard." I unlocked my door and quickly left.

# CHAPTER **52**

I SLIPPED out and saw that the signal light over booth four was red. Tiffannie was busy. Walking out to reexamine the wares, I checked again after a bashful looking man in a buttoned-up blue poplin suit and red bow tie paced from the dark corridor and out the front door.

The light over booth four shined green. Stepping inside, I locked the bolt and slid a five dollar bill through the slot. Again the curtain slid open. Behind the Plexiglas divider I saw a beautiful black female in a sofa chair. She reclined in an open black silk bathrobe laid against the inside of the chair. The only other thing she wore were bright red high heels, the bottoms of which were firmly planted against the lower left and right corners of the window. Tiffannie held a telephone in her left hand.

I sat on the bench and picked up the phone on my side.

"That will get you five minutes, babe. What can I do for you? Or should I say what can I do to myself for you?"

Studying the wall over Tiffannie's left shoulder, I focused my thoughts. The recorder silently wound tape in circles, taking it all in.

"Good evening." I slid a twenty through the slot and noticed her eyebrows perk. "I understand that this is somewhat unusual, but I have to talk with you about a man you know named Cleveland Barnes. I'm his attorney and this is the only place I knew to find you. If you would like to talk somewhere else I would be happy to accommodate you, but I really need to talk with you."

Tiffannie grimaced, sat up, crossed her legs, pulled the robe on, shut it, and tied the belt. Then she looked at me with a puzzled grin.

"What is your name?"

"Stuart Clay."

"Are you a lawyer?"

"Yes."

"Well, are you like the Royal Canadian Mounties? Always getting your man?" She frowned. Not angry, just intense and curious.

"You are decidedly not a man, Ms. Squires. I have a job and an obligation to do it. Would you prefer to meet somewhere else?"

"Hell no, whitebread." She laughed at me. "I've got to earn me a living too! You want to rent the mouth? You pay the standard rate. Talking to me will be one hundred bucks for ten minutes." She flicked her tongue at me and flashed a friendly grin.

I counted out five twenties and slid them through the slot. Satisfied, she smiled again.

"What can Miss Tiffannie's mouth do for you?" She grinned.

"It can answer questions."

"Yes, well, the mouth and me figured that much."

"Were you out in front of the Potomac Club on Sunday night? Two days ago."

"I was. There and a few other places. What of it?"

"Do you remember Cleveland Barnes being out there?"

"Who is he?"

"Cleveland Barnes. A homeless person, about fifty-five, white and dark hair Rasta locks and a beard. Panhandles around the Key Bridge."

"Cleavey. Yes, I know him. He was out there."

"Was he intoxicated?"

"How do I know, cracker boy? Cleveland is always drunk or something. Usual stuff, but old Cleveland does have a rap that he does and he is at least always high on that."

"What do you mean?" As if I didn't know by now.

"He talks to himself and goes from being a real blabber mouth to saying nothing at all. He lives in his own world, and believes in some big revolution coming or something. But I've never seen him hurt anybody. He is always nice to me."

"Did you know he was arrested and charged with the murder of a guy that had just come out of the Potomac Club?"

She laughed again. "They're fools! Cleavey is no murderer."

"I don't think so either. Do you remember how long he was out there with you?"

"Not really. I saw him by Goodfellas and over panhandling by the Georgetown Theater too. We were over by the Potomac Club between say two, two-thirty in the morning."

"What was he doing?"

"He was panhandling, collecting stuff. Doing what Cleavey does. Preaching."

"And you?"

"Just hanging out, doing what Tiffannie does." She pinched her lips matter-of-factly.

"Do you know a lady named Mona Day?"

"Moaning who?"

"Mona, not moaning. Mona Day."

"Now that doesn't ring any bells. Was she supposed to be out there?"

"I'm just asking."

Until this moment, Tiffannie had looked me straight in the eye. Now she studied her nails.

"I don't believe I ever heard of her. Where did you get that name?" Tiffannie eyed me briefly.

"She's a material witness in the murder. I'm sure the government has her name too. If you hear anything about her, please call me. She's important."

"No. Don't know her. I'll check around, but if I find something I want to be paid for it."

"Why am I not surprised?" I said, pulling out my written questions. "Did there come a time when you were with Cleveland in the vicinity of the parking lot to the side of the Potomac Club?"

"Yes."

"Okay, Tiffannie. I'm not trying to put words in your mouth.

There is a lot riding on this. Please answer me carefully. Give me your best memory of how things happened. Prior to the immediate time when you were by the parking lot, how did you meet up with Cleveland?"

She sat there with arms crossed, transformed from nude performer to grimacing witness. For several seconds she seemed to just frown at the wall of our little cube. I waited, saying nothing. Finally, she looked up at me.

"I ran into him up by that bank with the gold dome at the corner of Wisconsin and M Street. He was headed same way as me. We walked down toward the water on Wisconsin Avenue together and then turned up Bridge Street underneath the freeway. Cleavey's pushing his stupid cart clanging with cans. And that's it."

She studied the nails on her right hand.

"How about from when you got on Bridge Street up until you left Cleveland."

Tiffannie grimaced but continued.

"Alright, if you insist. We walked down Bridge Street past the club and saw that damned head on the meter. I saw that thing's milky eyes and bloody mouth and just about barfed!"

"What happened next?"

"What happened next? Tiffannie got her black ass out of Georgetown. That's what happened next. I don't need any trouble, mister."

"Did you see Cleveland go into the lot?"

She huffed and thought to herself.

"Yes. I think he started gabbing about something he saw in that lot, but I didn't see it and I just wanted to get away."

"Okay. That's pretty much what I thought. My information is that you were talking with Cleveland on Bridge Street by the Potomac Club parking lot, that the two of you discovered the dead guy's head, and that you ran off after that. Is that true?"

"That's what happened, but who told you that? Did Cleveland tell you that?"

"I can't say right now. Hold on."

I held my hand up, then filled in the date and time blanks on a subpoena that Cyndi had already prepared for Tiffannie. This moment could be tricky.

"Cleveland needs your help," I said, as I slid a completed

subpoena through the money slot. Mostly, people don't like to get subpoenaed. Sometimes they really throw a fit. Tiffannie had told me that she had no criminal record, but she probably had some kind of bad experience with the criminal system in her line of work. I feared she would start screaming. But I needed her one way or the other. I silently prayed that Tiffannie wouldn't make a scene. There had to be a bouncer in a joint like this and odds were that he packed heat. I didn't want that person thinking that I was trouble—though of course I was.

Tiffannie looked down at the papers just as the curtain started to pull shut.

"That'll be another twenty dollars," I heard from behind the curtain.

I counted out twenty more dollars and slid the bills through the slot. The curtain opened back up, revealing Tiffannie in the not-so-sexy act of reading her subpoena.

"This real?" She didn't look angry, just puzzled.

"As real as it gets." D.C. law permitted attorneys to serve subpoenas. I had probably served a thousand. The subpoena was completely lawful.

Tiffannie shrugged.

"Maybe I want to leave town for a few days."

"You can't leave town. That is a crime and the court will issue a bench warrant to bring you back." If I was lucky.

"Just for not showing up?"

"That's right. The subpoena is properly served and I'm going to file the copy tomorrow in the court jacket. You'll be subject to a bench warrant if you don't appear for the hearing. This is no game, Tiffannie. I need you. Cleveland Barnes is charged with murder and the government wants to get him."

She licked her lips, studying me intently.

"Tell me more about Moaning Day. I know a lot of women in the business and it surprises me that I don't know her." Tiffannie avoided my eyes again. "Is she black or white?"

"It's Mona, not Moaning. She's white. Blonde hair. About five feet, four inches with a slight Southern accent. We understand that she is a high-priced call girl working out of the northwest D.C. area."

"She must be out of my circle, but I'll ask around. This number good?" She pointed to my office telephone on the subpoena.

"Let me give you my cell phone." I pulled out a card with the cell number listed and slid it through the slot to Tiffannie.

She read the card for a moment and then looked up. "I'll help you with Cleavey if you want. He's a little crazy but he's no big killer. Let's talk about him."

And we did. For the next twenty minutes I plugged bills through the window, took notes, and hoped my recorder's batteries held up. Tiffannie was helpful. Expensive, but helpful. She'd shared sidewalks with Cleveland all over the district and never saw anything remotely resembling violent behavior. On the night in question, Tiffannie observed Cleveland at different times and different places in Georgetown over a period of hours. He pushed his shopping cart and trolled all over the Georgetown turf for throw-aways. Tiffannie had seen Cleveland out and about right up to the time of the murder, or so she said. This might be as close to an alibi as I could get.

I'd develop Tiffannie's testimony, amplify it, cast it in the context of Benny's bizarre demise, look for other folks who saw the two together. There had to be other witnesses, people who saw them together. Cyndi and I really had to talk to Samantha Myers. The space of time between her sighting of the head and Cleveland's presence there with Tiffannie had to be very short. Maybe she saw them there together.

Tiffannie's testimony would help my defense of Cleveland. He was out pilfering junk and happened to pilfer in the wrong place.

We finished our interview. I paused, studying my scantily clad witness. God knew I was no Samson—and so did I. Even so, Tiffannie could well be my *jaw bone* to use against the Philistines.

# CHAPTER 53

ANOTHER shoe would fall.

It happened every time, and I expected nothing less. Tiffannie seemed cooperative, but I'd caught her off guard. I smiled at her through the Plexiglas. This was all too easy.

Tiffannie hadn't had time to consider what would happen to her when she cooperated. To be honest, I'd counted on this element of surprise. But murder was like real estate in more ways than one. Excited buyers buy and often had remorse after everything was signed and sealed and the adrenaline wore off. Trouble is, witnesses who are caught off guard often suffer the equivalent of *buyer's remorse*—call it *witness' remorse*. First, the witness agrees to testify and gets excited about the prospect of testifying. Then the person realizes what they have bought into, how involved the process is, and how tedious and unrewarding the role of trial witness can be. Dangerous too. Thereafter, memories seem to conveniently falter as the witness consciously or unconsciously looks for ways to get from under the yoke of a subpoena to give testimony.

It always happened, in some degree or another, inevitable as tarnish on the shined silver of a well-prepared case. There is no cure. You just have to keep rubbing. Sometimes the witness had to be brought in the hard way, by a court enforcing the subpoena with a marshal's handcuff.

Federal law protects home buyers in the buyer's remorse circumstance with a seventy-two hour right to cancel the purchase. Fortunately for my case, witnesses have no similar protection. Tiffannie couldn't legally back out. That didn't mean she wouldn't try to find another way.

I protected myself from *witness' remorse* with a tape recording, which can itself be risky. Still I had to worry about Tiffannie disappearing. Someone in her line of work could easily vanish. I couldn't afford to let it happen.

I asked Tiffannie where she lived. She was highly entertained by the inquiry.

"Wherever it suits me." She smiled. "You can always get me here. You could say I'm on the staff."

"Will you be here the rest of tonight and tomorrow?"

"Yeah, and the next day too. This is my Monday through Thursday deal. Friday I'll probably go out for the evening."

"Right." I backed off. Fact was, I'd have her tailed until the preliminary hearing. If things went right, she'd never know.

I thanked Tiffannie again and left. There were several guys lingering outside the booths. They were the raincoat crowd, nurtured on muffled panting and the stench of sour sweat and stale ejaculate. I studied their faces in the half-light and moved out past the outer display racks. One of them could have listened to my conversation with Tiffannie, though it seemed like they were just doing their weirdo routine.

Walking out of Peepers, I clicked off the recorder and noticed Cyndi standing over by one of the benches in the open area across from the National Portrait Gallery. She'd wrapped herself in an old blanket like some street addict whacked into oblivion.

"Change for a quarter, mister?" She did her best street urchin.

"You got a deal, lady. What are you doing out here?" We walked back to the Oldsmobile.

"Thought you might need rescuing."

"Thanks for the back up. I was afraid of getting molested in that place."

Pulling the back door open, I got in. Cyndi followed me, then locked the door. We sat behind the darkened windows for a moment while I rubbed my face and took stock.

"Pretty raunchy joint." I sighed. "But we got Tiffannie, kiddo. She has some baggage to neutralize but we got her! Now I just hope she doesn't decide to hit the road."

Cyndi tossed her blanket into the back window and looked me in the half light. "What'd she say?"

"Enough to warrant an Alibi Notice if this goes to trial. Says that she ran into Cleveland at the corner of Wisconsin & M and walked with him down to the club, and that they discovered Benny's head together."

"Is she believable?"

"Believable enough. The woman is pretty articulate. She claims that she doesn't have prior convictions, but I need you to run a check on her. I'll do a motion to limit testimony to block prejudicial references to her line of work. The government will argue that it's relevant to explain why she was really out there, and it probably is, but we should win a limited protective order. Who knows? Maybe we'll get the whole tamale. Depends on the black robe we draw. Maybe tomorrow you should talk to the Georgetown student who found the head, Samantha Myers, and see if she might have passed Cleveland and Tiffannie on the sidewalk."

"Right."

Explaining the details of the interview, I stretched my legs out straight and tried to relax. The back seat of the Oldsmobile was roomy, but we were close together and I thought of the night before. Cyndi's face shined. After I'd talked for several minutes, I found myself tilting her chin up for a long slow kiss. Then I moved to the business at hand.

"There's one more thing."

"What? You sound worried."

"Not worried, but I know another shoe will drop. We've got to do surveillance on Tiffannie. Like, now. We can't leave her. We've got to have a twenty-four-hour stakeout until the Prelim. I'll get backup tomorrow morning, but that leaves me, or you and me, for tonight."

"I'll stick, Stuart. Sure."

"Let's take turns napping. Wouldn't surprise me if she bolted.

Plus, she might have something to hide. It's hard to sit here all night, but we got to."

"So we sit here. It's no problem for me to do the stakeout. You got some other clothes?"

"No."

"Why don't you just let me do it."

"No way. But one of us has to run back to the office. I need different clothes and we need some more batteries and tapes."

"And subpoenas," Cyndi added. "That was the last one you just served."

We were only four blocks away, but after dark it would be better if I, the big male, were the one walking these streets. "I should do it. Could grab some food too."

"If she left, how would I recognize her?"

"Looks like she is the only black lady in there. Tiffannie is about five feet seven-ish, long blonde highlights in her hair, built like something out of male fantasy. Kind of hard to miss."

"Don't get steamed on me, cowboy. Save it." She kissed me again.

We'd gone the whole day without discussing the night before. That was fine. We weren't ashamed, weren't in denial, weren't undermined as a team. Just busy.

"This place only has a front and side entrance," Cyndi said. "The back abuts another building on F Street. From here we can see both exits. I'll sit in the car with the doors locked. Bring me a foot long Philadelphia Cheese Steak sub with two Pepsis."

"Same dainty appetite. See you in twenty minutes. Be safe."

"I'm the one with the black belt. Remember?"

"There is that, now that you mention it. If anything breaks while I'm gone call me right away and I'll come back."

"Okie doke." She kissed me again.

I got out, headed south, then cut to the east. Turning left on D Street, I looked back and saw Cyndi's silhouette in the Oldsmobile.

Little did I know the size of the shoe that was about to fall.

# CHAPTER **54**

ENTERING my office building, I exchanged greetings with my friend William, a middle-aged guy with a shaved head who always seemed too overdressed and composed to make his living sitting here at the night desk. He read a dog-eared paperback titled The *Concrete Blonde.*

I got off the elevator on the seventh floor to find the Factory in a buzz. I overheard a room full of associates talking in exaggerated tones about a summary judgment response in a case involving an Egyptian freight company in an international labor dispute. The hall to my office was cluttered with numbered crates of legal exhibits piled amidst stacks of Domino's Pizza and Dunkin Donuts boxes and now-emptied coffee urns.

Old Bailey and Newgate Jail glistened from my computer screen as I walked in the door. I quickly undressed and loaded my suit coat, trousers, shirt, and tie onto the door hook. I opened the bottom drawer of my vertical file and pulled out a fresh set of night wear, black jeans, T-shirt, and soft soled shoes. Climbed into the night clothes. The phone could ring anytime and I wanted to be ready to get out of there.

I'd just started to sort a fist full of mail when Cyndi called.

"Time to boogie cowboy. Tiffannie came out in dark clothes like a round-assed bat out of hell. She got in a black Ford Explorer parked at the curb, license plate CXQ-299. She's headed west on H Street, NW. I'm following her now."

"Go. I'll catch up with you. I'll call you from a taxi."

The rush kicked in. So much for meal plans.

I flew out of the elevator at sub A level and ran through the parking garage, around the corner, to the Capitol Grill's entrance. A taxi idled close to the restaurant's front door while an older, well-nourished gentleman got out. I motioned to the turban-wearing driver and he waived me in.

"Where to boss?" My Sikh guide welcomed me into his mobile spot of worship. The cab air reeked of incense. I noticed a small shrine, a taped photograph of a waving swami on the front dashboard, and burning cones beneath the coffee cup holder. The driver stroked his long white beard, awaiting my instruction.

"Head west down Pennsylvania, take a right on Sixteenth and head north. Got to make a phone call to get the exact address."

"All right, boss."

I lowered the back window a tad, sniffed in a few breaths of fresh air, then flipped the phone open and dialed Cyndi.

"Where are you?" She answered on the first ring.

"Headed to Sixteenth on Penn. Where we going?"

"We're headed west on Massachusetts Avenue by Eighteenth."

"Just keep the phone on. Anybody with Tiffannie?"

"Nope. She's traveling solo and fast."

For the next twelve minutes Cyndi trailed Tiffannie and reported on her location. I prepaid my assistant a twenty, so he took my directions in stride. We picked up Massachusetts Avenue and cut northwest to Embassy Row. Meanwhile, Tiffannie turned by the National Cathedral and headed north up Wisconsin Avenue in the direction of Chevy Chase. She abruptly turned left by the Tenleytown Market and picked up Newton Street, a residential area that wound around the perimeters of the American University.

"She's parking at 30$^{th}$ and Newton," Cyndi said.

"Drive by. I'm almost to Wisconsin. Think she sees you?"

"Not at all. She's walking up to a single family house. 3223 Newton Street. Look, it's only two blocks in from the Tenleytown

Market. I think these are all student rentals. Wait, the front door is opening. Some tall, skinny white guy with short dark hair is letting her in."

"Maybe he's a customer? Could it be Shark? Without a wig or something?"

"No way. This guy's a beanpole."

"Then who could he be? Tiffannie told me she would be at Peepers all night. Either she lied or her plans changed."

"Don't know. I'm turning this off and having a closer look."

"Be careful."

The cab driver pulled into the Tenleytown Market parking lot. By my estimation the house was less than three blocks over. The phone rang again.

"Pay dirt, Stuart," Cyndi whispered. "You won't believe it."

"What?"

"I'm by a side window in the bushes. Tiffannie and the dark-haired guy are inside with Mona Day."

# CHAPTER 55

"THEY'RE arguing. I can't hear. The man is waving his hands. Making weird faces."

"Get across the street and wait for me. You're too damned close. I'm at the market now. I'm running to you."

"No, Stuart, I want to listen closer."

"Want nothing, dammit. Cut it out!" I shouted into the telephone. "Remember under the bridge? Last night? These guys are dangerous. Get out of there. We'll go back in together."

"Okay." The line went off.

I ran up Newton Street and ran to the address Cyndi gave me. Probably had to call Rhondo. First investigate.

The addresses were in the 2700 range, which meant that Cyndi had given me mistaken directions. I had five blocks to go. I cursed to myself and continued to jog, searching the street for Cyndi. Four minutes later I got to the 3200 block. Cyndi was nowhere to be seen.

I slowed down, walked past the house at number 3223. The two-story Victorian cottage had a basement level that protruded about two feet above ground level. Eyebrow windows jutted out of the front roof line. There were picture windows on the left side of the first floor. All the lights on the first floor were on.

There were plenty of dark pockets in the side yard. Must have been where Cyndi looked inside. No sign of her.

Tried Cyndi's phone again. No answer. I didn't want to go into the yard. I didn't have any choice. The next house on the street was all dark. I walked by it then walked down the left side into the back yard and back over toward 3223. From the right rear corner of the house I saw a dining room. The furniture looked worn, like something in student housing. Nobody there.

Still, no Cyndi. After two minutes, I stole across into the yard, trying to get a better look into the window. No sign of anyone. I looked toward the evergreens. Nothing.

I'd have to call Rhondo. I started to retreat toward the other house. A stinging bolt slapped my back and knocked me onto my face.

My head swam. Stunned for a moment, I rolled to my right and jumped up. Ambushed. My back and right shoulder muscles contracted fast and hard, into a lump of pain. Someone rushing me, but I managed a heel kick into the man's groin.

He grunted and I saw him fall back, clutching a wand phaser. Damn.

I walked forward and landed a toe kick into his ribs. He grunted again and grabbed at my right leg, still slow from the phaser's jolt.

I pulled away, but he jerked me and I fell onto him. Taking my left arm back, I punched at his throat, but he lowered his head and I got the left cheek instead.

I drew back to hit again when I felt the phaser prongs blast into my left leg.

I fell over, couldn't move. Someone stood over me. I tried to go into a body roll. A kick in the kidneys nearly caused me to pass out. Reeling in pain, I felt a wet cloth shoved over my nose and mouth. Hitting behind me with both fists, I tried to hold my breath and wrestle. Useless. A punch to my kidneys ratcheted pain through my body. I gasped and sucked in the sweet smelling chloroform.

The world went black.

# CHAPTER 56

BRIGHT lights. Inside, on a metal floor. He slapped my face repeatedly. Hurt so much. I lay on my back, both hands clamped into something. Felt like a truck had run over me.

"Wake up, Mason. Time to run that mouth." He slapped me again. Hard. I feigned sleep. The voice. Who was it? I knew this voice.

"Cut the crap, pal," he continued. "You've been out for an hour. The chloroform wore off. Open your damned eyes or you get a boot in the crotch."

I knew this voice! Was it Shark? No. Adrian? No. Somebody I'd met at court?

"Come on!" He kicked me full force in the groin. I yelled out and tried to roll over.

"Open your damned eyes." He jerked my head up by the hair and I looked into the eyes behind a mask. Madness behind a harlequin mask. Black and white sequin diamonds and rhinestones over the forehead and cheeks, a black cover that went down the neck and an elaborate headdress of peacock feathers. The man was over six feet tall, slender. Didn't look strong. He was.

"My eyes are open," I groaned.

"What were you doing outside that window?" He pushed me back. I slammed against a grooved metal floor. Squinting in the bright light, I stole a glance. We were in a windowless truck compartment. The cab was completely separate. Nothing in the truck bed but the two of us and glaring ceiling lights.

"Going to say it one more time before I smash your balls into dog food," he hissed.

"What did you say?"

"What were you doing outside that window?"

"Looking for my investigator."

"What was she doing?"

I took a loud breath in. "Just wait a minute," I cried. Try to think. No way to help Cyndi now.

"Following a witness. Did you see her?"

"Who? Who was the witness?"

"Tiffannie Squires. My investigator followed her there."

"Who else knows?"

"Knows what?"

"Knows that she followed Tiffannie to the house?"

"No one else."

"And who else did your investigator see there?"

"I have no idea."

His fist clobbered my right cheek and slammed into my nose.

"Don't get cute with me, Pal. She told me she saw Mona. She told you about it on the phone." He pulled my head up by the hair. "What I want to know is this. Did you tell anyone?"

"Tell anyone what? Don't know anyone named Mona." My head swam. I needed to concentrate, to figure out who...

"Listen, Lukie," the harlequin hissed. "What we have here is a breakdown in communication. Have another egg."

He slapped me full force.

"And another one."

My body exploded in pain as he landed a kick in my groin. I closed my eyes to a streaming bright red light and went into a convulsing fit. Harlequin grabbed me by the hair and pulled my face up to his.

"Did you tell anyone you saw Mona and where you saw her?"

"No," I cried. "Didn't have time. Ran out the door to follow

Cyndi. What did you do to her? You better not have hurt her."

"I don't believe you. Who else? Did you tell that Jamaican cop?"

"No one else." Blood dribbled out of my nose, over my lips, and fell off my chin. Gagging from the salty taste, I fought passing out. Then he kicked me again, pulled my hair up, off the truck bed, and shoved the blaring spot against my face.

"One last time, Perry Mason. Who else knows about the blonde?"

Who the hell was he? Who was under the mask? I knew this voice. I'll eat you someday!

He kicked me again.

"Nobody else. I swear." Squeezed my eyes tight. Not giving this punk anything else. "Nobody."

Something pierced my left forearm. A needle. I opened my eyes. Harlequin doubled and tripled. The compartment spun around like a lopsided top. Harlequin's whiney voice morphed into a slow motion baritone. Puffs of black smoke floated from his mouth, through the air, lifting us like a helium balloon into the great unknown. We floated into blackness.

# CHAPTER 57

THE escalator stairs ratcheted downward. I heard a ringing. So much noise! So many people. Ringing loud. How in God's world did I get here? I couldn't remember for the life of me how I'd got from Tenleytown to the fourth floor of the D.C. Superior Court. Yet here I was, going down on the escalator, looking out over the wide open lobby. Down through crisscrossing escalators. Down to the noisy, busy world below.

Distant faces came into focus. Attorneys, marshals, jurors, growing louder and more restless. Above were massive skylights and a north wall of glass. My vision followed the glasswork across the ceiling to the north wall, where the glass framed the top third of the front of the building. A groaning filled the air as this wall melted to the inner shape of a head. We people were electricity in this head, flashing and sparking into the outer darkness. Then I hovered outside, in the black sky, seeing the head glowing in the night, looking at the courthouse shining in the night, mounted on top of an old parking meter. It all exploded and glimmering bright glass shards passed by me, shot through me, streamed out across the universe into a black abyss.

And the ringing continued.

My eyes pulled open like rickety curtains on a broken down stage. Fully leaved branches hung above me. The fresh air blew across me. All was quiet except for the chirping of birds and the distant whir of highway traffic. Even the half-light of morning pierced me. Double vision without Johnny Walker Red? A new low.

My eyes shut. I forced myself to sit up. How could I move with all the stuff moving around?

Where was I? My cell phone wouldn't stop ringing. Bad headache. Where the hell was I? Tried to reach for the phone. Arm pushed through sorghum. Push dammit, push, I cried, wrestled for the phone in my pocket and flipped it open.

"Clay." The word traveled out like a gas bubble in the bottom of deep pool. I watched the bubble wobble and rise above me. My head swam and vision blurred in and out. The overhead leaves turned into faces, stared with disapproval. An angel warned me to be strong. Bad. Really bad. Be strong.

"God damn you, Stuart." The voice echoed in my ear. Deep in the water. Stuck. Someone up above, a dot of light, rippling. Screaming. "Been calling you since four o'clock this morning. It's almost seven! Where the hell are you?" Rhondo shrieked into the phone.

"Wait," I said, not recognizing the warbled meter of my own voice as another bubble rippled off into the liquid. I tried again to sit up.

"A second, man," I muttered, more clearly, falling back.

"What are you doing?"

"Can't talk yet." I drooled in a breath. "Wait."

"Don't you hang up, man. We're going try and get a trace started on the phone."

"Okay," I whispered, looking at myself, seeing caked blood and filth covering my shirt and arms. My trousers were torn. I had no shoes or socks on. I felt my face, knew it had to be grossly swollen. Both my arms showed many shades of blue, purple, and green.

"God dammit, where are you?" Rhondo asked.

I struggled to speak. Had to talk.

"On top of something. Beat up bad, man."

"Are you in a house somewhere or outside?

"You got to give me a second."

I glanced around. She stared down at me. An alabaster angel, holding hands open. Polished and unpolished markers, granite and other stone, some with statues and some without, jutted from rocky ground. Some with black wrought iron fences, some with white chains, many adorned with globed candles and flowers. The lines of markers traveled off, down a hill into a grove of trees, which, I realized, lined a bike path and a trail down to the Potomac River. I knew this place.

"Rhondo," I whispered. "I'm on top of a crypt in the Georgetown Cemetery. Don't know how I got here. Somebody beat the shit out of me. Shot me up with some sort of knock out drug."

"Need an ambulance, man? You sound pretty bad."

"I don't want that. No time. I think they got Cyndi too and I don't know where she is. I'm pretty scared because—"

"If you're well enough, you got to get down to the Triple Nickel now," Rhondo said. "I'm sorry. Cyndi's dead."

# CHAPTER **58**

"WHAT?" I gagged. The angel held her hands out. Please no.

"She's dead, man. A couple twenty-two slugs in her brain and somebody tossed her off the Fourteenth Street Bridge. I'm sorry, man. You got to get in here."

"Christ! Give me a second!" I closed my eyes. Trembled uncontrollably. How could she be dead? Flashing back two nights back, I saw Cyndi at my apartment. Beneath me. How could she be dead?

"You got to come in, man," Rhondo insisted. "You guys're doing stuff that's going to get you dead, too."

"I'm on a case, Rhondo."

"You're not going to defend anyone dead, man."

"Tell it to the judge. He got me into this." I worked my way up and leaned on the crypt, still fighting vertigo. Finally, I stood.

"Stuart, I got a bead on your cell phone. Why don't you just sit there? Let me come over with a few doctors."

"I'm sorry, Rhondo. Thanks for calling."

"You ass! Don't hang up!" Rhondo screamed. "Everybody's

looking for you including your boss. That guy Haskell has been calling me up and screaming. Press is camped out in front of your office building. They're also over by the MPD headquarters at 300 Indiana. Word on the street is that people are claiming this was an attack on Barnes' legal team because of the demonstrations. The chief's blood pressure is through the damned roof. He's paranoid that we're going to have a riot in front of the D.C. Superior Court that will spread—"

"Don't give a shit," I whispered. "Got to go do something, but I'll be in touch pronto."

"People are worried about you."

"Can't help it. Tell Lisa I'll be in later today. You're right. I got to give a statement, but it has to wait."

"You got to come in now, man."

"Can't."

"What you mean can't?" he blasted. "Your investigator is on a slab at the D.C. morgue and you can't come in? Listen, Jack. I just came back from telling Michael Oh that he'll never see his sister again. Know how that makes me feel to tell a close friend that our friend has been brutally murdered? God damn you Stuart, don't make it a double header for the monsters. You get in here now!"

I thought of her smiling dark eyes, her brilliant nasty wit, her wonderful body beneath me. I loved the luscious mystery that was her. Never got a chance to say so. Oh, Jesus. Dead?

"Sorry, Rhondo. No sugar-coating this one. I messed up. It's the business we're in. It's my damned fault."

I hung up.

# CHAPTER 59

FOR a long time I just sat and watched the morning light grow stronger. I didn't feel, couldn't feel. Feeling would come later. Much later.

I checked my messages. One from Jack Payne, two from Percy, another two from Fred Collins, and five from Bridgette Ginadio. All had to wait. I leaned on the crypt, tried to shake off the haze, tried to take stock of things.

Cyndi was dead. I had to accept it. Deal with it. To do that I had to get back to Tenleytown. Had to see that house again. Then I'd call the rest.

The angel by the crypt stood tall, marshaling, protecting, affirming the dignity of precious bones as they melded into dust. She gazed down at me. A minstrel tune crept into my head. "All night, all day, angels watching over me my lord." Maybe so. Maybe so. Where the hell was the angel for Cyndi? For that matter, where the hell was I?

She just should have waited. I should have never left her alone to begin with. In ten minutes I would have been back to Peepers.

Ten minutes changed destinies forever. No remedy. Nobody makes a death rattle go back on its word.

I broke.

A few minutes after eight that morning I stood and walked out of the cemetery. My body was filthy, bruised, and bloodied. Clothing hung off me in torn shards. I felt comforted by one existential truth. Money still talked and I had a pocket full of cash, about seven hundred dollars of walking around funds.

Shimmying down the bank on the eastern edge of the cemetery I walked out to Wisconsin Avenue and hailed a reluctant taxi. He looked distrustful, so I made up a story about getting mugged the night before. Close enough to true. We bee-lined to an Army-Navy store on the edge of the American University campus.

I procured blue jeans, an oversized hooded sweatshirt, ankle boots, and big dark glasses that, along with some calamine lotion, disguised much of my bruised face. Not exactly Bill Blass casual. It would do. The cashier kept staring at my swollen eye and cheek, suppressing shock at the cuts and the swollen green-purple thing that my face had become.

"Took a few jabs in an amateur boxing tournament." I yuck-yucked her up.

"You should see the other guy."

She said nothing. No smile. Nothing.

Putting the new stuff on in the dressing room, I coated my face in three layers of calamine, put on the glasses, and jammed my old clothes in the trash. Walking outside, I hailed another cab. I had her detour to a sub shop for a steak and cheese, coffee, and a small bottle of cabernet. I was desperately hungry, needed the coffee to wake up, and the wine to deaden my pain. Forget abstinence. All food and drink were consumed by the time we reached Newton Street.

Stepping out of the cab onto the quiet street, I spotted my Oldsmobile parked two blocks up and wondered for a moment. Maybe Cyndi could be asleep inside. Maybe they'd made a mistake. Before approaching the house I walked over and checked. Doors were locked and I saw no one inside. Cyndi's camera and my tape recorder sat on the floor of the passenger's seat where I'd put them the night before. My visit to the booths of Peepers seemed like ancient history.

I'd have to call Rhondo, Jack Payne and the others. First I

wanted to see the place. Needed to see if Mona Day had left any clues that would help explain what had happened.

My search was well advised. As a matter of fact, Mona had left a big clue behind. She had left her body.

# CHAPTER 60

THE house was as I'd left it, however I had left it. The front door was wide open. I walked four steps up to the covered front porch. The doorway was on the left side of the porch and light shined into the front room from a window at the far left corner.

She sat with a straight back, in an overstuffed beige easy chair, stained by two long flows of blood. Even in death Mona was gorgeous. Her eyes were open. Her face had a peaceful expression. She grasped a piece of paper with a typed note on it. Deep six inch slits ran down the length of both wrists. A bloody knife lay on the aged hardwood floor.

It seemed like at least a year since I'd explained to Cleveland that tampering with a crime scene was a felony. Easy to say, but I wanted to read that note. I really wanted to.

Dizziness surged over me again, but my higher voice and reasoning ability remained intact. It would be important to act the right way, to walk my talk, and just give up the impossible. No way could I feel right. I'd just have to act right and wait.

Pulling out my cell phone I hit Rhondo's number. He

answered on the first ring.

"You hung up on me, man."

"Got a body, Rhondo. Maybe it's a suicide. Doubt it. I'm at 3223 Newton Street right off of Nebraska Avenue west of Wisconsin. I'm at the open front door of a porch looking at the late Mona Day."

"Don't go in. We're on the way. You okay? You sound like you're about to fade."

"Of course I'm not going in. Think I'm crazy? God damn, Rhondo."

"How come you're there?"

"This is where Cyndi was last night. I followed her over here in a cab. By the time I got here she'd disappeared. This is where I got attacked."

"You might think about getting a lawyer, Stuart. Not that anybody would suspect you, but we got issues here. We got some serious talking to do."

"Kind of an understatement, don't you think? I'm going to back off the porch and sit on the yard. Could you send some medics over?" I started to reel again.

"People are already on the way. I'm out of here now."

Whatever adrenaline I'd mustered for the trip over here had been spent, challenged by the news of Cyndi's death, and now the death of Mona.

I passed out.

Some time later I awoke to nudges on my shoulder. Opening my left eye I beheld a 250-poundish paramedic with the name "Lucile" stitched into her shirt pocket. She'd arrived with the cavalry, an emergency squad, three other paramedics, four cruisers, eight cops, including Rhondo, Zeus Martin, and Byno Sanchez, lead investigator for the Mobile Crime Unit. Emergency lights blazed.

Byno dawned a full cover suit with a closed helmet, his Captain Video costume. He walked up the front steps of the house with a cassette recorder in his gloved hand.

Pretty soon the entire front, side, and backyard were staked out in yellow tape, press towers leered in, and the circus came to Newton Street. Fred Collins waved at me from the outer edge. I just couldn't move. I saw two helicopters buzzing around overhead.

"You got beat up pretty bad." Rhondo stood over me.

"Tell me something I don't know."

"You've got to debrief with the U.S. Attorney's office."

"I know. Have Lisa bring Cleveland from the jail. He has to release me with a signed disclosure and permission before I can talk."

"So we assumed. There's a come-up for transporting him this afternoon. Triple nickel."

I heard tires squeal and turned around to see a four-door black Lincoln pull up to the curb. I'd never been for a ride in one, but I recognized the car and the license plate "MITCH3" from the Mitchell & Strong fleet of leased cars. Percy slid out of the driver's side and ran over to the edge. I motioned to Zeus to let him come in.

"What the hell happened, Stuart? Your investigator got murdered? Her name and yours are all over the morning news. We've got a crowd of urchins outside our office."

"Hi, Percy. We got ambushed. Call Jack Payne for me. I got beat up pretty bad, man. Might need you to help me in court, later."

"Yeah, okay. Have any idea who did it?"

"Got a few ideas, but hang with me for a second. The Barnes case might be breaking here."

"How could that be?"

"Rhondo!"

We all turned around. Byno walked out on the porch and handed something in a plastic bag to Zeus. The paper from the dead woman's hand. Walking over to us, Zeus examined it through the plastic then handed the evidence to Rhondo. Zeus nodded to Percy and then went back to the edge of the porch, waiting for more. Rhondo read the note and handed it to me.

The typed, signed statement read as follows:

"I, Mona Day, admit that I killed Ben Batiste with an ax and a knife outside the Potomac Club on the night of July 27th. I acted alone. I did it to get his money and jewelry, which I have already sold. The street person had nothing to do with this. I can't live with the guilt."

I looked at the statement, looked at Rhondo, then bit my lip. What a crock this was. But I couldn't say what I knew; couldn't hurt my client. Without proof, I couldn't be the one casting doubt on Mona's note.

"It's time to dump the case, Rhondo." I sat down and rubbed the back of my neck. Percy and Rhondo stood over me as the parade of cops and techs roamed back and forth.

"Look at the record," I continued. "The woman in that chair left the club with Benny. I have a time stamped videotape that proves it and you have a copy."

Both men nodded.

"Benny died thirteen minutes after leaving the club." Closing my eyes, I lapsed into monologue. "She is the last person we know of that was with Benny before he took it in the neck. Now she, whoever she is, shows up dead. She clutches a statement indicating the means of death and the motive for murder. Now, maybe she murdered Benny and maybe she didn't. I can damned well assure you guys that Cleveland didn't kill her and he didn't kill Cyndi. And we all know that Benny was a made man and that when a made man gets whacked it is in all likelihood a hit. So why doesn't the government just get over it and cut Cleveland loose? You know bloody well that—"

"Just a second." He motioned. Zeus was running over from one of the squad cars.

"National Crime Index Computer has no record of a Mona Day. We're checking other data bases, but as of now that lady doesn't exist."

"So who is she, man? How did you know to come here?" Rhondo spoke quietly.

"Stuart," Percy jumped in. "You don't look very well and I don't think that—"

"Thanks, Percy. I know what you're going to say. We'll talk in a minute. Rhondo, my man, you got to cut me a little slack until I see Cleveland. I'll debrief, but I got to cover my bases with him. I'll have to get a written authorization because it could compromise him. Capisce?"

Rhondo studied me intently, shaking his head.

"Rhondo, come here!" Byno had pulled the respirator mask off the front of his helmet. He called from the front porch of the house. He held out two large clear bags. One held a butcher knife and the other a thin, silver ax.

# CHAPTER **61**

THE knife and ax gilded the lily in Cleveland's favor. My hunch was that they'd never find Mona's prints on either weapon. Within minutes, however, Byno proved me wrong. The only prints on either weapon were Mona's—whoever Mona was.

To expedite the inevitable I agreed to meet with various members of the U.S. Attorney's office, the MPD, and the FBI. Percy wanted to attend the meeting as a co-counsel and, practically speaking, to protect me from questions that might ask too much. I declined. Both Rhondo and Percy wanted to give me a lift to the U.S. Attorney's office. I declined.

Down the block on the other side of Newton Street I spotted my Oldsmobile sedan. The hide-a-key was under the front left bumper where I always left it. I asked Percy to follow me back to Judiciary Square in case I got the shakes again. I pulled slowly away from the curb and fought to stay focused on the mechanical task. Making a U-turn on Newport Street, I headed back to the Tenleytown Market. By the time I got to Wisconsin Avenue I felt more relaxed in my driving, and called Percy on my cell phone. At first, his line rang busy. In the rearview mirror I saw Percy holding his phone to his ear, talking to someone else. No sooner had I put my phone down than it rang.

"Stuart. Saw you on caller ID, but that was Jack and Haskell. They really think I should go with you to the meeting."

"Thanks for helping out, Percy. It's a pretty black day. I know you guys have my best interest at heart. Your going there might compromise the firm's interests. If I'm forced to withdraw we need to be able to tell the court with a straight face that a Chinese Wall can be built between you and me. You might have to be the lead lawyer because I might become your star witness."

"Chinese Wall?"

"You know. We have to isolate me from you because I'm no longer a detached lawyer in the case. And the less I elaborate the better off you are, Percy. Please explain to Jack. He has as much trial experience as I do. He'll understand."

"If you say so."

And I did say so. If someone else had to take over I wanted it to be a closely tied guy like Percy. I'd become the best fact witnesses that Cleveland's legal team could wish for, as long as they asked the right questions. I could tell them about Tiffannie, about the Harlequin, about the circumstances under which I came to Newport Street. All of that could be marshaled in Cleveland's favor.

"I have to go over to Fourth Street right now to the U.S. Attorney's office," I continued. "But we need to be ready to go to court. Don't mean to lay it on you heavy but—"

"Do it. By all means, Stuart. I mean what I said before."

"Good because I need to get through this day. You need to help me. First, ask Jo Ann to go into my office with the master key and get my suit and a new shirt off the back door. There should be a tie with the suit. I can't go to court looking like I just left a St. Patrick's Day celebration at the biker bar.

"Second, if we meet with the judge or go to court I need you with me. I'm still pretty woozy and might need some backup."

"That's fine. If you want me to take the lead on that."

"No. I don't want you to be the lead unless I have to step down to become a witness for Cleveland. But to be safe I think we need a canned motion for protective order to be filed if the government tries to squeeze me too hard. I know some things about what happened last night that might not help Cleveland's case. If need be, I'll assert attorney-client privilege to prevent from disclosing them."

"I can do that. I'll get on it."

"No, look. It's already done. Just go to my desktop computer in that little office when Jo Ann opens it up. Go into my word documents and look up the protective order motion and memorandum in the case of U.S. versus Paul Scranton. It's like in August of 2001. Just call up that document and create a new file for Cleveland Barnes. You can get the case heading off the other motions I filed day before yesterday. They're in the word documents. Nothing else needs to be changed." I paused for several seconds.

"What else, Stuart?" Percy sounded focused.

"Tell me what Jack and Haskell are saying."

"Jack just wanted to make sure that you're all right. I think Haskell is concerned too, but..." Percy stopped mid-sentence.

"But what?"

"This isn't the time to bring it up. He wanted to know if we needed to advise our carrier about Cyndi's death. He's concerned that the family might sue."

"What a bastard! My investigator gets murdered, I'm probably walking around with a concussion, and that miserable little twit is worrying about the firm's exposure to a negligence action. God damned twit bureaucrat."

"Don't get upset. Jack reigned him in."

"I'm about to talk to Cyndi's only family member outside of Tokyo. I'll tell Jack if there's the slightest hint of anything. Can you tell Jack and Haskell this and maybe intimate that Haskell is going to need some dental work if he speaks to me about it? Keep that miserable lizard away from me or I'll rip him a new one."

"Right. I just mentioned it to you because you asked, Stuart. Don't take it personally. You've got a lot going for you with the firm."

"I've got hell to pay is what I've got. And it's all personal all the time. Unless you didn't know, 'nothing personal' is a Washington, D.C. way of saying fuck you, though I'm sure you didn't mean it that way."

My vision blurred temporarily. I coasted to the curb and road up on the sidewalk, then braked to a halt.

"You okay?" Percy pulled in behind me.

"Just wait a second. No more about Haskell Eaton. I can't get worked up right now. You have no idea how much I hate him."

"Right."

I sat for several seconds wondering if I should cut this short and get to an emergency room for a scan or something. Hell with it. I pulled away from the curb again, beginning slowly and picking up speed. Finally, I turned left after the national cathedral, entered Massachusetts Avenue off the access road, and passed by several of the larger foreign embassies.

"Percy, I'm getting off now. I'll call you from the U.S. Attorney's office."

"Sure. Take care of your head. Do you need anything for pain?"

"What?"

"For pain. Do you need any meds? I got torn up in a car wreck a few years back and have some stuff if you need it."

"What do you have?" My suspicions flared.

"OxyContin. If you need something stronger, I could look around."

"No, I'm okay for now, thanks. I'll let you know if I need anything. Just please help me with the stuff I mentioned."

"Right. I'll talk to you later." He hung up.

I chugged in the direction of the U.S. Attorney's office, no longer looking in the rearview mirror, but rolling the word across my tongue again and again.

OxyContin?

# CHAPTER 62

DRIVING back toward Judiciary Square, I called Michael Oh and tried to explain what had happened. Not an easy conversation. Michael seemed too shocked to ask any hard questions. He didn't have to accuse me of anything. My greatest accuser stared back at me from the rearview mirror. Cyndi had assumed the risk of being an investigator. She ignored my entreaties to wait until I got to the house at Newport Street. All that seemed irrelevant.

Michael said something about it being Cyndi's karma to leave us the way she did. This seemed to give him a lot of comfort. Maybe so, but I decided that maybe it was my karma to die plugging the animal that hurt her. That would be acceptable, even fair. Maybe that's the only way I'd ever find peace again.

Michael asked me to handle the estate issues and, though I'm no estate lawyer, I knew how to do this work as well as any general practitioner. I'd certainly do it for Cyndi. I hung with Michael and called Gawler's Funeral Home to get arrangements started. I'd open an intestate estate action for her later in the week.

Passing through Dupont Circle I decided to delay a few

minutes and try to clear my head. I followed the circle around to New Hampshire Avenue and sped another nine blocks out, back around where it heads to Takoma Park, then turned right onto Georgia Avenue. I headed south, through an ocean of liquor stores, dilapidated row houses and already crowded street corners. Police cars were everywhere, lights always flashing, one of the chief's new initiatives. A bust went down by the Brown Sugar Palace. Waiting at a stop light, I studied a half dozen overdressed guys lying face down on the sidewalk, hands and feet bound by plastic cuffs. Everyday sights in my workaday world. I took some comfort in the appearance of the regularity of it all.

My discussions with Percy were really just a bunch of brain gas. The tide had turned in U.S. versus Barnes. With all of the new developments, it would only be a matter of time before they cut Cleveland loose. That wouldn't bring back Cyndi. It would free me to go back after whoever the killers were.

Georgia turned into Seventh Street, and I slid three blocks east to Fourth Street, and approached the Triple Nickel. Cars parked and double-parked by the U.S. Attorney's office. Busy prosecutors pulled boxlike litigation bags with built-in wheels past hot dog vendors already set to sell, past grand jury witnesses and morning traffic going into the building to give, take, or hear evidence, past attorneys who would get or give discovery, organize or dissect files, cops who would return or fill out warrants, prosecutors preparing for or running away to court.

With no hope of finding a space, I passed over a block to Third Street and found a broken meter in front of the Mitch Snyder homeless shelter. As usual, most people wouldn't park in front of a building with thirty or forty homeless people congregating on the sidewalk. I parked, locked away the camera and recorder beneath the passenger seat, and locked the Oldsmobile up and gave away a few bucks to a bedraggled guy sitting on the curb, promising a few more if he would watch my car while I was gone.

I pushed through the glass door at 555 Fourth Street. The sunglasses and calamine lotion apparently didn't disguise enough of my appearance. Perhaps something about the cauliflower ear, stitched cheek, and poorly disguised blue-green bruises alarmed the Deputy U.S. Marshals. Before I reached the bulletproof glass window two deputies reached approached me. "ID please." The one with the flat top and the mashed nose grimaced. I nodded as amiably as a guy looking like I did could nod, fished out the weathered card announcing my status as a member of the District of Columbia Bar, and asked them to buzz Lisa Stein.

Lisa came off the elevator, took a look at me and shuddered. Luckily we were on either side of the metal detector. At this juncture an empathetic embrace just didn't do it for me.

"I'm so sorry," Lisa said. Sure, the lady meant it.

Sorry seemed weeks away, pints of Guinness, and fingers of Jameson away—if I were to drink over it, which I might. But not now. Now was business.

"Thanks." I passed through the metal detector. For good measure a graying assistant passed his wand up and down my person. Wonder if these guys thought bruises might beep. On second thought, I needed to cut them a break. Strange looking people often do strange things.

Looking over at Lisa, I chastened myself for the cynical way that I'd come to regard her. Maybe I should just practice letting people off the hook. Lisa and I walked back in the direction of the elevator. Everything stopped in the lobby. Everyone stared at me. I started to get vertigo again but was able to stuff it.

"Let's go down." Lisa took my arm and led me to the elevator. She hadn't touched me in years. I remembered the last time, remembered her walking away from me the evening they'd found Tameka hanged.

The elevator door closed and Lisa still held my hand. We looked at each other, smelled each other's air. I brought her hand up and kissed it. We studied each other's faces for several seconds. She leaned over and kissed my lips.

"I still love you, Stuart Clay."

"Me too. But it doesn't matter a bit, does it? We all have our paths to walk. I always seem to mess up the lives of the people I love." I rubbed my face. "Just tell me who am I talking to, okay?"

She let go of my hand.

"Rhondo, Zeus, and two guys from the FBI field office are downstairs in the Debriefing Unit. Barnes is in a holding cell down the hall from us."

"Ain't that duckie? Maybe we can wrap this up." I saw no reason not to.

"Maybe. Does Cyndi have family?"

"Her brother Michael. He's an MIT wonk with a small IT

company. Out on the Dulles Corridor. Her father's dead. He was a friend of mine and Rhondo's. Rest of the family is out of touch in Tokyo. Looks like yours truly is doing the estate work."

"Jeez. It must be hard."

"I shouldn't have left her alone for five minutes. You go hunting something and forget about danger. She wouldn't pull back. Went hog wild after a witness and walked right into an ambush. I screamed at her, told her to get away from the house until I got there but she wouldn't pull back."

"Is this the house where they found the woman?"

I looked at Lisa, catching myself. I felt like a needy moron. The last thing I could do is share grief and information with a friend who happened to be opposing counsel.

"Christ, woman. I shouldn't have said anything. I got ethical issues five ways to Sunday. Let me get with Cleveland first. You didn't hear me, didn't hear what I said. Okay? You'll hear it later. Okay?"

"I wouldn't hurt you, Stuart."

"Often nobody plans to hurt anybody. Ever heard of unanticipated consequences? God damned unanticipated consequences?" I shook my head.

We continued the ride down in silence. The elevator doors opened onto B-3, the infamous zone of the Debriefing Unit.

First things first. I'd draft something in long hand for Cleveland to sign, something allowing me to talk to the U.S. Attorney, the police, and the FBI guys about our investigation. Lisa had handed me a manila folder containing a standard debriefing letter. Cleveland and I would both sign that too. Her letter had all sorts of standard gobbledygook thought up and inserted by a career bureaucrat who was wound a bit too tight. I used to think that with these guys around its amazing that the people's business ever got done. Lately, it occurred to me that maybe they were the ones who really knew the score. Maybe we can't be paranoid enough.

Lisa took me to the holding cell for Cleveland, nodded at the marshal, then disappeared into a conference room next door. The deputy asked to see my bar card and driver's license.

"Counselor, today you don't look like the young fellow in this picture." He handed me back my card. The man stood up slowly, then walked to the back of the room and unlocked a thick door, pushed it open, revealing the chained, manacled, and handcuffed man deposited behind a table.

Cleveland was clad in an orange jump suit and black lace-up boots. His pointy dark eyes shown through foliage of crows' feet, gray beard wire, and freshly washed Rasta locks. He stared straight at me. I felt an electric surge rush up my spine and considered how my life had changed in the last fifty-some hours.

"What's up, Snick? Just sitting down to some creamed corn beef on rice and some fatty jerked me up for the wagon here. What is this about?"

Cleveland's good humor and ease grated on me.

"There've been developments and we've got to talk. I think I might be able to get your case dropped."

"Oh baby!"

"Somebody else confessed to killing Batiste. Trouble is she's dead. The government isn't totally sure what to make of it. I have information that would probably convince them of her involvement. You have to consent to my talking about it."

"What does that mean?"

"We need to sign some special kinds of letters."

"Letters?"

And so it went.

In the minutes that followed, I explained what had transpired, what a debriefing interview was, why we were at the U.S. Attorney's office, and what the consent forms were about. To a certain degree it was like teaching algebra to a person who'd never learned to count. But Cleveland got the gist of it. Whether I deserved it or not, the guy seemed to trust me. My task was easier at this stage because it was I, not Cleveland, who had to be debriefed. It would get a lot stranger if we went to trial. The prosecution could conceivably move to disqualify me because I'd become a fact witness. Or the court could remove me without a motion from anyone if the judge got a sense that I'd crossed over the line and would be a source of live testimony. That was a known risk in the type of trial preparation that I did. My present posture seemed awkward and untidy but, nonetheless, undergoing debriefing was the right thing, for Cleveland, for Cyndi, and for the government too.

I had a simple agenda: Get Cleveland out of harm's way. Find who murdered my investigator. Hose them down. They could fall to the police or fall into hell's third basement when I fired a bullet through the heart of Cyndi's murderer. Either way was okay with me.

After fifteen minutes of going back and forth Cleveland seemed to show a basic understanding of what was taking place. He signed both forms and pretty much gave me carte blanche to say whatever I wanted. I had absolutely no intention of letting my prosecutorial brethren know this.

# CHAPTER **63**

LEAVING Cleveland, I nodded to the marshal in the outer room. I slid into a lavatory for a few minutes to douse my face with cold water, get the caked blood out of my hair and eyebrows, dab new coats of calamine lotion over the bruises. Then I walked down to the conference room.

"Morning, folks." I nodded at Lisa, Rhondo, Zeus, and two strangers. "I'm afraid that Cleveland doesn't trust me to do much of anything, but we can try anyway." As I made my announcement, I slid into a battered chair at the end of the square table. "He wants a guarantee that the government will dismiss his case with prejudice."

"Did you tell him the tooth fairy doesn't work here?" Lisa said.

"Listen, I'm too tired for posturing," I lied. "We've all got a job to do. You do your job and cut my man loose. I'll do my job and help you track a monster."

"What Monster, man?" Rhondo said. "By the way, this is Bruce Daniels and Marvin Ziglar from the Bureau." He pointed at the two agents and I leaned over and shook hands with the clean-shaven, middle-age white guys. Zeus too. Opening the manila folder, I slid a signed copy of the U.S. Attorney's form letter over to Lisa. I looked at Rhondo.

"To answer your question, I'll help you track the monster who killed my investigator Cyndi Oh, the hooker we just found known as Mona Day, and Benny Batiste. This case has only been going on for two days. The bodies are mounting up and it's liable to turn into a cottage industry at the rate they're going. Maybe we ought to cut to the real chase."

"The hooker confessed. You saw the note," Lisa said.

I studied her, remembering that she didn't know what Rhondo had told me.

"That's right, Lisa. She was involved in it. But I think we all suspect or know that there is another murderer out there. We all know it's not Cleveland. I daresay you and I both have cards up our sleeves that could help get that person a lot quicker. You saw Fred Collins' articles in the *Post,*," I continued. "And I have got to believe that everybody in this room knows that Benny was the subject of grand jury inquiries in New York. As a matter of fact, I have to believe that you guys probably know a hell of a lot more about Benny Batiste than I do. You probably know who really had a motive to off Benny. Am I right, Lisa?"

"Why don't we just begin with you helping us out with what you know?" Ziglar deadpanned.

"Before you shoot that down, Stuart, just listen to me," Lisa said. "Everybody wants to do the right thing here. Your client could find himself removed to U.S. district court and under the federal death penalty statute. You better cooperate."

I about fell over. Lisa was dead right on the money. I had to take this possibility seriously. I could use the mob card to try and spring my street guy. If I used it too well and didn't get my street guy off, he could find himself facing the death penalty in the U.S. district court. If the case got removed there, that would take the case away from Lisa's beat. Who knows what the next Assistant U.S. Attorney would be?

Common wisdom has it that D.C. juries wouldn't even give the death penalty to Jack the Ripper. But no sane defense lawyer risked the issue.

"I respect what you're saying," I said. "And it would give me great pleasure to cooperate with you. Cleveland won't let me, attorney-client privilege. He wants the case dropped."

"We're not in a position to drop the case," Lisa spoke.

"Then I guess we've got nothing to talk about and that's too bad. I want to see you spear the slime that killed Cyndi."

"Yes man," Rhondo began,"but—"

"But nothing, Rhondo," I snapped. "Let's get real here. It's just us in the room. Look at what we know. We know Benny had ties. We know Mona was with Benny when he left the club. We know somebody besides Cleveland killed Cyndi and beat me up."

"What did he look like?" Ziglar spoke again.

"I can't tell you squat without dismissal. And I want it with prejudice."

"Now you get real, Stuart," Lisa snipped. "Even if we dismissed, it would have to be without prejudice. Your guy had Batiste's shoes on and obviously went through his pockets."

Even if we dismissed? A crack in the armor.

"So what keeps you from dismissing today without prejudice and taking it to the grand jury next week." It could happen. A dismissal without prejudice meant without prejudice to reopening a criminal case. That generally didn't occur. Still it could. I had to hold out for the best result.

"Your privilege has limits," Lisa said. "We could go the court this afternoon. In fact, we will go to the court and seek an order. While you were talking with Barnes I scheduled an emergency hearing with Judge Robideaux for three o'clock today."

"That's fine. We ought to see the judge and you ought to dismiss the goddam case today!"

"If you don't help us, we'll seek an order moving the court to order your withdrawal on conflict grounds. Then we'll seek to compel you to disclose information in connection with Cyndi's murder and Mona Day's death. You can't just hide behind your privilege."

"That's great. You go girl. Don't forget to throw your pom-poms in the air when you file the motion. Maybe Robideaux will order me to talk and maybe he won't. If he tells me to do something I can't do maybe I'll get the cell next to Cleveland. Then, I assure you, Rhondo's boss will have to deal with Voodo-schmoodoo riots on the courthouse steps. Happ Duncan will be our mayor again for sure. Maybe he'll nickname you Pappa Legba for winning the bloody election for him!"

"Come on, Stuart." Lisa smacked her pen down on the Formica top.

"Come on nothing. Go ahead and lock me up," I snarled.

"You wouldn't let that happen."

"Do I look like a guy who can't take a punch?" I rubbed my cauliflower ear and glared at her.

We finagled back and forth for the next forty-five minutes. Just a little bickering among old chums, right?

Ultimately we reached an informal understanding. The deal seemed simple enough. I would tell them what I knew from the investigation. They would cut Cleveland a break and enter discussions about the possibility of a dismissal without prejudice. This appeared, and indeed was, a vague understanding that favored the government. Even so, experience told me to go with it. It wouldn't get any better. I had to go with it in order to find what they'd really offer.

I answered questions for several minutes, I told them about the trip under the bridge, the bridge people and Shark, about Mickey and the Tweedle Twins, the trip to Peepers, our tracking of Tiffannie Squires to Newton Street, and my close encounter with the man in the harlequin mask. Zeus and the FBI guys wrote down everything I said and asked frequent questions.

The oddest moment of the meeting came when I mentioned Zebra's statement about Shark and the long telephone calls. Everyone perked up all at once. Marvin Ziglar reached into a briefcase underneath the table, pulled out an accordion folder, and thumbed through it until he found what he was looking for.

"Is this him?"

Staring down at a nine by eleven inch side-view of a man in a business suit with short dark hair combed straight back. I started to say he was nothing like the man I'd seen when the facial features clobbered me.

"Yes," I answered. "His hair is way past his shoulders and he was bareback in jeans, but that's him."

"Carlos Moldano," Ziglar stated. "Ever hear the name?"

"Yes. Cyndi knew who he was."

"His brother was the president of Mexico. He's wanted there and here for over a hundred felony counts of murder and trafficking. Where did you seem him last?"

"Under the bridge the night before last. And I think Zebra said he was—"

I stopped speaking as Marvin Ziglar ran out of the room with his cell phone.

"I thought those guys got plastic surgery." I addressed Agent Daniels.

"Not this one. He's known for his vanity. He probably left town after you saw him. We'll see. But we'll try anyway."

"What the hell is he doing here?" Rhondo addressed the question to Daniels, who just shrugged his shoulders.

We continued talking for several more minutes and after a while Marvin Ziglar returned. I finally got to a point of having talked myself out. Rhondo started to tell me more details about the morning's crime scene search. He confirmed that the case against Cleveland had just gone to hell. I surmised the government would have had to cut Cleveland loose anyway. Byno and the assistant Mobile Crime Unit crime search techs found a quantity of evidence implicating Mona in the murder. This included both weapons with her prints all over them, blood residue that appeared consistent with Benny's, a dress spattered with same blood, and a letter from Batiste, signature and fingerprints verified, telling Mona that he looked forward to working with her routinely on certain "special projects" in the district. I shook my head, wondering how she could bestow sexual favors on this Bronx bull and then slice his head off. I'll never get used to the brutality and duplicity. I also wondered about what Benny's real relationship with Mona could have been. The suicide note claimed robbery as a motive for the killing. Mona and Benny weren't strangers and I didn't buy it.

Only the DNA tests could ultimately confirm the blood match on Mona's clothing and any residue on the weapons. Mona's guilt seemed a real good bet. It was certainly an accepted fact in this room.

For my client's sake, I went with the program. I didn't believe that Mona could have acted alone and it seemed like a joke to accept robbery as her motive. Equally troubling was Tiffannie Squires' disappearance from the scene last night. Where had she gone? Was she involved too? She had to be involved in some way or she wouldn't have made a beeline to our missing witness. I'd answer these questions as soon as Cleveland walked out of jail.

At the close of our meeting, Lisa gave me a copy of the signed notice of dismissal without prejudice prepared before our meeting ever started. She promised to make certain representations on the record at our three o'clock hearing. I'd have a few of my own. All in all, the government had no intention of pursuing a case against Cleveland without strong new evidence linking him to the murder. I explained everything to Cleveland before he was transported over to the bullpen to wait for the three o'clock hearing.

Walking back to retrieve my Oldsmobile, I thought over the meeting. It had gone well. There were limits. Lisa and Rhondo and the FBI guys were forthcoming about matters that affected Cleveland's innocence. Not on other matters. Lisa never mentioned a word about the Sewell family or Ruthie's possible involvements. The meeting focused on the information that seemed squarely in the public domain and, since Mona and the scene at Newport Street had to be included, Cleveland walked. I pressed them repeatedly, thinking that they had leads on whoever headed up the team fighting with Benny. They did. They weren't saying who. This omission proved to be tragic. If they had budged a little, just a little, we might have put it all together and could have prevented an awful lot of grief.

# CHAPTER **64**

AT 12:33 that afternoon I unlocked my Oldsmobile, got in and drove away from the front of the Mitch Snyder homeless shelter. I locked the doors, switched the noisy air conditioner to high, then tried to reach Percy at the office. His voicemail kicked in. I left a brief message about our three o'clock hearing in front of Judge Robideaux. I felt better, but still wanted and needed backup counsel.

A chanting vigil continued in front of the courthouse and I heard Amanda Sewell barking out some sort of speech. I blocked her out and turned left onto Sixth Street, then made a quick right onto the ramp that led into the parking garage beneath 603 Pennsylvania Avenue north building. Slowing at the attendant's booth, I handed a ten and a fiver to Thomas, an Ethiopian gent who worked the entrance with his partner Jorge. We'd become friends. They were entertained by the hours I kept. We chatted whenever one of my cases made it into the news and I'd given them each a bottle of merlot last New Year. Today Thomas seemed highly upset. He wagged his head back and forth in a continuing, "Mr. Stuart, Mr. Stuart! What happened, Mr. Stuart?" I held my hands up, then shook my head and drove down into the lower levels.

Pulling up the hood on my shirt and dawning the sunglasses, I jumped out and used my key card to access the entrance to the inner hall, then to the foyer leading into the gym. I grabbed a *Washington Post* off the table and headed straight through the door and into the locker room and shower area.

Several guys were working out. I moved through the outer gym areas so fast that no one had a chance to make inquiries. Near the lockers, I grabbed two fresh towels off a stack and locked myself in a toilet stall to undress and scan the newspaper.

Fred Collins had a front page article on Cyndi's death. A recent photograph showed Cyndi and I walking up to the metal detector leading into the halls of Paradise, happily toting large case files. The people in the photo seemed distant, gone forever now. They were.

I read far enough into the article to find that Cyndi had died of multiple gun shot wounds from a twenty two caliber pistol to the right ear and eye. Two burn marks at the base of her neck were thought to be caused by a stun gun. Rhondo and Zeus were, once again, assigned to the homicide investigation.

It hurt to read the article. It hurt not to read it. No stun gun had been found at Newport Street. I started to hyperventilate, struggled to shut my mind off, to erect a barrier against panic.

I folded the paper and put it down, had to put it down, had to suspend further scrutiny until after I finished with Cleveland. Had to block thoughts, to feel better.

For ten minutes I showered in the hottest water tolerable, washed every part of my body three times, and did a first draft of a shave on my grizzled snout with one of the disposable razors provided by the club management. I dabbed a new coat of lotion on my face, dressed, and put on sun glasses. Ducking out to the elevator, I rode up to the seventh floor without interruption.

Jo Ann met me in the firm's lobby. She gave me something resembling a motherly hug. I still felt utterly hollow. I thanked her and disappeared into my office. My freshly pressed suit, shirt, and tie were nicely laid out. Noticing the blinking message lights, I made another policy decision, to ignore both the message machine and the stack of pink slips left by Jo Ann. The one exception was for Fred Collins. I didn't listen to the messages but assumed that he had called, called his cell, and indicated that I'd give him an exclusive interview that evening. Hopefully he'd have something new for me. As to the rest of the callers, they could wait until after the three o'clock hearing.

I slipped across Indiana Avenue to purchase pancake makeup and beige powder at the CVS drugstore and a meatball sub sandwich with a monster-size coffee at Jack's Deli. Returning to my office, I applied the makeup cream and powder, then devoured the sub. As I finished up lunch at about 1:45, someone knocked on my office door.

"Hi, Percy."

I opened the hatch to my broom closet and Percy entered for the first time since he'd come to Mitchell & Strong.

"Stuart. You don't look so bad." He walked in with a yellow pad and Mont Blanc. I motioned him to the couch.

"I'm much improved." And, I thought, even my pancake pallor looked better than Percy's blotchy color.

"Glad to hear it. We need to talk about this hearing that's coming up. I've been through the file on everything several times, but you've got to brief me on what happened last night and this morning."

"Sure."

Now strengthened by lunch, a trip through the showers, and spruced up duds, I relayed the essential details of the last twenty-four hours. He took notes and seemed attentive, but I thought his eyes looked glassy. I wondered if he'd taken OxyContin. Resolved to look the drug up on the internet. One thing I didn't need is a backup counsel that slurred his words in court.

I brought Percy up to date on all of the things that I'd told Lisa and the others over at Fifth Street a few hours before. Again, I didn't share information about Cleveland's possible connection to the Spilotro family. It seemed irrelevant to the issues at hand. I was surprised by Percy's familiarity with the facts. He'd obviously spent a lot of time studying the files and precedent pertinent to Cleveland's case. We talked for over a half hour and, whatever Percy's personal situation involved, I couldn't help but be impressed with his command of detail. If I fainted in the courtroom it seemed like Percy could pick up the torch and run with it. That's what I needed.

We finished up around twenty after two. I started to think about the walk over to the court. Would we get through the demonstrators and media without incident? If Cleveland got released from the courthouse should I make a statement to the press?

"What about after today?" Percy's question jarred me from my thoughts.

"After today?"

"Yes. After today. Assume you get Cleveland out. Is that the end of this? I mean, I know you're devastated by the murder of your investigator. But this is a marvelous victory and I'd love to have you work on a few of the Diel projects. My concern is whether you will be able to jump into that after what's happened to you and your investigator?"

"Thanks for the offer. Probably I will." I studied my face in the reflection of a wall plaque. Looked like the pancake cover held up well. "I just have a few things to do for Cyndi's sake."

"Like what?" Percy looked interested. "Anything I can help with?"

"Not sure. Well, first I'm doing her probate stuff. That should be straightforward. But there are a few loose ends from the case that need to be followed up on."

"You're going to keep working the case?"

"Got to do it for Cyndi." I looked over at Percy now. "We haven't really gone into it because there's no reason to now, but Batiste's murder was part of a mob war. Cyndi and I got in the middle of it and got ambushed. Maybe that would have happened anyway, given the circumstances. Maybe it's part Cyndi's fault because I couldn't reign her in. Maybe I'm dead to rights guilty of stupidly exposing myself and her to deadly risk. The dust hasn't settled on that and I don't know what I think except that I owe it to Cyndi to find her murderer."

"You think you can do that?" Percy studied me intently.

"Damn straight I can. If it's the last thing I ever do, I can." I started to panic—trust no one! Just like in the elevator with Lisa. The day had been overwhelming and I found myself venting with still another person I shouldn't vent with. Percy cared about the case as a public interest matter and because his father cared about the case. I couldn't risk having him tell Haskell that I'd cracked up and turned into the Lone Ranger. I could hear Haskell preaching to me about how such an investigation was not in the firm's best interest. Jack Payne would back him up on that one.

"Please keep that remark here, Percy. I wouldn't compromise the firm or spend firm time on this. It's a personal thing."

"Oh, I understand. Please."

"Thanks. Not sure I do," I replied "It's been one hell of a twenty-four hours and I'm not really thinking so clearly about what's next. Maybe we should just get over to court."

"Right. I'll go get my coat." Standing up, Percy stumbled slightly then went off down the hall. Another wave of dizziness hit me and I put my head back to rest for a few minutes until he returned.

I put my suit jacket and sunglasses on, grabbed a manila folder with a yellow pad inside of it, and left my office. Jo Ann seemed stunned at my appearance but smiled at us from behind her receptionist's counter, observing me leave the office with my new-found chum.

I grabbed several candies from Jo Ann's little bowl, thinking that the sugar might help with the ebb and flow of vertigo. The elevator went down, and we headed out and east across Sixth Street and approached the halls of Paradise.

The gris-gris chanters seemed to be having a shift change. I saw Happ Duncan shaking hands with Amanda Sewell. He took her bullhorn in hand and waved to the crowd. A number of older, conservatively dressed folks had entered the fray since I'd driven by earlier and it seemed like the crowd was growing in size and intensity.

No one seemed to notice us as we walked by. With my suit and sunglasses I didn't look so different from a lot of middle-aged white lawyers going in and out of the courthouse. That would change in a little while when I approached the microphone, hopefully with Cleveland standing beside me, and gave a statement to the press.

# CHAPTER **65**

"RUTHIE, its Stuart Clay."

"Lawyer Clay. What is going on? I saw the papers and—"

"Don't mean to cut you off, maam, but I've got to get into the courtroom in just a second. Several things have happened. The government has decided to drop the charges against Cleveland."

"Praise Pappa Legba. Praise our gris-gris on that court! It worked. I knew it would work."

"Right." I smirked at myself in the reflection of the small glass window to the inside of the courtroom. "Ruthie, it's been a rocky couple of days." No reason to go into details. "I think Cleveland should be out within a few hours."

"Lord, Lord, lawyer Clay. I can't get over there that fast. How are we going to do this?"

"I've already thought about it. I'm bringing him to your house. Hopefully he'll stay there for a while."

"Well, that's wonderful. What time is his case up?"

"In five minutes, before Judge Robideaux. My assistant is in the court waiting for the judge. It should be a brief matter;

however, the judge is still in a murder trial so it's hard to say when the hearing will take place. I'll have my cell phone with me before we leave and I'll give you a call."

"What happened today?"

"I'll explain it to you when Cleveland and I see you."

I clicked my phone shut, then walked over to a water fountain to down some ibuprofen. Ruthie had seemed very excited about Cleveland's release and had announced various plans to make Cleveland comfortable at her house. Then I could get on with business.

I called Fred Collins again and got his voicemail once more. Too bad. With only a minute to go, I quickly left word that Cleveland would probably be released around four P.M., and I planned to make a statement and answer questions in front of the courthouse. I would still give Fred an exclusive on the story leading up to Cyndi's death.

Peeking through the narrow windows to the courtroom, I saw the jury hadn't been dismissed in Judge Robideaux's murder trial. I left a quick message for Bridgette Ginadio. Overall, I'd rather just take her questions and Fred's because they were smarter and easier to interact with.

I pushed open the doors to courtroom 316 and took a seat in the back row. Percy, Lisa, and Rhondo were already there. Judge Robideaux had ended the taking of testimony for the day. He busily admonished the jury about what they shouldn't do that evening: (a) talk about the case at home; (b) visit the crime scene; (c) discuss the case with another juror; (d) read newspaper articles about the case. I'd always suspected that these rules were frequently and shamelessly violated. Even so, the dour litany went on for several minutes. I'd heard it before dozens of times and knew the judge could probably recite it in his sleep. I could.

After several minutes, the judge dismissed the jurors, had a discussion with counsel, spoke briefly to the defendant, and adjourned trial till the next day. Though the defendant wore a suit and tie, the marshal handcuffed his hands behind has back and started to walk the fellow back to the lockup The defense attorney handed the marshal a wooden hanger that, no doubt, would be returned with the defendant's suit after he changed back into the one-piece orange prison garb.

The courtroom emptied out, counsel left the lectern area, and our case was called. Percy and I walked to the counsel table at the right of the lectern. Lisa took the left side. The marshals brought out Cleveland minus his manacles and handcuffs. He took a place between Percy and me.

The dismissal of U.S. versus Barnes transpired with a whimper, not a bang--about as dramatic as slurping a Styrofoam cup of seltzer water after a night on the town. Judge Robideaux looked as if he had the weight of the world on his shoulders. I suspected he wouldn't have agreed to hear us today without the intervention from a high level at the U.S. Attorney's office. The case against Mona was overwhelming. The demonstrators portrayed Cleveland as a martyr and soon the present carnival atmosphere outside might turn into serious civil disobedience. Spike Armstrong twisted everyone's arm to do whatever could be done to diffuse the situation and all involved appreciated the serious need to act quickly. Still, very few people outside of this courtroom of seven people knew we were about to pull the plug.

After Genevieve Mason, the courtroom clerk, called the case and read the case number out for the record, Lisa announced her name and title for the court reporter taking down every spoken word for the record. Percy and I did the same and, after the marshals nudged Cleveland, he announced his name. Looking over, I noticed that this time Cleveland wore black leather boots with the shoestrings removed.

Lisa tendered her notice of dismissal to the court. The judge took the papers and sat yawning while Lisa made representations for the record regarding the intentions of the United States. The government moved to dismiss charges without prejudice against Cleveland Barnes, the man who'd stolen the dead guy's shoes.

Judge Robideaux briefly inquired of counsel then looked through the file and knitted his brow. He asked Cleveland if he understood the proceedings that were taking place. I tensed up, suddenly realizing that the judge could, in theory, postpone the hearing if he thought that Cleveland was too out of it to understand that the charges were being dismissed. That seemed at once patently absurd and then patently possible as I considered what the case jacket and clerk's notes must reflect about the case.

My head spun. I glanced over at Cleveland. He seemed to be dreaming, barely responding to the court's inquiries that were, on the one hand, quite summary in nature but, on the other hand, necessary in order to establish his understanding of this hearing. Was Cleveland lost in fantasies of Mabutek and the wonder of Georgia in 1835? Feeling lightheaded, I turned left, locking onto Lisa's lips, her tensed lips, moving up and down, launching words like kids blowing bubbles that wobbled out like shouts in a tunnel. They drifted across the room, glistening bubbles with rainbow reflections dancing across their surfaces, floating through space. They wobbled slowly, upward in the direction of Judge Robideaux. He studied them, stared down at us, ate tums from an oversized bottle, and strained to look alert, to suppress his wariness and exhaustion.

The courtroom glowed and disappeared, went black. Somehow I was not there, went to another world, on my back in the truck. I stared up at the Harlequin. Cyndi's murderer. Sequins glistened as he pulled me up by the hair and punched me again, inflicting more pain, screaming in that hateful voice. That familiar voice. Who the hell was this?

By God, I'd find out!

# CHAPTER 66

THE courthouse nurse stood over me with his gym bag full of stuff, asking if I wanted an ambulance. No way. Where was I? Still in court. I'd fallen into the lectern. Just a little lightheaded. Got a lot on my plate, I told him. Percy helped me stand up.

The clerk called judge's chambers. Judge Robideaux hurried back to the bench and sympathetically inquired about my condition. As I was well enough to function, the marshal brought Cleveland back out. Apparently, my blackout helped expedite the proceeding whatever Cleveland's state of mind. Fine with me. The judge summarily granted motion to dismiss without prejudice. He told me to get some rest. A court order, he said. Genevieve Mason announced, "This honorable court stands adjourned until July 28th at 9:00 A.M." Clenching his bottle of Tums, Judge Robideaux hurried off and the clerk announced adjournment. The marshals took Cleveland back to the lockup for the processing of the release order and clearing of holds.

Lisa and Percy pleaded with me, wanting to drive me home. I declined. I wanted to, indeed had to, collect Cleveland, deliver him to Ruthie, and call it a day.

Lucky for me all holds on Cleveland were dropped by the court. The marshal service would cut Cleveland loose at the courthouse.

I had to ascertain how and where release would actually occur. Found that Cleveland would be loose downstairs. He would come out through the bullpen.

Thanking Percy for his assistance and declining his offer to stick with me, I headed for the U.S. Marshal's block to wait for Cleveland's release.

I sat in the outer entrance to the bullpen, across from the bulletproof half window where the Marshal sat. Had it really been less than three days? More like a lifetime ago. My reality had been altered. But my true job still lay ahead. I would figure it out, would juggle facts until the Rubik's cube fell into place. I'd find the monster who killed Cyndi Oh, and he would either surrender to the authorities or I would kill him myself. No third option existed for me.

Today there were other requirements. I had to collect Cleveland, then ceremonially end the case by delivering him to his loved ones. This was my practice in cases with a minor or an impaired client. It provided a sense of completion. I hoped that Cleveland would stay put, maybe pine for Mabutek in the safety of his sister's back yard.

After about forty-five minutes, Cleveland stumbled out of the bullpen like a dazed prodigal son beholding the fat calf of freedom. He wore a slap happy smile across his face.

"You have done it, Snick. You have done it!"

"Yup." I'd done it all right. Hurrah for me.

"Cleveland, I'm going to take you to Ruthie's place. She wants you to stay there until you at least get some more clothes and a few days of rest. She says to tell you that she'll make crawfish stew."

"Oh, babie. It's Cleveland's day for sure." He rubbed his chin. "Where is your investigator?"

I looked at Cleveland, incredulous. He had no idea what had happened.

"She had another assignment," I lied.

"You thank her for me. You guys are pretty amazing. I got locked up once for shoplifting underwear and served more time than this."

"Right."

We walked down the hall of the C level together, Cleveland in his orange jump suit and black boots and I in my gray pinstriped suit with black sunglasses. While the rest of the court was fairly empty by now the C level still buzzed with the flurry of the three o'clock session of arraignment court in C-10. People recognized us and gave us leeway in the hall. I felt a surge of strange emotions and my eyes welled up with tears. Had to stop this before we got outside. Taking the escalator up to the JM level I saw the CJA Administrator Howard Reynolds riding down on the other end with another lock-up list in his hand. He looked over at me and made a loud whistling noise, shaking his head in disbelief.

We walked out the door and I noticed Lisa and Percy talking off to the side of the crowd. I quickly took Cleveland over to Happ Duncan. I tapped Happ's shoulder. He turned around, seeming somewhat annoyed. I put my hand up to his ear.

"Smile, guy. This is Cleveland Barnes beside me. The case is dismissed," I whispered. "You can have a photo opportunity if you'll let me talk for a second."

Adaptable fellow that he was, Happ didn't miss a step, didn't ask anything, and simply broke into a wide smile. He put one arm around me and the other around Cleveland and held it for at least thirty seconds while people looked on and chattered among themselves and a whisper spread through the crowd. Then Happ stepped forward and spoke into the bullhorn.

"The halls of justice have heeded our cry. I am here to tell you that I stand with Cleveland Barnes, a free man! And with his attorney Stuart Clay. This is indeed an auspicious moment and one that the citizens of our nation's capitol will remember next November. I thank our city's judges for seeing to it that justice is done in this case. I thank my brethren before this court today for holding a vigil for justice, a vigil for freedom, a vigil in the name of what is fair and what is decent, a vigil to free Cleveland Barnes."

The crowd broke into applause and shouts and Happy D held up his hands to quiet the exuberant.

"I'd like to turn this people's pulpit over to the man who has held the faith and diligently represented Cleveland Barnes, a lion and a crusader in the halls of justice. Here is attorney Stuart Clay."

I reached down into my tired gut and grabbed for a cup of advocacy.

"Good afternoon, ladies and gentlemen. About three days ago the man standing to my left in the orange jump suit was arrested on a city street in Georgetown because of a misunderstanding that has now been cleared up. I'm glad that has happened. I'm glad that Cleveland Barnes is now a free man.

"I'm not here to point fingers or find fault with our court system, the U.S. Attorney's office, or the police department. They, like the rest of us, are trying to do the right thing and the right thing is not always easy to do.

"What I can say is that our system of justice has worked in this case. Mr. Barnes received what I hope will be viewed as effective legal representation. The citizens of this city and the surrounding areas have been free to bring their concerns to the steps of this courthouse.

"The court and arms of government have processed this case expeditiously and have moved with great dispatch to end the case against Mr. Barnes once another individual stepped forward to take responsibility for the murder of Benny Batiste. It is a day for the citizens of this city to be proud that justice has been done. It is a day of celebration."

The crowd applauded and a contingent of "Happy D supporter for D.C." chants filled the air. I didn't mind being seen as a Happy D—it might help. I just wanted to get my message out.

"As you may know from the news reports today, this case has been touched by tragedy with the death of my investigator, Ms. Cyndi Oh, a dedicated investigator and Yale graduate who decided to perform a stint of criminal investigation before she returned to earn her law degree. I do not have words to express the personal sorrow and devastation I now experience because of her death.

"Suffice it to say that I am deeply saddened by Ms. Oh's death and am eager to see her murder solved. I would like to announce that I will pay a $10,000 reward to anyone who provides information leading to the arrest and prosecution of the person or persons responsible for the murder of Cyndi Oh."

The crowd went silent. I feared I might black out again. A surge of strength rose in me and I knew that I'd be all right. My message delivered, I spoke in a conversational tone now.

"The murder of Cyndi Oh was a terrible tragedy. I'd like to

240

call upon all of you to help solve this crime.

"I know many of the reporters present have questions and I'll be happy to answer what ever I can. Please direct your questions to me as I would like for Cleveland Barnes to maintain his right to silence." I gave Cleveland a quick *get it fella?* stare. For once he just nodded to me deferentially.

"Mr. Clay, how did this happen so quickly?" Fred Collins asked. "One moment we're hearing about preparation for an upcoming preliminary hearing and the next moment we see Mr. Barnes released. Please explain."

"Please call me Stuart. Thanks for the question. I think it's fair to say that this happened quickly because everybody did their job. We had excellent leads to work with because of the forensic investigation by the police and medical examiner and the defense investigation in the case. We were hot on the trail of the real murderer of Benny Batiste and I guess the pressure of this took its toll on that person."

"Do you believe the confessing party, Ms. Day, acted alone?" Fred followed up.

"I'm not sure, Fred. Given the work you've done and reported in the *Washington Post*, it is reasonable to ask the question that you are asking. I hope the police will pursue this. Understand that my job was to vindicate the rights of Cleveland Barnes. My job is finished.

"What I will continue to do is search for the person or persons responsible for the murder of Cyndi Oh. If that person or those persons are listening today, let me put you on notice. You can run, but you can't hide. There isn't enough land on the earth or water in the oceans for you to get away from me. Catching you..." My voice started to break up. "Catching you is the primary purpose of this attorney's life from this day forward."

I stood silent for a moment, thankful that I'd not removed the sunglasses.

After several moments had passed, Bridgette Ginadio spoke up.

"Isn't it, in fact, likely that there is another person involved in the murders? How else do you explain the murder of Ms. Oh? Wasn't she murdered in Mr. Barnes' case?"

"Excellent point, Bridgette. I don't have the answer to your question. I will reiterate that there is a $10,000 cash reward for information leading to the conviction of the person or persons responsible for the murder of Cyndi Oh."

The questions went on. I answered anything that I could and when possible, I repeated the offer of ten grand for information to track down the dirt bag that killed Cyndi. Sounded like I was rich. I wasn't. I'd have to cash out my IRA. Fine. I'd happily do it.

In retrospect it all seems odd since, after all, the killer had been right under my nose.

# CHAPTER 67

WE walked down the Indiana Avenue sidewalk to Sixth Street and then crossed the street and entered the ramp to the parking garage. I nodded to Thomas in the attendant's kiosk. He emerged momentarily to inform me that I looked much better now than a few hours back. Cleveland followed me down through the garage to the Olds sedan, still sitting in the space by the garage entrance to the firm's gym.

We got into the car and pulled up the ramp and out of the garage. Waving to Thomas, I drove on to Sixth Street and turned left. We headed in the direction H Street.

Cleveland asked me to stop at a hot dog stand. I obliged, thinking he wanted a victory dog or some such artery clogging morsel. But no. Batting a doleful grin he inquired as to whether I would spring for a pack of menthol 100s. Why not?

We drove in silence. Cleveland chain smoked and stared out the open window, laughing to himself and muttering in fits and starts. The catfish were jumping in his own private Idaho, or New Columbia, or Georgia, or wherever he resided. I took it in stride.

I understood how a jailed man felt when it was over, when the rudeness ends, when you get to return back into your own subjectivity. Even in my battered state, I couldn't begrudge Cleveland his euphoria.

We turned right on H Street and progressed across town to the point where it became Benning Road. I thought of how recently I had made this trip with Cyndi. I understood, but didn't—saw, but from a distance. I was seeing reality and yet took protection in a tunnel vision of autopilot busy-ness.

The trip seemed to go quicker than before. As we pulled into 46th Place, I felt myself starting to nod again. Maybe I shouldn't have driven, but it was all too much. I just wanted to sleep. I wanted to dump off my cigarette-puffing compadre, drive back to Chinatown, climb up the stairs, open and lock the door, and lie on the closest private floor I could find.

We pulled up to Ruthie's house and again I felt an acute sense of dread and danger. I knew instantly I'd made a mistake. I'd risked too much, and now had to get in and out again. What if Adrian was the harlequin and waited inside? Just speculation, but one thing I remembered. LaWayne packed heat. Looking at the elaborate security devices around the property I had to ask myself a simple question that hadn't occurred to me before. Was all of this security to keep the bad guys out? Or to protect the bad guys inside? I just didn't know.

I wanted to cut and run. Wish I had a gun. I left it at the office. Damn me, I'm a brainless do-gooder. Something occurred to me. I reached into my side bin on the Oldsmobile's door, took out a pocket knife I kept there. Stuck it in my left back pocket on the inside of my wallet. But that wasn't enough. I didn't want to go in there.

"Cleveland, I want to just drop you off here. You know where you are, right?"

"Yeah, man. That's fine."

Smiling LaWayne walked into the yard at Ruthie's. He seemed very glad to see Cleveland, opened the electronic driveway gate, and walked out to us. Cleveland put his window down and reached out to shake LaWayne's hand. Then LaWayne pulled his right hand up to shake but instead aimed his pistol at my head.

"Into the driveway, pal. Some folks want to talk to you."

I raised my eyebrows at him.

"You aren't stupid enough to shoot me here."

"Want to bet? We own this cul-de-sac. I could cut your stinking white body to pieces and feed you to the dogs in this cul-de-sac. Nobody would see it. Care to find out?"

If I went in that house I might never get out alive.

I floored the car and spun around, throwing LaWayne off balance as I fishtailed and headed to G Street. As I approached, a black Ford Explorer pulled broad side into the intersection. Adrian Sewell and two men I'd never seen before jumped out. Each of the men aimed a semiautomatic rifle at me.

"Out now!" Adrian barked.

"Why?"

"Out now or you're dead meat!" A spatter of bullets emptied into my Oldsmobile. I got out. They pointed back to Ruthie's and we walked. LaWayne stood up and dusted himself off, then smiled at me.

"Like I was saying, lawyer Clay. We'd love for you to come in and have some of our fine chicory coffee. Just walk this way."

# CHAPTER **68**

LAWAYNE led us into the house, then engaged the alarm.

Cleveland walked in front of me as we trudged up the stairs. He turned around and stopped. Why was he looking at me so oddly? A fist slammed into my kidneys from behind. I fell forward into the stairs. Before I could react, my arms were pinned back and a powerful arm reached from behind and clamped a chloroform soaked pad over my face and lips. I pulled my right heels and pulled a heel kick into the back of LaWayne's gajones. Fighting for consciousness, I heard him curse, felt a powerful hand slap my right ear. The world went black.

*"I love ritual." the Harlequin said. "It brings back something we've lost, something we need." He walked up close and held up his video cam as the men screamed and pled, begged for mercy, begged for life. A woman chanted in French.*

*"Mo Batayu, Mo Batayu..."*

*The Harlequin shrieked as I fell forward, tumbling down the escalator steps, back inside the courthouse. Glancing up, I saw Cleveland standing at the top, snickering at me.*

*"Mo Batayu, Mo Batayu…"*

*"Please, man. No. I beg…"*

*Who said that? A loud thump sounded. More loud thumps.*

*"Mo Batayu, Mo Batayu…"*

*Cleveland and the Harlequin stood at the top of the escalator steps. Cold shrieks frosted the glass ceiling of the courthouse, heads rolled down the escalator steps, rolled toward me.*

I awoke from a garbled blackout, gasping for breath, fighting to hold my head away from the dusty, moldy surface beneath me.

How long had I been out? Didn't know. Must be night or else I was underground. Pulled my face off a concrete slab in a half-lit area. What was it? Smells of hay and animal dung filled my nostrils. A barn? My hands were tied back, bound tightly with some kind of bristly twine. How long had I been here? I remembered Ruthie's house, LaWayne, Adrian's arrival, and Cleveland's sneering laugh. Hard to remember since then. Seemed like a long time. The inside of my right arm ached and I knew I'd been spiked, given intravenous shots and probably more than one for it to hurt like this.

Had to get away from this place before they came back. Reaching with the tops of my fingers, I felt the knife still there, where I'd put it between my wallet and the inside of my trouser pocket. No one in sight, but behind me an annoying grinding sound. Dirty moist air emanated the odor of hay and animals, made me itch. An occasional bray or snort cut the grinding. As my eyes adjusted I studied the scene. Windows covered with cheap shades confirmed the outside darkness; two dim bulbs twenty feet up on the wall lit the room. Following the light down the wall, I saw a ten-foot square trough full of hay and a tree stump. To the left were rows of stalls occupied by several horses that were facing each other. To my right was a huge mound of fresh hay and a wall of riding tackle. I looked back at the trough and light bulbs as my eyes continued to focus. I saw blood spatters in the trough and massive black stains in the hay. I struggled to look behind me.

"Hello, Snick," Cleveland spoke.

Rolling over on my side, I spotted him. Cleveland rubbed a round sharpening stone back and forth over the blade of a large silver ax. He grinned. I slid the knife out with my left hand and opened the blade.

"Took three hits last time, boss. Got to do better. Not respectful to take so long."

"What are you talking about, Cleveland?" I began to cut the rope.

"The heads, man. When I chopped off them heads. I wanted to show proper respect, but it's hard to do it right." He laughed. "Guess I need practice, huh?"

"What?"

"Come on, boss. Get real." He smirked. "Turnabout is fair play. They were bad guys. Now, I don't know what they want to do about you. But you got some answering to do too. Remember? You shot me."

"Cleveland, I met you three days ago for the first time. "

"Don't jive me, Snick. I've been waiting since 1835 to get you. Since the riot." He stomped over and bore down on me, the thin silver ax in his right hand. "Since you killed me!"

# CHAPTER 69

TERROR raged up my spine and out my arms. Was he going to murder me now?

"Slow it down, man. I'm the guy that got you out of jail. Remember? Tell me when I did this. Tell me when I killed you."

"Lafayette Park in 1835. Don't think I'll forget. Don't think my people will forget it."

Oh, Christ. How did I get here? I kept cutting the rope, thread by thread. Slow going.

Cleveland burst into laughter.

"Maybe it's all just a game. Huh, Snick? Maybe next time we'll be on the same side or I'll be white and you will be black. After all, you all right. You are my lawyer!"

Ruthie and Adrian pushed through a side door on the barn. Both seemed strangely transformed, hard faced and with soiled clothes. The dignified older woman and smiling prodigal son were eclipsed by others, strangers with malice pouring out of their faces.

"Why am I here?" I spoke. "What did I do?"

"Quiet, you dead thing!" Ruthie snapped at me. "Got nothing more to say to you. You got to wait for him if you want to beg for your damned life. We tried to help you, but you wouldn't leave those girls alone. Stupid girls and stupid lawyer! Stupid. Go messing with things that are none of your damned concern. What it get you? You hurt my business, damn you. You should have left Tiffannie and Mona alone!" She shook her finger at me.

"Wait for whom? You know those girls are why Cleveland got out. What are you saying?"

"That's what you think, dead thing. You could have just waited until we set it up and everything would have been fine. Nobody wanted to kill that girl you got with you. You damned fool. Instead she died. Mona had to die too. What did it get you? Why didn't you let us help? Why did you have to be such a smarty-assed lawyer?"

Exasperated, I shook my head at the glowering woman. What was she talking about? Who was going to set what up? Who were *they,* anyway?

"Ruthie, I've got no idea what you're talking about. I think—"

"I don't care what you think, dead thing. Save it." She stomped over to Cleveland."

Ruthie leaned over to Cleveland, cupped her hand, and whispered in his ear. He laughed like an excited child, and stroked the hand. Then he picked up the silver ax again, glowering at me. The witch's familiar was back with his ruler.

"Adrian?" I shifted over to look at him. "What is this? Why am I here? Can't you do something?"

"Hey, it's not me, man. It is not up to me or her." Adrian held up the palm of his hands and looked at me with a half smile, a weak smile. "Nothing personal. You did all right." He walked down the right hand side to a stall and started pulling a large trunk out across the straw.

"Did all right? I got Cleveland out. What's the problem? Why do you have to pull me into whatever this is?"

"Because you weren't going to leave it alone, man. You just wouldn't let up. That's what he said."

"He who?"

Adrian ignored my question and maneuvered the trunk to push open the door. Seconds later, a taller figure walked in through the open door. He remained in the shadows. For several seconds, I studied the silhouette standing back in the dark.

"Who are you?" I called out. "What do you need with me?"

Silence, for several seconds more. I heard a rustling noise and then a sniffing sound. He turned from me and lit a cigarette, cupping his hand over a lighter's flick. Couldn't see the face. Watched a red glow as the silhouette sucked and blew smoke across the room. A thick odor of marijuana overlaid the manure and hay.

"You know, Stuart, a man just can't get good help these days," the voice spoke at me. "It's pretty pathetic when the guy in charge of the circus has to do his own damned wet work to get it right."

I suddenly realized who the voice belonged to. It made no sense whatsoever.

"What's that got to do with me?"

"Too damned much, that's what. These fools mess up. Next thing I know Perry Mason is ready to bring in Lieutenant Tragg and pee on my rainbow. Now, you know I can't let that happen."

"If I'm so awful, why didn't you kill me before? Why'd you let me live?"

"You aren't awful, just misdirected. Thought I could draft you. You're supposed to be a defense attorney, not a do-gooder. Actually, you're more Ralph Nader than Perry Mason—and, believe you me buddy, I don't have time for do-gooder BS."

"Why are you doing this?"

"What's it matter to you? All you need to know is that I'm death to you." He sucked on the reefer and I heard seeds crackling. "That's all you should care about, you goddam trouble-maker. Why didn't you just take the help offered to you and stay away from the street?"

"Because that's not how I do it."

"Then I guess you'll just have to pay the price for it!"

"Why? What's in it for you?" I repeated myself.

"Oh, you might say I'll become the head of mergers and acquisitions, business development, and client relations all rolled into one. Plus I get to whack anybody I want. Now there's one hell of a perk."

Percy Diel walked out of the shadow.

# CHAPTER 70

PERCY leered at me, glassy eyed and shaky, a horrific rendition of the lawyer I'd talked with hours before. Track marks ran like red demon snakes up both his bare arms. His white shirt and suit pants were ruined, stained with dirt and blood smears. I had to speak, had to keep him talking.

"You aren't dumb enough to kill me!"

"I'm not dumb enough not to." Percy toked the roach and held it, then smoke spurted out from his throat and dribbled out over his thin lips.

"You've done a great job for us, but your world view is flawed."

"My world view is flawed? You're going to kill me because my world view is flawed?"

"That's right. I wanted to use you. Wasn't that goddam obvious? I sat in your miserable little office to draw you in. But no. You told me you wouldn't let up. Then you give a goddam press conference offering a reward for my capture. And what's that do for me? How long until you find me?"

"Maybe never. Anyway, the fat lady hasn't sung. I'm adaptable and I did just give a press conference with Cleveland. People saw me leave my office with Cleveland in my passenger seat."

"Big deal. They didn't see me. The only people who know who I am are in this room. Well, one other, but he got the hell out of dodge after you stumbled into him under the bridge. And it's going to stay that way minus one—and that would be you. Nobody's going to find you, not ever. Your piece of garbage Oldsmobile is taking a trip to the Shenandoah State Park as we speak. I understand a lot of depressed people go up there to commit suicide. Aren't found for years. I guess a guy whose sweet-assed chicky investigator got popped might decide to take a trip out that way. What do you think?"

"Go to hell!" I shouted. Got to keep cutting the rope.

"And you too, *Ralph Nader* Mason!" he yelled back. "Like I said. You just can't get good help. Either they don't follow instructions or they run off like you, half-cocked and trying to save the whole damned world."

He walked over to the straw trough, searching for something as he continued talking.

"You know, Stuart. Haskell is right about you. You're just an overgrown kid playing cowboy, still believing in the tooth fairy of justice. You're pathetic."

"When did Haskell say that?"

Had to keep him talking. Needed time to cut the rope. When he stopped talking I'd be dead.

"After he briefed me on his meeting with Jaworski." Percy reached into a mound of hay, searching, then pulled out a burlap sack, and opened it. Percy sighed with satisfaction. He saunter-staggered back, then hugged Ruthie and rubbed his hands over her hips. He staggered toward me.

"What fun. I love these rituals. You should see the pit in back Stuart." He laughed. "Well, you will see it. A work of art. True art." He came at me again, blasting my face with scotch breath.

"Tell me why I'm here, Percy Diel."

"I already told you. I'm not dumb enough to let you go. I got to take you out because you're a stupid do-gooder. It would just be a matter of time until you came after me."

"What a delicacy!" Percy declared. He pulled open the bag.

"I'm happy you sprang Caliban because I need my rituals and Cleveland's the man. But you're a rude boy, Stuart. You slept through the party."

He reached in and yanked out, what? Oh, God! Gagging, I squeezed my eyes shut, then opened again. Percy dangled three severed heads by their hair. Mickey Jaworski, Tweedledum, and Tweedledummer. He dropped Jaworski and picked him up with the other hand.

"They were your enemies, Percy. I'm not. What makes you think I'd ever have found you? What makes you think I'll tell anyone about you? I want to work on the mall project and I don't care what you do after hours."

Percy staggered forward and nearly fell, then began to giggle.

"You don't even believe the crap yourself, Stuart, so don't insult my intelligence. Sorry. Let us just say that progress requires sacrifices. Right, guys?" He smirked at the lifeless faces, at their wide open stares. Tweedledum's mouth drooped and a large, silver coin fell out. Percy chuckled. Adrian walked over without talking, picked the coin up and put it back in the head's mouth. "A piece of eight!" Percy declared. The stoned eyes flickered with madness as he put the Tweedles back in the bag. Percy clutched Mickey's head by the fuzz, holding the head inches from my face. I strained to turned away, block Percy's view of my hands.

"This one gave a better scaffold speech than Louis XVI. But those mean Parisians, Robespiere, Madame Marie Laveaux, and Caliban, they weren't persuaded." He motioned to Adrian, Ruthie, and Cleveland, then tried to move Mickey's stiffened chin up and down.

"That's right, Stuart." Percy's words barked in an accent while he tried to move the chin. Mickey's milky dead eyes were inches away from own. "I stuck my head where it didn't belong and what do you think happened?" Percy put the head away.

"Would you believe these carved melons are going back to New York wise-guy central in an ice chest? Wrapped in gold tin foil with a big pink bow?"

"That's your business, Percy. As long as you don't involve me in it, I don't care."

Percy sighed again, then plunked down beside me and patted my back. His head fell forward to raised knees.

"That's a hoot, Stuart. You're such a wise-ass. 'Tis a shame to kill a mocking lawyer," he slurred. "But you just know too much. And you'll never stop. Stalwart defender of the good. You legal beagle you. But I'll tell you a secret thing, Stuart. You're too much of a goddam moralist to be a top notch defense lawyer. Haskell and I both know that." He rubbed his head and looked at me.

"Is Haskell in on this, too?"

"Oh, hell no. That retentive twit doesn't know me from Andy Hardy. I could have been Al Capone Diel. It's my name he loves. I mean it's like this, Clay. We appreciate your work. That's why I whispered in Jack Payne's ear and got you hired in the first place. I thought we might need someone like you down the line. Then when Cleveland got busted, Adrian and I both remembered the great job you did for Abdul Orleans. The kid blew away a competitor in broad daylight and you got him off scot-free. And you didn't balk at my money, did you?"

"*Your* money?"

"Who do you think paid the tab, Perry Mason? The tooth fairy? We have been at this for a while. Since I was out in Prince George's County getting Adrian's punks off. How else do you think we met? See, when I first met Adrian, his father had already worked with the New York guys for over twenty years, bringing in smack and coke powder, then crack to D.C. But the New York crowd got complacent. Pathetic fat guys watching the *Godfather* and trying to muster the Corleone spirit. That's all crap. We got something better.

"We're bringing in Carlos Moldano from Mexico. Bet you didn't know that's who you met under the goddam Key Bridge! His men are here now, working through the Georgetown projects. The one I was going to have you work on. Oh, darn it. Have to find someone else now. Anyway, Moldano knows how to work. He doesn't need to watch the Mystery Channel to find a model. He is the model. He is the original. He'll eat those New York geezers alive."

"Give me the chance to work with him. I can do better."

"Stuart, you owe me," Percy interrupted. "I started whispering in Jack Payne's ear about our need for someone—who just happened to suit your credentials. Good relations with the court, noblesse oblige and all that shit. Old Jack, there's another suck-up. He got the message.

"And it's good you were in place. Mona was supposed to control Cleveland and look what happened. He took those shoes and that other stuff as his goddam trophies. He has been a lot of trouble, that New Columbian. It's a good thing he's good at what he does. Death by axe. Really satisfies a deep need in me to see that. Better this time than Batiste. The fat guy was too stoned to know what was going down and that's half the fun. It's so eloquent. There's a certain nostalgia to it, like it harkens back to a time when life was simpler, sweeter. And it sends the right message to all the competition, too."

"And your father? Did you jive him too, into funding this case? Is that why he wanted the firm involved?"

"That was all a crock I made up for Haskell and Jack. My father has no idea who Cleveland Barnes is. I haven't spoken to him in months. I'm not even sure he remembers who I am." Percy's voice rose. He rubbed his tracks. "That old bastard never had any use for me. 'Not visionary enough to carry the family mantle,' he said. His only son, his one damned child. He spent my whole life using this face to itch his overachieving ass. But just wait. Payback is a bitch. I have lots of plans for Cleveland! Before I'm done, that old-bastard excuse for a father will have his head mounted on a pike!"

# CHAPTER 71

I STUDIED the profile of Percy's face. Slowly I cut my bindings. No noise. Was he passing out?

"Well." Percy shook himself out of a stupor and sat up suddenly. "We got to get this show on the road."

"Glad to know I've served the cause of justice with Abdul Orleans," I said. I stared at him carefully as the blade ripped back and forth behind my back. "Percy, how'd you get me appointed?"

Silence. Percy looked down at the horses, ignoring me.

"I don't know," he finally answered. "Adrian did what he did. It was up and up. Somebody whispered to somebody. You know that courthouse better than I do."

"So where is my reward?"

Ruthie walked over, picked up the burlap bag with the three heads inside, and headed for the door. She leaned down and whispered something into Percy's ear. He looked up at her, shaking his head no, then kissed her hand and squeezed her. Ruthie motioned to Cleveland. He rose slowly, axe still in hand. Ruthie took it from him. The two left and I heard her calling to

257

Adrian. Two car engines started and I watched the black Ford Explorer and Ruthie's Cadillac drive past the door and leave.

Still sitting beside me, Percy leaned over again. He looked like he might pass out.

"Look, why clip me now?" I asked. "You want me to be your boy, that's something we can work out."

Percy sighed, staring at me like a difficult child that wouldn't eat his spinach.

"Come on, Clay. It's like this. Nothing personal."

"Fine. Why am I here?"

"Christ! When your investigator saw Mona with Tiffannie, she sealed her death warrant. When she told you about it she sealed yours. You've made it clear you are Ralph Nader-Mason. Ruth and Wendell owned Peepers, though they set it up through some dummy corporation in Delaware. The police probably won't be able to track it. They also owned the whorehouse on Newport Street.

"Whorehouse?"

"What did you think it was, stupid? A Hare Krishna temple? Now the place is empty and it will stay that way. Shipped all the girls out of state. Nobody will ever claim ownership and the city will take it for taxes someday. I don't think anyone will be able to trace that place either, but you know the connection and you just got on television and declared war on us. So to make a long story short, you are not an acceptable risk, Nader-Mason.

"Ruth works for me, now. She's my girl." He smiled. "Finger licking good, son. I'm going to keep my Voodoo girl and merge empires. I can't let you walk. First time in my life I've found something good and you aren't going to ruin it!" he screamed. "You got to go. Mona goes. Tiffannie goes. I had half a mind to do you last night but—" Percy broke into hysterical laughter again. "But we needed you in court today to spring the idiot Caliban. Isn't that a hoot?"

Percy fell back looking at the barn ceiling, then he continued. "We tried to stay involved, tried to steer you away from us. But no. Dudley Do-Right had to ride in and those damned girls helped you. They should have both been killed."

"Is Tiffannie dead?" Got to keep him talking. "Is Tiffannie dead?" I repeated.

"Tiffannie? Jesus, she ought to be. Damned woman ran her

stupid lip, led you straight to Tenleytown."

"Who killed Cyndi?"

"Who do you think?" he quipped. "Not bad for an amateur, huh?" Percy's mood darkened. He spoke in sharp, precise tones. "I took the bitch out myself and I'm proud of it. Damage control, Nader-Mason. It's your team or mine now. And the people on my team who help you are dead meat. Tiffannie is a traitor. She worked for Ruth and Ruth works for me. But I'll find the bitch and I'll cut her head off. You should have left it alone."

He stumbled up and staggered toward the door. Looking back, he snickered.

"Its time for your trip to the lime pit room at the Hoffa hotel! Let's go." Reaching under his shirt, Percy pulled a .22 pistol out of his waistband. He pointed the pistol at my head.

"Stand up, Mason, or I'll pop you here and call the sanitation crew to take you out back!"

# CHAPTER 72

STARING into the barrel of the .22 pistol, I swung my body around into an upright position and sat up. Turned to my left to keep my back to Percy. I bent the knee and stood, swinging my weight onto it and bringing my right knee up too.

Percy staggered up and over to the door. I still had my arms behind me.

"We're about ready, Nader-Mason." Percy blew into the pistol. "Going to need to get you out back here in a second. You act right I'll take you out nice and quick. No humiliation." He motioned to the open door that he had come in through. "Come on, it's time. You got to walk out to the lime pit room or I'll shoot you now. Try and mess with me and I'll call back Caliban to cut your head off. He won't buck me because he's already mad. I told him he could do it to you, but I changed my mind."

"Where'd they all go? What happened to Adrian and Ruthie?"

"No need for them to be here and see anything. She was the master of ceremonies when Jaworski and his assistants were, as they say, sanctioned by the court. She put a wonderful spell on all three before Caliban sent them to hell. Now are you going to walk or do I have to drag you?" Percy stared at me impatiently.

"Let me think a moment."

How to delay? I panicked inside a tunnel of disbelief. A horse whinnied in the last stall. Waves of shock started to run down my back. My eyes shot to the door and I pulled them away. Had to focus. What should I do?"

"So tell me about your father. Morton Diel. Does he really hate your guts or what?"

"Oh, come on Stuart!" Percy whined. "You can't drag this on."

"No really, tell me about it."

"Drag or walk, Nader-Mason? Last chance."

"I'll walk. I'll walk."

Percy leaned against the doorway, aiming the gun at me, waiting for me to pass him.

"Walk directly out and to the left now. We go in back of the barn to a big hole. It will be filled with concrete tomorrow. The new barn extension going over you."

Percy gripped my left arm from behind and started to bring the pistol up to my back. Before he could raise the pistol, I stomped down on his foot, hard. Percy screamed out in pain and rage, then tightened his grip. I spun around quickly to the right, snapping the thread that held the rope and jabbed his right arm with the back of my right elbow. The gun went flying across the room. As I completed my turn, I came up behind Percy and punched his left kidney. He ran for the pistol. I followed close behind. He stooped to pick the gun up. I drove my pocket knife into the back of his shoulder. Kicked him over. He rolled over and groaned, and I picked up the gun and aimed it at him.

"You shouldn't have messed with me, Mason. Cleveland's going to deliver the court's sanction now. After I blow your knees out." Percy pulled a smaller gun out of his right boot and pointed up at me from where he lay.

"Drop the gun or I'll blow you away, Percy." I pointed the pistol at his head.

"You pussy-faced do-gooder," he slurred. "I'm not afraid of you, Mr. ACLU pussy. You couldn't kill anybody." He cocked back the trigger. "I'm going to plug you so full that—"

My pistol spit three shots. A shot whizzed by my ear. I fired again. A red dent appeared on Percy's forehead. He fell back, head tilted to the right. Blood ran from his nostrils, mouth, and left eye. Percy's right eye gazed away, into the land of the dead.

# CHAPTER **73**

"GLAD you got him, lawyer-boy." A stall door creaked open. Tiffannie Squires walked out of the shadows.

I stared. Said nothing.

"Told myself I'd stop him, but I didn't know if I had it in me."

Her tall silhouette move into the light. She clutched a weathered plank, but tossed it in the hay after studying Percy.

"His highness is dead," she announced, as she leaned over, pulled open his fingers, and took the gun. She stuck it in the back of her jeans.

"Whose side are you on, lady?" Still had two shots left.

"Really, I would have stopped him," she said. "But come on, now. We don't have much time."

I stared at her in disbelief.

"Much time for what?" I stammered. "Where the hell did you come from?"

"I followed you. From court to Ruthie's, then to here."

"Here?"

"Diel family stables. We're right off Rock Creek Parkway."

"You've been here the whole time?"

"Yeah. I snuck in from the parkway. You might say I've done a lot of work in this barn. Percy liked me with the horses. Called me his Catherine." She smirked. "So I came in the back entrance just when those grease balls got the blade."

"You didn't try to stop it?"

"How could I do that with Ruthie, Cleveland, Percy, and Adrian holding court? Anyway, the grease balls deserved it. But not you. Now we've got to get out of here before Ruthie gets back." She kicked Percy's hand in disgust. "Fine with me, you know. One down, three to go. Come on, lawyer-boy. We got to get out of here."

I'd killed a man. Felt nothing. Maybe relief. Exhaustion.

Tiffannie stepped over, offered her hand. I stood up shakily.

"Why'd you run away last night, then come back to help me?" Didn't trust this woman.

"Percy killed Mona, and I'm getting even." She steered me out the door, over to a narrow path. "I'm a working girl. I love people with my body. I don't hurt anyone unless helping somebody get off is a crime. Now move it. Adrian will be back after he takes those heads away. No telling who else might show up."

We walked for several minutes in the dark. A few times I had to stop and put my head down as the drugs they'd shot into me fought against my adrenaline. Tiffannie braced me and we moved toward a distant light.

After several minutes, I sat and rested. Tiffannie watched me, saying nothing.

"I don't get you, lady," I whispered. "How'd you get hooked up with these crazy people?"

She studied me for a moment, then spoke.

"Sewells and Ruthie got shops all over town. Run women and who knows what else, like places advertised as a massage house and we know what gets massaged, like where Mona worked." Her eyes began to fill with tears, and then she shook her head and grabbed me, pulling me to my feet.

We hurried off into the darkness, down a narrow foot trail and into the woods. I could see by the light of the half moon. Still I stumbled and tripped, pushed my bruised legs through their machinations. I saw no sign of other people around, but the trees and bushes around us were dense enough for an army to hide in.

After several minutes, Tiffannie steered me off the trail into the underbrush and urged me on.

"How well did you know Mona?" We reached a ten-foot chain-link fence that stretched out on either side as far as could be seen.

"Down this way." She ignored my question, jerked me toward an opening cut in the fence, shoved me through, and then followed. We pushed through more brush and trees.

"I knew Mona as well as anybody knows anybody in this business. She was okay. Just some preacher's daughter from Georgia, ran away cause the good reverend couldn't keep his zipper up."

"Why'd you tell her about my visit? Didn't you know that they'd hurt Mona?"

"The girl messed up with Cleveland, but I thought she would be okay because that long hair Spanish guy had one on for her. She laid low and then he split after you flushed him out. Percy went nuts when he found out you went under the bridge looking for Mona, wanted to kill enough people to shut it all up. What kind of fool would use Cleveland anyway? Mr. Cool couldn't hold a candle to old man Wendell. Too stoned out to plan a clean hit."

She pulled me off to the right, down a steep grade. We came out of the thicket, into a clearing. I saw pavement in the distance. A dim street light cast down to a table and stone barbecue pit. Then it hit me.

We were at the picnic stop in Rock Creek where they'd found Tameka Starnes' hanging body.

Tiffannie's black SUV sat under a street lamp. She pressed something inside her front pocket and a dash light flickered as the door locks clicked open.

"I'm saving your lawyer ass, so you got to help me. Adrian's got boys all over D.C."

"Deal," I said, but before I could get in, a bolt shot through my chest and I fell across the hood of the SUV, and then onto the asphalt. I heard a voice.

"Tiffannie, stand away from that dead thing. Stand away from that wad of Clay!"

# CHAPTER 74

RUTHIE sprang around me and jabbed the crackling taser rod into Tiffannie's left breast.

"Stand away from the dead thing, girl!" she screamed as Tiffannie fell, touching her thigh with the rod. I rolled away, pulled my gun out and shot twice. Missed. I threw the empty gun away, stumbled to my feet and ran to the tree by the barbecue grill.

"What did you do to my pet, you dead thing? Where is Percy?"

"Percy's dead. Give it up, Ruthie."

"He's not dead. You're the dead thing. It's written you are dead. They will take you to the world below!" Ruthie pointed the taser at me.

Dizziness engulfed me. A voice spoke inside, saying that Ruthie told the truth. Time to give way, go on to other things, lie down. I thought of Cyndi. Now my time to die? Yes, the voice inside said.

"Lie down, dead thing. Back to the dirt with you."

She pointed at me with both hands now and I felt the force of, of what? I didn't know.

Ruthie slowly moved forward and walked past where Tiffannie lay. I saw light reflect on the knife that Ruthie held in her left hand. She'd cut my throat. I could see it, could feel it, could taste the blood in my mouth. I felt immobilized, like a lump with no will, made to wait while my destiny was delivered. Then it came to me.

"Did your people hang Tameka Starnes there?" I motioned to the tree.

"Quiet, dead thing!" she howled. "You join that traitor now."

I jerked away, over to the barbecue pit. Up in the tree, Tameka appeared. She stared down out me, hanging in the lamplight by a green garden hose.

"Not yet, Stuart," Tameka said. She disappeared.

Ruthie ran at me. I reached into a bed of ashes, grabbed handfuls of charcoal soot and threw them into her face. I blocked the knife and taser with my left arm, and pulled Ruthie forward as I drove my right fist into her stomach. She withered and dropped.

I patted Tiffannie's face, struggling to awaken her from a stupor. Reaching underneath her, I grabbed Percy's gun. Tiffannie sat up. Confused at first, she helped me bind Ruthie with a tow rope and duct tape from the back of her SUV. I called Rhondo on her cell phone.

For the second time that day, an army of police, medics, and crime scene technicians swarmed to my side. The police found three headless corpses in a lime-laced grave. Soon Ruthie, Adrian, and Cleveland were all in custody.

Later that night, I debriefed again at the Triple Nickel with Rhondo, Lisa, and her boss, an array of blue suits I'd never laid eyes on before, and U.S. Attorney Margery Foxwell. They learned a lot from me and, this time, I learned a few things from them.

Recent investigations in New York and the District of Columbia provided documentary evidence proving a thirty-year relationship between the Sewell Family and the Spilotro organization's drug traffickers. Wendell Sewell had a certain genius in his methods, kept a low profile, and stayed off the radar screen of law enforcement authorities. After Wendell's first stroke, Adrian took over and immediately did things that attracted police attention. Authorities also suspected that new movers had entered the scene, and that Adrian had struck ties with a local crime lord with ties to Mexico. However, no one had a clue that Percy Diel led this group.

An eyewitness fingered Percy as the person who stood outside a large white truck and dumped a wrapped object off the southern portion of the Fourteenth Street Bridge. Because of uncertainty about the cause and time of Cyndi's death, Percy might have been charged with murder and received the death penalty under Virginia law. But I beat them to the punch. That seemed like a just result to me.

Truth is, the police correctly assumed that Cleveland had ties to the Sewells, and, therefore, was involved in Benny's murder. In some ways, Percy pegged me right. I believed in the tooth fairy of justice, and justice had prevailed notwithstanding my naïve values. I saw it now. True justice, like nature, was red in tooth and claw.

Cleveland would probably spend the rest of his life at the John Howard Pavilion of St. Elizabeth's Hospital. Ruthie and Adrian faced multiple life terms without parole. Though the heads were never recovered, Tiffannie emerged from the Witness Protection Program long enough to testify—and received a new life from the program. I appeared as a witness against Ruthie and Adrian and testified that I'd seen them leave the barn with the heads of Mickey and his assistants in a bag.

During a recess in the trial, Adrian's lawyer appeared outside the courthouse before a barrage of cameras, and used Mickey Jaworski's line: "Everyone deserves a lawyer. Everybody."

Wonder what Mickey would say now?

I failed Cyndi as I'd failed Tameka, though it wasn't for lack of trying. Evil walked on two legs, and this stranger snuck in whenever he could. Nothing came easy. I saw only one guiding star.

We saved ourselves from the darkness by finding our jobs and doing them, whatever the cost. In a world turned upside down, this was the only pure thing, the only way to rise up from the confusion, the only way to affirm our dignity.

So I'd go back out to the streets of Washington, D.C., where the ghosts of the past and the hopes of a new world raged through the fountainhead of human reality, out into the present. I could get caught in the current and be thrown over. That risk came with the territory in this city I loved and the court where I made my living.

It was another day in Paradise. Another day to be grateful.